NAUSEA

OTHER BOOKS BY JEAN-PAUL SARTRE
PUBLISHED BY NEW DIRECTIONS

Baudelaire (a critical study)
The Wall (short stories)

Nausea
(*La Nausée*)

Jean-Paul Sartre

Translated from the French by Lloyd Alexander

Foreword by Richard Howard

Introduction by James Wood

A NEW DIRECTIONS PAPERBOOK

Translator's note: I wish to express my sincere thanks to Mrs. Violet Hammersley for her work in revising and correcting certain passages of this work.

La Nausée was first published in 1938 by Librairie Gallimard. First published in the U.S. in 1952 as a New Directions New Classic (cloth) and in 1959 as New Directions Paperbook 82. Reissued in 2007 with a foreword by Richard Howard and again in 2013 with an additional introduction by James Wood.
Manufactured in the United States of America

Library of Congress Cataloging-in-Publication Data
Sartre, Jean-Paul, 1905–1980.
[Nausée. English]
Nausea / Jean-Paul Sartre ; translated from the French by Lloyd Alexander ;
foreword by Richard Howard ; introduction by James Wood.
pages cm — (A New Directions paperbook)
ISBN 978-0-8112-2030-9 (alk. paper)
I. Alexander, Lloyd, translator. II. Title.
PQ2637.A82N313 2013
843'.914—dc23   2012050355

10 9 8

New Directions Books are published for James Laughlin
by New Directions Publishing Corporation
80 Eighth Avenue, New York 10011

A FOREWORD TO *NAUSEA*

Richard Howard

When the thirty-one-year-old Jean-Paul Sartre, a refractory philosophy teacher in Le Havre ("it is one thing to enjoy talking with your students and giving lectures, it is quite another to see yourself as a *prof* surrounded by other *profs* giving magisterial lectures and maintaining discipline in class: I didn't like my colleagues, I didn't like the atmosphere of the *lycée*"), having already published an essay *L'Imagination* with Alcan in 1936, submitted his first novel *Melancholia* to Gallimard later that same year, it was rejected, despite a favorable reader's report by Jean Paulhan; in an interview some thirty-five years later, Sartre remarked: "I took this hard: I had put all of myself into a book I worked on for many years; it was myself that had been rejected, my experience that had been excluded." Sartre had begun writing what he called his "factum on contingency" at the age of twenty-six, and was subsequently to acknowledge influences ranging from Valéry and Céline to Rilke's *Notebooks of Matte Laurids Brigge*; he was convinced of his novel's worth through and beyond the prestige of its derivations.

Resubmitted to Gallimard in April 1937 with powerful recommendations from Charles Dullin and Pierre Bost, Sartre's novel was at last accepted, though the title was judged "inadequate," as were certain "raw" episodes in the text—Roquentin's transactions with chambermaids in the Hotel Printania, details of low life in Bouville (*mudville*, after all), and scenes of Roquentin's past. Sartre agreed to cuts, and suggested an alternative title: *The Extraordinary Adventures of Antoine Roquentin*, supplemented (and contradicted) by a *bande publicitaire* that would confess (or exult): "There are no adventures." I treasure this suggestion as the sole example I can come up with of an eighteenth-century "libertine" irony in Sartre's entire oeuvre. This too-playful formula (after all, the work had originally been called *Melancholia*!) was also rejected, and finally Gaston Gallimard himself came up with a title which famously prevailed for the novel itself (and in some thirty translations the world over: how deceived we should be, as the French say when they mean disappointed, if confronted today by a novel with that original, all-too-human, sentimental or psychiatric appellation). Though Gaston Gallimard's title has remained more closely identified with the author than that of any other of his fictions or plays, Sartre as well as Simone de Beauvoir had reservations about "nausea," apprehensive that such title would inspire a "naturalistic" reading of his experimental metaphysical novel. But what actually happened is that the word somehow changed its meaning because of the novel title: capitalized and clearly in reference to the novel, "Nausea" no longer evokes physical malaise to the point of vomiting, but is a nickname for existential anguish.

La Nausée was published the following April, and Sartre's only book of short stories, Le Mur, written during the same years as the novel, was published in February 1939. It is these two works (of both Lloyd Alexander is the fortunate and gifted English translator, though I cannot resist the collegial privilege of pointing out that in a list of Anny's personal stage properties on page 136, "shawls, turbans, mantillas, Japanese masks, pictures of Épinal," the last item will necessarily confront the non-French reader with an enigma unless it is explained that *images d'Épinal* are not representations of a cotton-manufacturing town in NE France just south of Nancy, but old-fashioned conventionalized figures on printed fabrics, often affectionately collected and reproduced as illustrations in sentimental children's books), and especially the novel in the reader's hands, which afford Sartre his place as a decisive figure in modem fiction: within a decade of its publication La Nausée became a sort of modern classic, without thereby losing—in the minds of its enormous readership—its virulence, its emotional charge, its abiding fascination. This, on the one hand, because of its realistic power (Sartre was right about the effect of this particular kind of post-Zola treatment, but wrong to fear that it would damage a reader's appropriate response to his essential, or rather his existential enterprise), for *Nausea* is indeed a primary document of the everyday life and social anxiety of the 'thirties; but on the other hand, in formal terms and on account of its philosophic-fictional problematics, the work marks out a new and extremely influential departure for fiction, and was immediately taken by many French critics as the index of a "liberation" for the French novel (of course, as Alain Robbe-Grillet has reminded us some three decades later, all novels need to be liberated: literature is its own oppressor and must be its own emancipator).

Indeed it is by such novelistic problematics (narrative ambiguity; disintegration of character, repudiation of psychology; sportive experimentation of style) that *Nausea* inaugurated and was followed and favored by a healthy proportion (however dubious that adjective) of the French novels of the second half of the twentieth century.

In the procession of Sartre's literary works, *Nausea* would seem to occupy a privileged site: it is the "founding" work on which all subsequent texts may be said to *rest*, however fitfully—significantly, this first novel has never been disowned or disestablished by its author—and it is a work of experiment and transition informing all his productions to come, even as it is retrospectively modified by them. At some thirty years' distance, it is answered, complemented and opposed by *The Words*, which immediately upon publication was cited as Jean-Paul Sartre's other most decisive literary triumph. The author himself unhesitatingly acknowledged a preference for the earlier work; in an interview with the dogged editors of the Pléiade edition of Sartre's novels, he remarked: "Ultimately, I stand by one thing, which is *Nausea.* . . . It's the best of what I've done."

Perhaps not incidentally, the exhaustive scholarship which Messers Contat and Ribalka have provided in their splendid edition and on which I have drawn to a very minor extent (in comparison to the documentary riches they afford) offers a diverting illumination with which to conclude these prefatory observations. A *roquentin*, they tell us, has as its primary meaning in the *Larousse Dictionary of the Nineteenth Century*: "A name formerly given to songs composed of fragments of other songs and linked together as in a cento, so as to produce bizarre effects by changes in rhythm and abrupt breaks in the succession of thoughts." They note that *Nausea* continually refers to other ways of speaking, even as it rejects them, and that Antoine Roquentin himself appears to be a man who listens to and copies others' discourse in order to reconstitute it, half seriously, half comically, in his diary. Sartre himself, they add, was familiar with this meaning of "roquentin," but assured them it had had no influence on the composition of his text nor on the choice of his hero's name.

INTRODUCTION

James Wood

I.

In a lecture delivered in 1945, Jean-Paul Sartre described existentialism as "the attempt to draw all the consequences from a position of consistent atheism." *Nausea*, which appeared seven years earlier, in 1938, represents an early installment in this process of atheistical traction. It thus belongs alongside Camus's novel *The Stranger*, and his philosophical essay *The Myth of Sisyphus*; books which likewise commit themselves to the prosecution of difficult consequences, and which, like *Nausea*, are only partially convincing in the responses or solutions they propose to the realization that, after God, life is without meaning.

Nausea, then, belongs to a rare genre—or several rare genres. It is one of the few books devoted to the logical exploration of a world without meaning. It is a philosophical novel which, if it does not quite propose philosophical arguments in the formal sense, discusses and dramatizes them. In addition, it is one of those books—like *The Prelude*, or Rilke's novel *The Notebooks of Malte Laurids Brigge*—which becomes the document of its own making. That is to say, in such books, the writer-narrator talks about writing, and exhorts himself to write a great, solving work: only slowly do we realize that we are reading that very work. The self-exhortation is the literary achievement, if we can only see it. Sartre ends *Nausea* by making the narrator, Antoine Roquentin, pledge to write something that would be "beautiful and hard as steel and make people ashamed of their existence.... A book. A novel."

Sartre's novel also prefigures the French *nouveau roman* and the work of Beckett. His narrator has a shadowy, fictive quality. He is in the port town of Bouville (i.e. Mudtown; possibly based on Le Havre, where Sartre taught for several years), where he is working on a historical work, about the life of the Marquis de Rollebon, an eighteenth-century diplomat and traveler. He goes for walks in the town; watches his solidly bourgeois fellow-citizens; writes his book; goes to the library; has occasional encounters with a man he has nicknamed the Self-Taught Man; thinks about his former lover, Anny, and so on. He seems to be a real enough character, and even tells us that he is thirty years old. Yet whenever Roquentin talks about his past, it has the studied randomness and the glamorous opacity of espionage. He is a spy from the world of nothingness. For instance, he talks carelessly about having been in an unlikely number of places: Shanghai, Moscow, Algiers, Meknes, Saigon, Aden, Hanoi, Angkor. "When she [Anny] was in Djibouti and I was in Aden"; or "Six years ago ... I decided to leave for Tokyo"; or "the same discouragement I had in Hanoi—four years ago when Mercier pressed me to join him." We hardly believe that Roquentin was ever in Hanoi; and nor, we suspect, did Beckett, who may have borrowed the name, Mercier, for his novel *Mercier and Camier*.

Sartre flourishes this fictive quality, and Roquentin, of course, does not believe in his past anyway. When he abandons his work on Rollebon, he writes: "How can I, who have not the strength to hold to my own past, hope to save the past of someone else?" The reader senses that Sartre wants to alert us to Roquentin's fictionality, to let us know, in the style of Beckett and the *nouveau roman*, that Roquentin is a thoroughly unstable invention who has no real past outside the words of his creator. This is not just a literary game. As Beckett does, Sartre uses the fictionality of his fiction to ask us to reflect on the fictionality—or at least, the arbitrariness—of reality itself. *Nausea*'s very subject is the randomness, the contingency, the superfluity, of the world; where better to begin than with Roquentin's own randomness, his contingency as an invented character? It is as if Sartre is saying to us "How can you expect my character to be solidly real, to be anything other than obviously imaginary, when everything is contingent anyway? My character has been deformed out of reality by his own nihilism, his own metaphysical nothingness."

Nevertheless, Roquentin, while never a character of great depth in the traditional sense, and while always shadowy, has enough vitality—the vitality of his creator—to interest and involve us. Roquentin, like Dostoevsky's Underground Man, is a sufferer and a militant. He is at war with the town in which he lives, at war with the regulars at his café, at war with Anny and the Self-Taught Man, and at war with himself, or with pieces of himself. For the two principal characters with whom he interacts, Anny and the Self-Taught Man, arc in some way Antoine's doubles. (A further borrowing, perhaps from Dostoevsky.) He ridicules the Self-Taught Man, who is laboring through his education by reading the library's books alphabetically, author by author. The Self-Taught Man is ridiculous because he is a soft-hearted humanist, and because he has got all his knowledge from books. Yet there is nothing to suggest that Roquentin is not equally as impoverished, and merely hiding his poverty behind a panoply of place names. When the Self-Taught Man comes to Roquentin's room, to look over the photographs of Roquentin's supposedly wide travels, he is handed only a packet of "photographs" (never explicitly linked to Roquentin, and not necessarily taken by Roquentin) of "Spain and Spanish Morocco." Anny, too, is a kind of alter ego of the narrator. Near the end of the book, when Roquentin finally meets Anny again, she laments, in words similar to Roquentin's, that "it isn't good for me to stare at things too long," and continues: "in London, we had separately thought the same things about the same subjects, almost at the same time."

Roquentin is a solipsist, trapped in a terrible echo-chamber of the self, haunted by the sonics of his inflamed personality. But alongside his Dostoevskyan anger, and his Céline-like contempt for the bourgeois masses, Roquentin is visited by a deeper, more philosophical ailment: he falls into bouts of what he calls his "Nausea." These are episodes in which, afflicted by his sense that there is "absolutely no more reason for living," he is simultaneously alienated from and over-immersed in reality. He is overcome in a café, in a street, in his study. He feels that "nothing seemed true, I felt surrounded by cardboard scenery which could quickly be removed.... I murmured: 'Anything can happen, anything.'" Reality begins to lose its familiar outlines. Words, for instance, no longer seem to refer to their referents. At one point, Roquentin realizes that the seat he is on is a seat only by name: "it could just as well be a dead donkey.... Things are divorced from their names. They are there, grotesque, headstrong, gigantic, and it seems ridiculous to call them seats or say anything at all about them: I am in the midst of things, nameless things."

Yet, while reality begins to melt from him, it also becomes viscous. Suddenly, he is plunged into the thick heavy abundance of existence. In his periods of nausea, Things—a pebble, a beer glass, a tree, his own hand—oppress Roquentin with their heavy contingency and their awful superfluity. He feels his own flesh as mere lazy, vegetating fat. Why does this flesh exist? Why does the tree exist? Why are there so many trees, all of them producing leaves and branches and roots? In the town park, Roquentin is overcome by a sense of humans as "a heap of living creatures ... we hadn't the slightest reason to be there, none of us, each one, confused, vaguely alarmed, felt in the way in relation to the others. *In the way*: it was the only relationship I could establish between these trees, these gates, these stones." And he continues: "I, too, was *In the way."* This obstructive superfluity does not strike him as, in some way, part of the mysterious generosity of life (as religionists, and even some scientists, argue that nature's crooked abundance, its beautiful excess, could only come from God). Far from it. The abundance of life strikes him as "dismal, ailing, embarrassed at itself." He looks again at the trees, and decides that they did not want to exist but are unable to kill themselves. So they go on, like good little bourgeois, performing "all their little functions, quietly, unenthusiastically."

Roquentin concludes that nothing is simply itself. "The simplest, most indefinable quality had too much content, in relation to itself, in its heart.... The essential thing is contingency. I mean that one cannot define existence as necessity.... All is free...."

The episode in the park, which occurs towards the end of the novel, represents one of its climaxes, and is certainly the novel's longest and finest passage of philosophical essayism. But the novel has prepared us for this, for Roquentin has been falling in and out of smaller bouts of nausea throughout the story. One of his fiercest apprehensions, linked to, but less generalized than his sense of life's pointlessness, concerns his awareness that life's occurrences are random. Life resembles the pack of cards which he sees earlier in the novel. When we play at cards, we invest each card with a useless significance; for what is more random than that fine King of Hearts, say, which we hold in our hands? "Mighty king, come from so far, prepared by so many combinations, by so many vanished gestures. He disappears in turn, so that other combinations can be born, other gestures, attacks, counterattacks, turns of luck, a crowd of small adventures."

Roquentin sees the randomness of his own life, and indeed mournfully wallows in it. Finding, by chance, a copy of *Eugénie Grandet* open at page 27, he starts reading the novel, which he has never read before, at page 27. At another moment he goes out for a walk, and comments: "I go out. Why? Well, because I have no reason not to." If most people's lives are positively structured by randomness without their knowing it, Roquentin's life has become negatively structured by randomness, for he knows that it has become impossible to choose one course of action over another, and he is immobilized by it. Later, he announces, ironically: "I am free: there is absolutely no more reason for living ... this freedom is rather like death." He is free only in the sense that he could do anything at all; but he is not really free, because to be able to do anything at all is to be able to do nothing, since meaningful differentiation between choosing and not choosing has been lost.

Sartre sees that we structure life by absences, by nullity. Take words, for instance. We call a tree a "tree" partly by rejecting all the other names a tree could possibly have (cat, ball, dog, trombone, and so on). We stay in, one morning, partly because we *think* we cannot go out (I must get this introduction finished this morning!). We choose someone to love only by not choosing to love millions of others; yet we canonize our entirely random decision by ignoring, indeed inverting, its randomness, and enrobing ourselves in the garments of inevitability: we like to say, "we were *made* for each other," or "fate picked the two of us out."

But when life is properly seen to be random, excruciatingly experienced as random, as Roquentin experiences it, this tenuous structure of rejection and choice, of absence and presence, has disappeared and has been filled up by random presence, by superfluity, pointless plenitude. When one sees life as truly random, one can, as Roquentin fears, "do *anything*." But it would be a mistake to imagine that *this* is then freedom, while those who do not see life's randomness are still stupidly unfree. Is Roquentin free, because of what he now knows? Not at all. He is no freer than his blind fellow citizens. He can do everything but nothing. He is "free" only in the sense that he is really unfree; he is "alive" only in the sense that he is really dead.

Perhaps there *is* some consolation, however, in having pierced the veil of this terrible paradox of freedom. The citizens of Bouville, whom Roquentin watches going about their everyday business, are still veiled in ignorance of their arbitrariness. They are as unfree as Roquentin, yet they hide the terrible imprisonment of their existences by unthinkingly getting up, going out to work, relaxing on Sundays, and so on. They wrongly imagine that they have chosen this form of life, when of course it has chosen them.

Roquentin visits the local art gallery, and looks at the portraits of the town notables, the burghers who have made it what it is. These he calls "the Bastards" (*les Salauds*). He is filled with revulsion. These pompous civilians imagine that their lives have meaning, and they believe that these paintings solemnize and preserve their imperishable achievements. They are merely examples of what Sartre would later call "*mauvais foi*" or "bad faith": they have concealed from themselves the awful dilemma of their existences.

The scene in the gallery is perhaps the only weak one in the book. It is too long, too heavy-handed, and somewhat cruel. Roquentin looks at the portrait of Rémy Parrottin, by Renaudas. And then a bourgeois couple enters the gallery, impressed by precisely what revolts Roquentin. The man exclaims: "Parrottin of the Academy of Science ... by Renaudas of the Institute. That's History!" We are supposed to laugh at this man's mindless veneration, his respect for musty institutions. This man is clearly a walking dictionary of *idées reçues*. Yet instead, we feel the fat hand of didacticism; we feel Sartre urging us to agree with Sartre. There is something a little propagandistic about the scene (as Sartre's later novels would become increasingly didactic). Of course, the mockery of the bourgeoisie is a fine French tradition; but Sartre here lacks Flaubert's delicacy, and the scene perhaps reminds us of another moment in a gallery, in *Sentimental Education*, when Frédéric is walking his uneducated mistress, Rosanette, through a room in the palace at Fontainebleau. Gazing vacantly around her at the portraits, Rosanette absurdly pronounces: "All this brings back memories!" Her comment is foolish, yet its helplessness, and its absurd comedy, stir our sympathy and make Rosanette human. The man who says "That's History!" is not really human, he is Sartre's victim.

The scene perhaps prefigures that later Sartre who, after the Second World War, became increasingly political and increasingly intolerant of what he saw as bourgeois or Western softness. Though this later Sartre had complicated relations with orthodox Marxism, his own brand of Marxist existentialism had oddly uncomplicated relations with Western capitalism: he simply believed that violent revolution should sweep capitalism away. He denounced the Russian invasion of Hungary in 1956, but argued that only socialism, not the bourgeois notions of justice and human rights, could condemn it. In 1961, in his introduction to Franz Fanon's *Les Damnés de la Terre*, he wrote: "*Il faut tuer. Abattre un Européen, c'est faire d'une pierre deux coups, supprimer en même temps un opprimeur et un opprimé.*"—"It is necessary to kill. To shoot down a European is to kill two birds with one stone, to eliminate at the same time an oppressor and an oppressed." One cannot help reflecting on the irony that the celebrated philosopher of freedom, the great atheist, maintained an almost religious faith in an ideology that vandalized the very face of freedom.

In fact, Sartre was largely unpolitical during the 1930s (he did not vote), and *Nausea* is political only, as it were, at its margins. Still, Sartre intends us to register that the town's notables are not only myopics of bad faith, but representatives of France's right wing. Roquentin lingers over a portrait of Olivier-Martial Blévigne, who broke a town dock strike in 1898, who was an anti-Dreyfusard (i.e.

a conservative or anti-Semitic opponent of Dreyfus's innocence) and whose face "resembles Maurice Barrés," the President of the League of Patriots. Blévigne's biography fairly screams "conservative"; again, we may feel that Sartre's hammer is a little heavy here. But perhaps something subtler is intended. For though his novel seems to be set in the 1920s, Sartre may mean us to ponder the conservative ideology that had been burgeoning throughout the 1930s, and that would bloom, in some quarters, into Nazism and collaborationism a few years after the publication of *Nausea*. The Nazified intellectual Robert Brasillach, for instance, who was executed in February 1945 for his wartime collaboration with the Germans, had written in 1931, in his book on Virgil: "the land we are part of is above all this well-worn landscape, these well-seasoned words, the supreme ease we feel in rediscovering a street corner, the corner of a sentence, the corner of a memory." These sentences appear in a chapter entitled "*La Terre et les Morts*" ("The Soil and the Dead"), taken from Maurice Barrés's novel of that name. For the likes of Brasillach, a France of ancient custom and inherited principle was threatened by atheists, republicans, leftists, rootless Jews, governmental bureaucrats, and a writer like Sartre. It is not hard to see that, within this context, Roquentin's apprehension of life's randomness has a specific political charge, whether he knows it or not (he appears not to). For in Roquentin's unanchored world, there can be no such thing as "well-seasoned words," or the pleasure of an old street corner. In Roquentin's world there are only Things without names, and the terrifying, endless rediscovery of the entirely arbitrary. No street corner has any justification over another one. Custom dissolves into nothingness.

II.

Nausea appeared five years before Sartre's great book *Being and Nothingness*, and its philosophical adventures presage that later work. In both works, freedom is the issue at stake. Roquentin sees the terrible unfreedom of most people's lives. He believes himself to be free, but his freedom is without value, because his sense of life's randomness has robbed him of meaningful choice. Perhaps only at the end of the novel, when he appears to choose art and the life of the artist, does he make a meaningful, free choice. *Being and Nothingness* systematized the anguished paradoxes and ironies of *Nausea*. In it, Sartre argues that the self must be understood in relation to the world of things. The self wants to have the unthinking solidity of things (what Sartre calls the "*en-soi*," or "in-itself"). But the self is never simply itself, it is always "for itself," or "*pour-soi*." The self is nothing, has no meaning, though it is the source of all meanings. It desires to coincide with the unfree, unconscious nature of the *en-soi* but is unable to. Put more simply, the self is entirely free, unstable, and impermanent, and knows this. From this sense of absolute freedom is born anguish, a sense of dread. Thus the self will try to hide its liberty from itself, in acts of bad faith. Bad faith is the best proof, argues Sartre, that we are indeed free and that we know it.

Sartre's vision of humans as alone and perpetually deciding what kind of humans they will become—his sense of the doom and the responsibility of this burden—was popular in a Europe poisoned by war and stupefied by, shamed by, questions of responsibility and free will. In the political context of the post-war, it was as if Sartre's whole philosophy revealed that one is *never* simply—as the Nazi phrase had it—"acting on orders." His thought is both optimistic and anguished. It is anguished because he sees that we are sentenced by our freedom, imprisoned by it (since it makes us afraid); optimistic because Sartre believed that we *are* truly free and can indeed make free choices. Roquentin is in some sense a prototype of Sartre's later notion of the self. He is a *pour-soi* colliding with the *en-soi* of his surroundings, and he knows this. But his self-awareness seems to offer him no actual freedom. Not because, like his fellow-citizens, he runs away from freedom, but because he appears to having nothing to *do* with his freedom, nothing to commit it to. In some sense, his freedom has been corroded by his sense of his own freedom. (This paradox is best found in Sartre's comment that the French were most free while occupied by the Nazis.)

Only at the end of the novel does a chink of hope glance on this hero. Sitting in a café, about to depart for a new life in Paris (an utterly random and pointless gesture), he asks to hear again his favorite song, "Some of These Days." He scoffs, in his bourgeois-bating way, at the idea that music "consoles." Those idiots who go to hear Chopin or Wagner and emerge "refreshed"! But he begins to think about this melody sung by a black woman and written by a Jew. The tune is untouchable, in a sense. There is a scratch in the café's record, but the tune plays on, unaware of the scratch. This is because the melody exists beyond its record player, beyond the instruments that play it. "It is beyond ... it does not exist, because it has nothing superfluous: it is all the rest which in relation to it is superfluous. It *is*." The melody stays the same. And what about the man who wrote it? Doesn't Roquentin envy this man a little? Doesn't he wish that he himself had written this tune? Such people, he thinks, are a little like the dead, or the heroes of novels: "they have washed themselves of the sin of existing." Might it be possible to "justify your existence then? Just a little?" He reflects that this is the first time for years that he has been moved by the idea of a man.

Roquentin wonders if he could do the same as the man who wrote the tune. Not in music, but in the realm of art. Not a history book, because that is about what has existed, and existence is pointless, is not necessary. But perhaps an invented story, about something that has never existed: "It would have to be beautiful and hard as steel and make people ashamed of their existence.... A book. A novel." Roquentin's revelation is moving, because Sartre is delicate, artistically delicate. He stretches Roquentin's argument with himself over several pages, he does not hustle things. We believe in it as a process of thought.

Whether we believe in it as *thought* is another question. If this is Sartre's "solution" to the realization of pointlessness, and we must take it as such, it seems gestural only. Nor does it escape Roquentin's own earlier dismissal of those who take "consolation" in art. What is this but a bourgeois consolation in art, yet one merely performed at a slightly higher intellectual level than the passively bourgeois?

Camus reviewed *Nausea* when it appeared and, while dazzled by the book, disliked its philosophy. He did not make explicit his objection, but one can surmise that he disliked Sartre's fatalism. For Camus, the realization that life is absurd is the beginning of a stoic battle against that absurdity. Camus concluded, in *The Myth of Sisyphus*, that it was not acceptable for the absurd person to commit suicide, but that to live, and live rebelliously, "with my revolt, my freedom, and my passion," was the best way of both acknowledging and rejecting death. Sartre by contrast, at least in this novel, has got beyond—or never reaches—such a state of flushed challenge. In the park, Roquentin thinks about killing himself, but comes to the perfectly logical conclusion that given life's randomness, suicide too would be random, and thus meaningless: "But my death itself would have been superfluous." In other words. Roquentin is already dead, so why bother killing himself? Certainly, this would have seemed intensely fatalistic to Camus.

Although Camus argued that after God we create our own meaning, one feels that he never really believed in self-determination as absolutely as Sartre did. Camus continued to live under a religious shadow, wherein the battle was always with the terms handed to us by life—a secular version of man's battle with the Gods. Life was a religious sentence for Camus; he never quite relinquished the idea that meaning has left a residue of itself in the world. Sartre found Camus's religiosity frustrating, and said so; it was, along with political differences, one of the reasons for the break between the two men in the early 1950s. Sartre, though his language is sometimes religious, never had any time for religion. Camus was a tragic religionist, really; Sartre was, as he described himself, "a providential atheist."

Yet for all their differences, Camus and Sartre resemble each other most powerfully in the "solutions" they propose to the meaninglessness of existence. Roquentin thinks of writing a novel, and Camus tells us that we must fight life with our revolt, our freedom, and our passion. Are Camus's terms really any more stringent than Sartre's? Recall that Camus, in *The Myth of Sisyphus*, suggests that, in an effort to outwit the absurd, we might live various roles: as writer, as conqueror, as seducer, as actor. Is Roquentin any different, really? He fancies himself something of a traveler (whether he has actually been anywhere or not): thus, a conqueror. He fancies himself something of a lover, telling us cynically about the *patronne* of the café with whom he sleeps. He places his faith in the life of the writer. And his former lover Anny argues that when she was an actor, on the London stage, she experienced a series of "perfect moments," moments wherein she briefly outwitted the dragging arbitrariness of things. So *Nausea*, in fact, moves through most, if not all, of Camus's proposed categories of "salvation."

If Camus and Sartre resemble each other in this area, it is because it is impossible to "solve" the dilemma of the realization that "one cannot define existence as necessity," or that "there is absolutely no more reason for existing." Since both thinkers conclude that we must continue to live, both are pushed to logical contradiction: both have to furnish non-arbitrary or necessary reasons for continuing to live in an arbitrary or non-necessary world. Inevitably, they lack the theological consistency of another great thinker active at this time, Simone Weil, who believed in God and in the incarnation of Christ.

Both Sartre and Camus arrived at the idea that this life must be lived, in Camus's phrase, without appeal. But neither can prove that this *must* be the case. They can only suggest it, describe a suggestion. Both, finally, are forced into the realm of the gestural, the metaphorical. This is appropriate in the novel, for it is the language of art. It is not the language of the actual so much as of the possible—where "possible" means potential. It is the realm of active utopia. Camus, to my mind, was the deeper thinker, even if never the abler philosopher: his politics paid attention to actual conflict and did not fawn at the heels of tyranny and extremism; his philosophy, because it was so tinged with theology, encodes within itself a greater sympathy towards failure; because Camus stressed the struggle with life's terms rather than the pure capacity to choose, his thought touched, and touches, more lives than Sartre's. Paradoxically, though Sartre was not religious, he had an almost religious faith in man's ability to be free, to choose. This can give his work an unworldly air, and gives his later politics an unworldly monstrousness. Camus, the more religious thinker, was actually much more realistic about the tragic, constrained, Sisyphean nature of our ordinary daily imprisonment. Camus asked us to fight that imprisonment, if necessarily wearily and repetitively; Sartre hoped that we could simply explode the prison.

NAUSEA

Editors' Note

These notebooks were found among the papers of Antoine Roquentin. They are published without alteration.

The first sheet is undated, but there is good reason to believe it was written some weeks before the diary itself. Thus it would have been written around the beginning of January, 1932, at the latest.

At that time, Antoine Roquentin, after travelling through Central Europe, North Africa and the Far East, settled in Bouville for three years to conclude his historical research on the Marquis de Rollebon.

THE EDITORS

UNDATED PAGES

The best thing would be to write down events from day to day. Keep a diary to see clearly—let none of the nuances or small happenings escape even though they might seem to mean nothing. And above all, classify them. I must tell how I see this table, this street, the people, my packet of tobacco, since *those* are the things which have changed. I must determine the exact extent and nature of this change.

For instance, here is a cardboard box holding my bottle of ink. I should try to tell how I saw it *before* and now how I[1] Well, it's a parallelopiped rectangle, it opens—that's stupid, there's nothing I can say about it. This is what I have to avoid, I must not put in strangeness where there is none. I think that is the big danger in keeping a diary: you exaggerate everything. You continually force the truth because you're always looking for something. On the other hand, it is certain that from one minute to the next—and precisely *à propos* of this box or any other object at

[1] Word left out.

all I can recapture this impression of day-before-yesterday. I must always be ready, otherwise it will slip through my fingers. I must never[2] but carefully note and detail all that happens.

Naturally, I can write nothing definite about this Saturday and the day-before-yesterday business. I am already too far from it; the only thing I can say is that in neither case was there anything which could ordinarily be called an event. Saturday the children were playing ducks and drakes and, like them, I wanted to throw a stone into the sea. Just at that moment I stopped, dropped the stone and left. Probably I looked somewhat foolish or absent-minded, because the children laughed behind my back.

So much for external things. What has happened inside of me has not left any clear traces. I saw something which disgusted me, but I no longer know whether it was the sea or the stone. The stone was flat and dry, especially on one side, damp and muddy on the other. I held it by the edges with my fingers wide apart so as not to get them dirty.

Day before yesterday was much more complicated. And there was also this series of coincidences, of *quid-pro-quos* that I can't explain to myself. But I'm not going to spend my time putting all that down on paper. Anyhow, it was certain that I was afraid or had some other feeling of that sort. If I had only known what I was afraid of, I would have made a great step forward.

The strangest thing is that I am not at all inclined to call myself insane, I clearly see that I am not: all these changes concern objects. At least, that is what I'd like to be sure of.

10.30[1]

Perhaps it was a passing moment of madness after all. There is no trace of it any more. My odd feelings of the other week seem to me quite ridiculous today: I can no longer enter into them. I am quite at ease this evening, quite solidly *terre-à-terre* in the world. Here is my room facing north-east. Below the Rue des Mutilés and the construction-yard of the new station. From my window I see the red and white flame of the "Railwaymen's Rendezvous" at the corner of the Boulevard Victor-Noir. The Paris train has just come in. People are coming out of the old station

[2] Word crossed out (possibly "force" or "forge"), another word added above, is illegible.
[1] Evidently in the evening. The following paragraph is much later than the preceding ones. We are inclined to believe it was written the following day at the earliest.

and spreading into the streets. I hear steps and voices. A lot of people are waiting for the last tramway. They must make a sad little group around the street light just under my window. Well, they have a few minutes more to wait: the tram won't pass before 10.45. I hope no commercial travellers will come to-night: I have such a desire to sleep and am so much behind in my sleep. A good night, one good night and all this nonsense will be swept away.

Ten forty-five: nothing more to fear, they would be here already. Unless it's the day for the man from Rouen. He comes every week. They reserve No. 2, on the second floor for him, the room with a bidet. He might still show up: he often drinks a beer at the "Railwaymen's Rendezvous" before going to bed. But he doesn't make too much noise. He is very small and clean with a waxed, black moustache and a wig. Here he is now.

Well, when I heard him come up the stairs, it gave me quite a thrill, it was so reassuring: what is there to fear in such a regular world? I think I am cured.

Here is tramway number seven, *Abattoirs-Grands Bassins*. It stops with a clank of iron rails. It's leaving again. Now loaded with suitcases and sleeping children, it's heading towards Grands Bassins, towards the factories in the black East. It's the next to the last tramway; the last one will go by in an hour.

I'm going to bed. I'm cured. I'll give up writing my daily impressions, like a little girl in her nice new notebook.

In one case only it might be interesting to keep a diary: it would be if . . .[1]

---

[1] The text of the undated pages ends here.

Monday, 29 January, 1932:
Something has happened to me, I can't doubt it any more. It came as an illness does, not like an ordinary certainty, not like anything evident. It came cunningly, little by little; I felt a little strange, a little put out, that's all. Once established it never moved, it stayed quiet, and I was able to persuade myself that nothing was the matter with me, that it was a false alarm. And now, it's blossoming.

I don't think the historian's trade is much given to psychological analysis. In our work we have to do only with sentiments in the whole to which we give generic titles such as Ambition and Interest. And yet if I had even a shadow of self-knowledge, I could put it to good use now.

For instance, there is something new about my hands, a certain way of picking up my pipe or fork. Or else it's the fork which now has a certain way of having itself picked up, I don't know. A little while ago, just as I was coming into my room, I stopped short because I felt in my hand a cold object which held my attention through a sort of personality. I opened my hand, looked: I was simply holding the door-knob. This morning in the library, when the Self-Taught Man[1] came to say good morning to me, it took me ten seconds to recognize him. I saw an unknown face, barely a face. Then there was his hand like a fat white worm in my own hand. I dropped it almost immediately and the arm fell back flabbily.

There are a great number of suspicious noises in the streets, too.

So a change *has* taken place during these last few weeks. But where? It is an abstract change without object. Am I the one who has changed? If not, then it is this room, this city and this nature; I must choose.

* * * * *

I think I'm the one who has changed: that's the simplest solution. Also the most unpleasant. But I must finally realize

[1] Ogier P . . . , who will be often mentioned in this journal. He was a bailiff's clerk. Roquentin met him in 1930 in the Bouville library.

that I am subject to these sudden transformations. The thing is that I rarely think; a crowd of small metamorphoses accumulate in me without my noticing it, and then, one fine day, a veritable revolution takes place. This is what has given my life such a jerky, incoherent aspect. For instance, when I left France, there were a lot of people who said I left for a whim. And when I suddenly came back after six years of travelling, they still could call it a whim. I see myself with Mercier again in the office of that French functionary who resigned after the Petrou business last year. Mercier was going to Bengal on an archeological mission. I always wanted to go to Bengal and he pressed me to go with him. Now I wonder why. I don't think he was too sure of Portal and was counting on me to keep an eye on him. I saw no reason to refuse. And even if I had suspected that little deal with Portal, it would have been one more reason to accept with enthusiasm. Well, I was paralysed, I couldn't say a word. I was staring at a little Khmer statuette on a green carpet, next to a telephone. I seemed to be full of lymph or warm milk. With angelic patience veiling a slight irritation, Mercier told me:

"Now look, I have to be officially fixed up. I know you'll end up by saying yes, so you might as well accept right away."

He had a reddish-black beard, heavily scented. I got a waft of perfume at each movement of his head. And then, suddenly, I woke from a six-year slumber.

The statue seemed to me unpleasant and stupid and I felt terribly, deeply bored. I couldn't understand why I was in Indo-China. What was I doing there? Why was I talking to these people? Why was I dressed so oddly? My passion was dead. For years it had rolled over and submerged me; now I felt empty. But that wasn't the worst: before me, posed with a sort of indolence, was a voluminous, insipid idea. I did not see clearly what it was, but it sickened me so much I couldn't look at it. All that was confused with the perfume of Mercier's beard.

I pulled myself together, convulsed with anger, and answered dryly:

"Thank you, but I believe I've travelled enough, I must go back to France now." Two days later I took the boat for Marseilles.

If I am not mistaken, if all the signs which have been amassed are precursors of a new overthrow in my life, well then I am terrified. It isn't that my life is rich, or weighty or precious. But I'm afraid of what will be born and take possession of me—

and drag me—where? Shall I have to go off again, leaving my research, my book and everything else unfinished? Shall I awake in a few months, in a few years, broken, deceived, in the midst of new ruins? I would like to see the truth clearly before it is too late.

Tuesday, 30 January:

Nothing new.

I worked from nine till one in the library. I got Chapter XII started and all that concerns Rollebon's stay in Russia up to the death of Paul I. This work is finished: nothing more to do with it until the final revision.

It is one-thirty. I am eating a sandwich in the Café Mably, everything is more or less normal. Anyway, everything is always normal in cafés and especially the Café Mably, because of the manager, M. Fasquelle, who has a raffish look which is positively reassuring. It will soon be time for his nap and his eyes are pink already, but he stays quick and decisive. He strolls among the tables and speaks confidently to the customers.

"Is everything all right, Monsieur?"

I smile at seeing him thus; when his place empties his head empties too. From two to four the café is deserted, then M. Fasquelle takes a few dazed steps, the waiters turn out the lights and he slips into unconsciousness: when this man is lonely he sleeps.

There are still about twenty customers left, bachelors, small-time engineers, office employees. They eat hurriedly in boarding-houses which they call their *"popotes"* and, since they need a little luxury, they come here after their meals. They drink a cup of coffee and play poker dice; they make a little noise, an inconsistent noise which doesn't bother me. In order to exist, they also must consort with others.

I live alone, entirely alone. I never speak to anyone, never; I receive nothing, I give nothing. The Self-Taught Man doesn't count. There is Françoise, the woman who runs the "Railway-men's Rendezvous." But do I speak to her? Sometimes after dinner, when she brings my beer, I ask her:

"Have you time this evening?"

She never says no and I follow her into one of the big rooms on the second floor she rents by the hour or by the day. I do not pay her: our need is mutual. She takes pleasure in it (she has to have a man a day and she has many more besides me) and thus I purge myself of a certain nostalgia the cause of which I know too well. But we hardly speak. What good is it? Every man for himself: besides, as far as she's concerned, I am preeminently a customer in her café. Taking off her dress, she tells me:

"Say, have you ever heard of that apéritif, *Bricot?* Because there are two customers who asked for some this week. The girl didn't know and she came to ask me. They were commercial travellers, they must have drunk that in Paris. But I don't like to buy without knowing. I'll keep my stockings on if you don't mind."

In the past—even a long while after she left me—I thought about Anny. Now I think of no one any more. I don't even bother looking for words. It flows in me, more or less quickly. I fix nothing, I let it go. Through the lack of attaching myself to words, my thoughts remain nebulous most of the time. They sketch vague, pleasant shapes and then are swallowed up: I forget them almost immediately.

I marvel at these young people: drinking their coffee, they tell clear, plausible stories. If they are asked what they did yesterday, they aren't embarrassed: they bring you up to date in a few words. If I were in their place, I'd fall over myself. It's true that no one has bothered about how I spend my time for a long while. When you live alone you no longer know what it is to tell something: the plausible disappears at the same time as the friends.

You let events flow past; suddenly you see people pop up who speak and who go away, you plunge into stories without beginning or end: you'd make a terrible witness. But in compensation, one misses nothing, no improbability or story too tall to be believed in cafés. For example, Saturday, about four in the afternoon, on the end of the timbered sidewalk of the new station yard, a little woman in sky blue was running backwards, laughing, waving a handkerchief. At the same time, a Negro in a cream-coloured raincoat, yellow shoes and a green hat, turned the corner of the street and whistled. Still going backwards, the woman bumped into him, underneath a lantern which hangs on a paling and which is lit at night. All at once there was the paling smelling strongly of wet wood, this lantern and this little blonde woman in the Negro's arms under a sky the colour of fire. If there had been four or five of us, I suppose we would have noticed the jolt, the soft colours, the beautiful blue coat that looked like an eiderdown quilt, the light raincoat, the red panes of the lantern; we would have laughed at the stupefaction which appeared on those two childish faces.

A man rarely feels like laughing alone: the whole thing was animated enough for me, but it was a strong, even a fierce, yet pure sensation. Then everything came asunder, there was nothing left but the lantern, the palisade and the sky; it was still rather beautiful. An hour later the lantern was lit, the wind blew, the sky was black; nothing at all was left.

All that is nothing new; I have never resisted these harmless emotions; far from it. You must be just a little bit lonely in order to feel them, just lonely enough to get rid of plausibility at the proper time. But I remained close to people, on the surface of solitude, quite resolved to take refuge in their midst in case of emergency. Up to now I was an amateur at heart.

Everywhere, now, there are objects like this glass of beer on the table there. When I see it, I feel like saying: "Enough." I realize quite well that I have gone too far. I don't suppose you can "take sides" with solitude. That doesn't mean that I look under my bed before going to sleep, or think I see the door of my room open suddenly in the middle of the night. Still, somehow I am not at peace: I have been *avoiding* looking at this glass of beer for half an hour. I look above, below, right and left; but I don't want to see *it*. And I know very well that all these bachelors around me can be of no help: it is too late, I can no longer take refuge among them. They could come and tap me on the shoulder and say, "Well, what's the matter with that glass of beer?" It's just like all the others. It's bevelled on the edges, has a handle, a little coat of arms with a spade on it and on the coat of arms is written "Spartenbrau," I know all that, but I know there is something else. Almost nothing. But I can't explain what I see. To anyone. There: I am quietly slipping into the water's depths, towards fear.

I am alone in the midst of these happy, reasonable voices. All these creatures spend their time explaining, realizing happily that they agree with each other. In Heaven's name, why is it so important to think the same things all together. It's enough to see the face they make when one of these fishy-eyed men with an inward look and with whom no agreement is possible, passes them. When I was eight years old and used to play in the Luxembourg gardens there was a man who came and sat in a sentry-box, against the iron fence which runs along the Rue Auguste-Comte. He did not speak but from time to time stretched out his leg and

8

looked at his foot fearfully. The foot was encased in a boot, but the other one was in a slipper. The guard told my uncle that the man was a former proctor. They retired him because he used to come, dressed up as an academician, to read the school term marks. We had a horrible fear of him because we sensed he was alone. One day he smiled at Robert, holding out his arms to him from a distance: Robert almost fainted. It wasn't this creature's poverty-stricken look which frightened us, nor the tumour he had on his neck that rubbed against the edge of his collar: but we felt that he was shaping thoughts of crab or lobster in his head. And that terrified us, the fact that one could conjure thoughts of lobsters on the sentry-box, on our hoops, on the bushes.

Is that what awaits me then? For the first time I am disturbed at being alone. I would like to tell someone what is happening to me before it is too late and before I start frightening little boys. I wish Anny were here.

This is odd: I have just filled up ten pages and I haven't told the truth—at least, not the whole truth. I was writing "Nothing new" with a bad conscience: as a matter of fact I boggled at bringing out a quite harmless little incident. "Nothing new." I admire the way we can lie, putting reason on our side. Evidently, nothing new has happened, if you care to put it that way: this morning at eight-fifteen, just as I was leaving the Hotel Printania to go to the library, I wanted to and could not pick up a paper lying on the ground. This is all and it is not even an event. Yes —but, to tell the whole truth, I was deeply impressed by it: I felt I was no longer free. I tried unsuccessfully to get rid of this idea at the library. I wanted to escape from it at the Café Mably. I hoped it would disappear in the bright light. But it stayed there, like a dead weight inside me. It is responsible for the preceding pages.

Why didn't I mention it? It must be out of pride, and then, too, a little out of awkwardness. I am not in the habit of telling myself what happens to me, so I cannot quite recapture the succession of events, I cannot distinguish what is important. But now it is finished: I have re-read what I wrote in the Café Mably and I am ashamed; I want no secrets or soul-states, nothing ineffable; I am neither virgin nor priest enough to play with the inner life.

There is nothing much to say: I could not pick up the paper, that's all.

I very much like to pick up chestnuts, old rags and especially papers. It is pleasant to me to pick them up, to close my hand on them; with a little encouragement I would carry them to my mouth the way children do. Anny went into a white rage when I picked up the corners of heavy, sumptuous papers, probably soiled by excrement. In summer or the beginning of autumn, you can find remnants of sun-baked newspapers in gardens, dry and fragile as dead leaves, so yellow you might think they had been washed with picric acid. In winter, some pages are pounded to pulp; crushed, stained, they return to the earth. Others quite new when covered with ice, all white, all throbbing, are like swans about to fly, but the earth has already caught them from below. They twist and tear themselves from the mud, only to be finally flattened out a little further on. It is good to pick up all that. Sometimes I simply feel them, looking at them closely; other times I tear them to hear their drawn-out crackling, or, if they are damp, I light them, not without difficulty; then I wipe my muddy hands on a wall or tree trunk.

So, today, I was watching the riding boots of a cavalry officer who was leaving his barracks. As I followed them with my eyes, I saw a piece of paper lying beside a puddle. I thought the officer was going to crush the paper into the mud with his heel, but no: he straddled paper and puddle in a single step. I went up to it: it was a lined page, undoubtedly torn from a school notebook. The rain had drenched and twisted it, it was covered with blisters and swellings like a burned hand. The red line of the margin was smeared into a pink splotch; ink had run in places. The bottom of the page disappeared beneath a crust of mud. I bent down, already rejoicing at the touch of this pulp, fresh and tender, which I should roll in my fingers into greyish balls

I was unable.

I stayed bent down for a second, I read "Dictation: The White Owl," then I straightened up, empty-handed. I am no longer free, I can no longer do what I will.

Objects should not *touch* because they are not alive. You use them, put them back in place, you live among them: they are useful, nothing more. But they touch me, it is unbearable. I am afraid of being in contact with them as though they were living beasts.

Now I see: I recall better what I felt the other day at the seashore when I held the pebble. It was a sort of sweetish sickness. How unpleasant it was! It came from the stone, I'm sure of it, it passed from the stone to my hand. Yes, that's it, that's just it—a sort of nausea in the hands.

Thursday morning in the library:

A little while ago, going down the hotel stairs, I heard Lucie, who, for the hundredth time, was complaining to the landlady, while polishing the steps. The proprietress spoke with difficulty, using short sentences, because she had not put in her false teeth; she was almost naked, in a pink dressing-gown and Turkish slippers. Lucie was dirty, as usual; from time to time she stopped rubbing and straightened up on her knees to look at the proprietress. She spoke without pausing, reasonably:

"I'd like it a hundred times better if he went with other women," she said, "it wouldn't make the slightest difference to me, so long as it didn't do him any harm."

She was talking about her husband: at forty this swarthy little woman had offered herself and her savings to a handsome young man, a fitter in the Usines Lecointe. She has an unhappy home life. Her husband does not beat her, is not unfaithful to her, but he drinks, he comes home drunk every evening. He's burning his candle at both ends; in three months I have seen him turn yellow and melt away. Lucie thinks it is drink. I believe he is tubercular.

"You have to take the upper hand," Lucie said.

It gnaws at her, I'm sure of it, but slowly, patiently: she takes the upper hand, she is able neither to console herself nor abandon herself to her suffering. She thinks about it a little bit, a very little bit, now and again she passes it on. Especially when she is with people, because they console her and also because it comforts her a little to talk about it with poise, with an air of giving advice. When she is alone in the rooms I hear her humming to keep herself from thinking. But she is morose all day, suddenly weary and sullen.

"It's there," she says, touching her throat, "it won't go down."

She suffers as a miser. She must be miserly with her pleasures, as well. I wonder if sometimes she doesn't wish she were free of this monotonous sorrow, of these mutterings which start as soon as she stops singing, if she doesn't wish to suffer once and for all, to drown herself in despair. In any case, it would be impossible for her: she is bound.

Thursday afternoon:

"M. de Rollebon was quite ugly. Queen Marie Antoinette called him her 'dear ape.' Yet he had all the ladies of the court, but not by clowning like Voisenon the baboon: but by a magnetism which carried his lovely victims to the worst excesses of passion. He intrigues, plays a fairly suspect role in the affair of the Queen's necklace and disappears in 1790, after having dealings with Mirabeau-Tonneau and Nerciat. He turns up again in Russia where he attempts to assassinate Paul I, and from there, he travels to the farthest countries; the Indies, China, Turkestan. He smuggles, plots, spies. In 1813 he returns to Paris. By 1816, he has become all-powerful: he is the sole confidant of the Duchess d'Angoulême. This capricious old woman, obsessed by horrible childhood memories, grows calm and smiles when she sees him. Through her, he works his will at court. In March 1820, he marries Mlle de Roquelaure, a very beautiful girl of eighteen. M. de Rollebon is seventy; he is at the height of distinction, at the apogee of his life. Seven months later, accused of treason, he is arrested, thrown into a cell, where he dies after five years of imprisonment, without ever being brought to trial."

I re-read with melancholy this note of Germain Berger.[1]

It was by those few lines that I first knew M. de Rollebon. How attractive he seemed and how I loved him after these few words! It is for him, for this mannikin that I am here. When I came back from my trip I could just as well have settled down in Paris or Marseilles. But most of the documents concerning the Marquis' long stays in France are in the municipal library of Bouville. Rollebon was the *Lord of the Manor of Marmommes*. Before the war, you could still find one of his descendants in this little town, an architect named Rollebon-Campouyre', who, at his death in 1912, left an important legacy to the Bouville library: letters of the Marquis, the fragment of a journal, and all sorts of papers. I have not yet gone through it all.

I am glad to have found these notes. I had not read them for ten years. My handwriting has changed, or so it seems to me; I used to write in a smaller hand. How I loved M. de Rollebon that year! I remember one evening—a Tuesday evening: I had worked all day in the Mazarine; I had just gathered, from his correspondence, of 1789–90, in what a magisterial way he duped

[1] Editor's Footnote: Germain Berger: *Mirabeau-Tonneau et ses amis*, page 406, note 2. Champion 1906.

Nerciat. It was dark, I was going down the Avenue du Maine and I bought some chestnuts at the corner of the Rue de la Gaîté. Was I happy! I laughed all by myself thinking of the face Nerciat must have made when he came back from Germany. The face of the Marquis is like this ink: it has paled considerably since I have worked over it.

In the first place, starting from 1801, I understand nothing more about his conduct. It is not the lack of documents: letters, fragments of memoirs, secret reports, police records. On the contrary I have almost too many of them. What is lacking in all this testimony is firmness and consistency. They do not contradict each other, neither do they agree with each other; they do not seem to be about the same person. And yet other historians work from the same sources of information. How do they do it? Am I more scrupulous or less intelligent? In any case, the question leaves me completely cold. In truth, what am I looking for? I don't know. For a long time, Rollebon the man has interested me more than the book to be written. But now, the man . . . the man begins to bore me. It is the book which attracts me. I feel more and more need to write—in the same proportion as I grow old, you might say.

Evidently it must be admitted that Rollebon took an active part in the assassination of Paul I, that he then accepted an extremely important espionage mission to the Orient from the Czar and constantly betrayed Alexander to the advantage of Napoleon. At the same time he was able to carry on an active correspondence with the Comte d'Artois and send him unimportant information in order to convince him of his fidelity: none of all that is improbable; Fouché, at the same time, was playing a comedy much more dangerous and complex. Perhaps the Marquis also carried on a rifle-supplying business with the Asiatic principalities for his own profit.

Well, yes: he could have done all that, but it is not proved: I am beginning to believe that nothing can ever be proved. These are honest hypotheses which take the facts into account: but I sense so definitely that they come from me, and that they are simply a way of unifying my own knowledge. Not a glimmer comes from Rollebon's side. Slow, lazy, sulky, the facts adapt themselves to the rigour of the order I wish to give them; but it remains outside of them. I have the feeling of doing a work of pure imagination. And I am certain that the characters in a novel would have a more genuine appearance, or, in any case, would be more agreeable.

Friday:

Three o'clock. Three o'clock is always too late or too early for anything you want to do. An odd moment in the afternoon. Today it is intolerable.

A cold sun whitens the dust on the window-panes. Pale sky clouded with white. The gutters were frozen this morning.

I ruminate heavily near the gas stove; I know in advance the day is lost. I shall do nothing good, except, perhaps, after nightfall. It is because of the sun; it ephemerally touches the dirty white wisps of fog, which float in the air above the construction-yards, it flows into my room, all gold, all pale, it spreads four dull, false reflections on my table.

My pipe is daubed with a golden varnish which first catches the eye by its bright appearance; you look at it and the varnish melts, nothing is left but a great dull streak on a piece of wood. Everything is like that, everything, even my hands. When the sun begins shining like that the best thing to do is go to bed. Only I slept like a log last night, and I am not sleepy.

I liked yesterday's sky so much, a narrow sky, black with rain, pushing against the windows like a ridiculous, touching face. This sun is not ridiculous, quite the contrary. On everything I like, on the rust of the construction girders, on the rotten boards of the fence, a miserly, uncertain light falls, like the look you give, after a sleepless night, on decisions made with enthusiasm the day before, on pages you have written in one spurt without crossing out a word. The four cafés on the Boulevard Victor-Noir, shining in the night, side by side, and which are much more than cafés—aquariums, ships, stars or great white eyes—have lost their ambiguous charm.

A perfect day to turn back to one's self: these cold clarities which the sun projects like a judgment shorn of pity, over all creatures—enter through my eyes; I am illuminated within by a diminishing light. I am sure that fifteen minutes would be enough to reach supreme self-contempt. No thank you, I want none of that. Neither shall I re-read what I wrote yesterday on Rollebon's stay in St. Petersburg. I stay seated, my arms hanging, or write a few words, without courage: I yawn, I wait for night to come. When it is dark, the objects and I will come out of limbo.

Did Rollebon, or did he not, participate in the assassination of Paul I? That is the question for today: I am that far and can't go on without deciding.

According to Tcherkoff, he was paid by Count Pahlen. Most of the other conspirators, Tcherkoff says, were content with deposing and imprisoning the Czar. In fact, Alexander seems to have been a partisan of that solution. But Pahlen, it was alleged, wanted to do away with Paul completely, and M. de Rollebon was charged with persuading the individual conspirators to the assassination.

"He visited each one of them and, with an incomparable power, mimed the scene which was to take place. Thus he caused to be born or developed in them a madness for murder."

But I suspect Tcherkoff. He is not a reasonable witness, he is a half-mad, sadistic magician: he turns everything into the demoniacal. I cannot see M. de Rollebon in this melodramatic role or as mimic of the assassination scene! Never on your life! He is cold, not carried away: he exposes nothing, he insinuates, and his method, pale and colourless, can succeed only with men of his own level, intriguers accessible to reason, politicians.

"Adhèmar de Rollebon," writes Mme de Charrières, "painted nothing with words, made no gestures, never altered the tone of his voice. He kept his eyes half-closed and one could barely make out, between his lashes, the lowest rim of his grey iris. It has only been within the past few years that I dare confess he bored me beyond all possible limits. He spoke a little in the way Abbé Mably used to write."

And this is the man who, by his talent for mimicry? . . . But then how was he able to charm women? Then there is this curious story Ségur reports and which seems true to me.

"In 1787, at an inn near Moulins, an old man was dying, a friend of Diderot, trained by the philosophers. The priests of the neighbourhood were nonplussed: they had tried everything in vain; the good man would have no last rites, he was a pantheist. M. de Rollebon, who was passing by and who believed in nothing, bet the Curé of Moulins that he would need less than two hours to bring the sick man back to Christian sentiments. The Curé took the bet and lost: Rollebon began at three in the morning, the sick man confessed at five and died at seven. "Are you so forceful in argument?" asked the Curé, "You outdo even us." "I did not argue," answered M. de Rollebon, "I made him fear Hell."

How did he take an effective part in the assassination? That evening, one of his officer friends conducted him to his door. If he had gone out again, how could he have crossed St. Petersburg without trouble? Paul, half-insane, had given the order that after nine o'clock at night, all passers except midwives and doctors were to be arrested. Can we believe the absurd legend that Rollebon disguised himself as a midwife to get as far as the palace? After all, he was quite capable of it. In any case, he was not at home on the night of the assassination, that seems proved. Alexander must have suspected him strongly, since one of his official acts was to send the Marquis away on the vague pretext of a mission to the Far East.

M. de Rollebon bores me to tears. I get up. I move through this pale light; I see it change beneath my hands and on the sleeves of my coat: I cannot describe how much it disgusts me. I yawn. I light the lamp on the table: perhaps its light will be able to combat the light of day. But no: the lamp makes nothing more than a pitiful pond around its base. I turn it out; I get up. There is a white hole in the wall, a mirror. It is a trap. I know I am going to let myself be caught in it. I have. The grey thing appears in the mirror. I go over and look at it, I can no longer get away.

It is the reflection of my face. Often in these lost days I study it. I can understand nothing of this face. The faces of others have some sense, some direction. Not mine. I cannot even decide whether it is handsome or ugly. I think it is ugly because I have been told so. But it doesn't strike me. At heart, I am even shocked that anyone can attribute qualities of this kind to it, as if you called a clod of earth or a block of stone beautiful or ugly.

Still, there is one thing which is pleasing to see, above the flabby cheeks, above the forehead; it is the beautiful red flame which crowns my head, it is my hair. That is pleasant to see. Anyhow, it is a definite colour: I am glad I have red hair. There it is in the mirror, it makes itself seen, it shines. I am still lucky: if my forehead was surmounted by one of those neutral heads of hair which are neither chestnut nor blond, my face would be lost in vagueness, it would make me dizzy.

My glance slowly and wearily travels over my forehead, my cheeks: it finds nothing firm, it is stranded. Obviously there are a nose, two eyes and a mouth, but none of it makes sense, there is not even a human expression. Yet Anny and Vélines thought I looked so alive: perhaps I am too used to my face. When I was little, my Aunt Bigeois told me "If you look at yourself too long in the mirror, you'll see a monkey." I must have looked at myself even longer than that: what I see is well below the monkey, on the fringe of the vegetable world, at the level of jellyfish. It is alive, I can't say it isn't; but this was not the life that Anny contemplated: I see a slight tremor, I see the insipid flesh blossoming and palpitating with abandon. The eyes especially are horrible seen so close. They are glassy, soft, blind, red-rimmed, they look like fish scales.

I lean all my weight on the porcelain ledge, I draw my face closer until it touches the mirror. The eyes, nose and mouth disappear: nothing human is left. Brown wrinkles show on each side of the feverish swelled lips, crevices, mole holes. A silky white down covers the great slopes of the cheeks, two hairs protrude from the nostrils: it is a geological embossed map. And, in spite of everything, this lunar world is familiar to me. I cannot say I *recognize* the details. But the whole thing gives me an impression of something seen before which stupefies me: I slip quietly off to sleep.

I would like to take hold of myself: an acute, vivid sensation would deliver me. I plaster my left hand against my cheek, I pull the skin; I grimace at myself. An entire half of my face yields, the left half of the mouth twists and swells, uncovering a tooth, the eye opens on a white globe, on pink, bleeding flesh. That is not what I was looking for: nothing strong, nothing new; soft, flaccid, stale! I go to sleep with my eyes open, already the face is growing larger, growing in the mirror, an immense, light halo gliding in the light. . . .

I lose my balance and that wakes me. I find myself straddling a chair, still dazed. Do other men have as much difficulty in appraising their face? It seems that I see my own as I feel my body, through a dumb, organic sense. But the others? Rollebon, for example, was he also put to sleep by looking in the mirror at what Mme de Genlis calls "his small, wrinkled countenance, clean and sharp, all pitted with smallpox, in which there was a strange malice which caught the eye, no matter what effort he made to dissemble it? He took," she adds, "great care with his coiffure and I never saw him without his wig. But his cheeks were blue, verging on black, owing to his heavy beard which he shaved himself, not being at all expert. It was his custom to wash his face with white lead, in the manner of

Grimm. M. de Dangeville said that with all this white and all this blue he looked like a Roquefort cheese".

It seems to me he must have been quite pleasing. But, after all, this is not the way he appeared to Mme de Charrières. I believe she found him rather worn. Perhaps it is impossible to understand one's own face. Or perhaps it is because I am a single man? People who live in society have learned how to see themselves in mirrors as they appear to their friends. I have no friends. Is that why my flesh is so naked? You might say—yes you might say, nature without humanity.

I have no taste for work any longer, I can do nothing more except wait for night.

5.30:

Things are bad! Things are very bad: I have it, the filth, the Nausea. And this time it is new: it caught me in a café. Until now cafés were my only refuge because they were full of people and well lighted: now there won't even be that any more; when I am run to earth in my room, I shan't know where to go.

I was coming to make love but no sooner had I opened the door than Madeleine, the waitress, called to me:

"The patronne isn't here, she's in town shopping."

I felt a sharp disappointment in the sexual parts, a long, disagreeable tickling. At the same time I felt my shirt rubbing against my breasts and I was surrounded, seized by a slow, coloured mist, and a whirlpool of lights in the smoke, in the mirrors, in the booths glowing at the back of the café, and I couldn't see why it was there or why it was like that. I was on the doorstep, I hesitated to go in and then there was a whirlpool, an eddy, a shadow passed across the ceiling and I felt myself pushed forward. I floated, dazed by luminous fogs dragging me in all directions at once. Madeleine came floating over to take off my overcoat and I noticed she had drawn her hair back and put on earrings: I did not recognize her. I looked at her large cheeks which never stopped rushing towards the ears. In the hollow of the cheeks, beneath the cheekbones, there were two pink stains which seemed weary on this poor flesh. The cheeks ran, ran towards the ears and Madeleine smiled:

"What will you have, Monsieur Antoine?"

Then the Nausea seized me, I dropped to a seat, I no longer knew where I was; I saw the colours spin slowly around me,

I wanted to vomit. And since that time, the Nausea has not left me, it holds me.

I paid, Madeleine took away my saucer. My glass crushes a puddle of yellow beer against the marble table top, a bubble floating in it. The bottom of my seat is broken and in order not to slide, I am compelled to press my heels firmly against the ground; it is cold. On the right, they are playing cards on a woollen cloth. I did not see them when I came in: I simply felt there was a warm packet, half on the seat, half on the table in the back, with pairs of waving arms. Afterwards, Madeleine brought them cards, the cloth and chips in a wooden bowl. There are three or five of them, I don't know, I haven't the courage to look at them. I have a broken spring: I can move my eyes but not my head. The head is all pliable and elastic, as though it had been simply set on my neck; if I turn it, it will fall off. All the same, I hear a short breath and from time to time, out of the corner of my eye I see a reddish flash covered with hair. It is a hand.

When the patronne goes shopping her cousin replaces her at the bar. His name is Adolphe. I began looking at him as I sat down and I have kept on because I cannot turn my head. He is in shirtsleeves, with purple suspenders; he has rolled the sleeves of his shirt above the elbows. The suspenders can hardly be seen against the blue shirt, they are all obliterated, buried in the blue, but it is false humility; in fact, they will not let themselves be forgotten, they annoy me by their sheep-like stubbornness, as if, starting to become purple, they stopped somewhere along the way without giving up their pretentions. You feel like saying, "All right, *become* purple and let's hear no more about it." But now, they stay in suspense, stubborn in their defeat. Sometimes the blue which surrounds them slips over and covers them completely: I stay an instant without seeing them. But it is merely a passing wave, soon the blue pales in places and I see the small island of hesitant purple reappear, grow larger, rejoin and reconstitute the suspenders. Cousin Adolphe has no eyes: his swollen, retracted eyelids open only on a little of the whites. He smiles sleepily; from time to time he snorts, yelps and writhes feebly, like a dreaming dog.

His blue cotton shirt stands out joyfully against a chocolate-coloured wall. That too brings on the Nausea. The Nausea is not inside me: I feel it *out there* in the wall, in the suspenders, everywhere around me. It makes itself one with the café, I am the one who is within *it*.

On my right, the warm packet begins to rustle, it waves its pair of arms.

"Here, there's your trump—what are trumps?" Black neck bent over the game: "Hahaha! What? He's just played trumps." "I don't know, I didn't see . . ." "Yes I played trumps just now." "Ah, good, hearts are trumps then." He intones: "Hearts are trumps, hearts are trumps, hea-arts are trumps." Spoken: "What is it, Sir? What is it, Sir? I take it!"

Again, silence—the taste of sugar in the air at the back of my throat. The smells. The suspenders.

The cousin has got up, and taken a few steps, put his hands behind his back, smiling, raising his head and leaning back on his heels. He goes to sleep in this position. He is there, oscillating, always smiling: his cheeks tremble. He is going to fall. He bends backwards, bends, bends, the face turned completely up to the ceiling, then just as he is about to fall, he catches himself adroitly on the ledge of the bar and regains his balance. After which, he starts again. I have enough, I call the waitress:

"Madeleine, if you please, play something on the phonograph. The one I like, you know: *Some of these days.*"

"Yes, but maybe that'll bother these gentlemen; these gentlemen don't like music when they're playing. But I'll ask them."

I make a great effort and turn my head. There are four of them. She bends over a congested old man who wears black-rimmed eyeglasses on the end of his nose. He hides his cards against his chest and glances at me from under the glasses.

"Go ahead, Monsieur."

Smiles. His teeth are rotten. The red hand does not belong to him, it is his neighbour's, a fellow with a black moustache. This fellow with the moustache has enormous nostrils that could pump air for a whole family and that eat up half his face, but in spite of that, he breathes through his mouth, gasping a little. With them there is also a young man with a face like a dog. I cannot make out the fourth player.

The cards fall on the woollen cloth, spinning. The hands with ringed fingers come and pick them up, scratching the cloth with their nails. The hands make white splotches on the cloth, they look puffed up and dusty. Other cards fall, the hands go and come. What an odd occupation: it doesn't look like a game or a rite, or a habit. I think they do it to pass the time, nothing more. But time is too large, it can't be filled up. Everything you plunge into it is stretched and disintegrates. That gesture, for instance, the red hand picking up the cards and fumbling: it is all flabby. It would have to be ripped apart and tailored inside.

Madeleine turns the crank on the phonograph. I only hope she has not made a mistake; that she hasn't put on *Cavalleria Rusticana*, as she did the other day. But no, this is it, I recognize the melody from the very first bars. It is an old rag-time with a vocal refrain. I heard American soldiers whistle it in 1917 in the streets of LaRochelle. It must date from before the War. But the recording is much more recent. Still, it is the oldest record in the collection, a Pathé record for sapphire needle.

The vocal chorus will be along shortly: I like that part especially and the abrupt manner in which it throws itself forward, like a cliff against the sea. For the moment, the jazz is playing; there is no melody, only notes, a myriad of tiny jolts. They know no rest, an inflexible order gives birth to them and destroys them without even giving them time to recuperate and exist for themselves. They race, they press forward, they strike me a sharp blow in passing and are obliterated. I would like to hold them back, but I know if I succeeded in stopping one it would remain between my fingers only as a raffish languishing sound. I must accept their death; I must even *will* it. I know few impressions stronger or more harsh.

I grow warm, I begin to feel happy. There is nothing extraordinary in this, it is a small happiness of Nausea: it spreads at the bottom of the viscous puddle, at the bottom of *our* time—the time of purple suspenders and broken chair seats; it is made of wide, soft instants, spreading at the edge, like an oil stain. No sooner than born, it is already old, it seems as though I have known it for twenty years.

There is another happiness: outside there is this band of steel, the narrow duration of the music which traverses our time through and through, rejecting it, tearing at it with its dry little points; there is another time.

"Monsieur Randu plays hearts . . . and you play an ace."

The voice dies away and disappears. Nothing bites on the ribbon of steel, neither the opening door, nor the breath of cold air flowing over my knees, nor the arrival of the veterinary surgeon and his little girl: the music transpierces these vague figures and passes through them. Barely seated, the girl has been seized by it: she holds herself stiffly, her eyes wide open; she listens, rubbing the table with her fist.

A few seconds more and the Negress will sing. It seems inevitable, so strong is the necessity of this music: nothing can interrupt it, nothing which comes from this time in which the world has fallen; it will stop of itself, as if by order. If I love this beautiful voice it is especially because of that: it is neither for its fulness nor its sadness, rather because it is the event for which so many notes have been preparing, from so far away, dying that it might be born. And yet I am troubled; it would take so little to make the record stop: a broken spring, the whim of Cousin Adolphe. How strange it is, how moving, that this hardness should be so fragile. Nothing can interrupt it yet all can break it.

The last chord has died away. In the brief silence which follows I feel strongly that there it is, that *something has happened.*

Silence.

Some of these days
You'll miss me honey

What has just happened is that the Nausea has disappeared. When the voice was heard in the silence, I felt my body harden and the Nausea vanish. Suddenly: it was almost unbearable to become so hard, so brilliant. At the same time the music was drawn out, dilated, swelled like a waterspout. It filled the room with its metallic transparency, crushing our miserable time against the walls. I am *in* the music. Globes of fire turn in the mirrors; encircled by rings of smoke, veiling and unveiling the hard smile of light. My glass of beer has shrunk, it seems heaped up on the table, it looks dense and indispensable. I want to pick it up and feel the weight of it, I stretch out my hand . . . God! That is what has changed, my gestures. This movement of my arm has developed like a majestic theme, it has glided along the song of the Negress; I seemed to be dancing.

Adolphe's face is there, set against the chocolate-coloured wall; he seems quite close. Just at the moment when my hand closed, I saw his face; it witnessed to the necessity of a conclusion. I press my fingers against the glass, I look at Adolphe: I am happy.

"*Voilà!*"

A voice rises from the tumult. My neighbour is speaking, the old man burns. His cheeks make a violet stain on the brown leather of the bench. He slaps a card down on the table. Diamonds.

But the dog-faced young man smiles. The flushed opponent, bent over the table, watches him like a cat ready to spring.

"*Et voilà!*"

The hand of the young man rises from the shadow, glides an instant, white, indolent, then suddenly drops like a hawk and presses a card against the cloth. The great red-faced man leaps up:

"Hell! He's trumped."

The outline of the king of hearts appears between his curled fingers, then it is turned on its face and the game goes on. Mighty king, come from so far, prepared by so many combinations, by so many vanished gestures. He disappears in turn so that other combinations can be born, other gestures, attacks, counterattacks, turns of luck, a crowd of small adventures.

I am touched, I feel my body at rest like a precision machine. I have had real adventures. I can recapture no detail but I perceive the rigorous succession of circumstances. I have crossed seas, left cities behind me, followed the course of rivers or plunged into forests, always making my way towards other cities. I have had women, I have fought with men; and never was I able to turn back, any more than a record can be reversed. And all that led me—*where?*

At this very instant, on this bench, in this translucent bubble all humming with music.

And when you leave me

Yes, I who loved so much to sit on the banks of the Tiber at Rome, or in the evening, in Barcelona, ascend and descend the Ramblas a hundred times, I, who near Angkor, on the island of Baray Prah-Kan, saw a banyan tree knot its roots about a Naga chapel, I am here, living in the same second as these card players, I listen to a Negress sing while outside roves the feeble night.

The record stops.

Night has entered, sweetish, hesitant. No one sees it, but it is there, veiling the lamps; I breathe something opaque in the air: it is night. It is cold. One of the players pushes a disordered pack of cards towards another man who picks them up. One card has stayed behind. Don't they see it? It's the nine of hearts. Someone takes it at last, gives it to the dog-faced young man.

"Ah. The nine of hearts."

Enough, I'm going to leave. The purple-faced man bends over a sheet of paper and sucks his pencil. Madeleine watches him with clear, empty eyes. The young man turns and turns the nine of hearts between his fingers. God! . . .

I get up with difficulty; I see an inhuman face glide in the mirror above the veterinary's head.

In a little while I'll go to the cinema.

The air does me good: it doesn't taste like sugar, it doesn't have the winey odour of vermouth. But good God, how cold it is.

It is seven-thirty, I'm not hungry and the cinema doesn't start until nine o'clock; what am I going to do? I have to walk quickly to keep warm. I pause: behind me the boulevard leads to the heart of the city, to the great fiery jewels of central streets, to the Palais Paramount, the Imperial, the Grands Magasins Jahan. It doesn't tempt me at all: it is apéritif time. For the time being I have seen enough of living things, of dogs, of men, of all flabby masses which move spontaneously.

I turn left, I'm going to crawl into that hole down there, at the end of the row of gaslights: I am going to follow the Boulevard Noir as far as the Avenue Galvani. An icy wind blows from the hole: down there is nothing but stones and earth. Stones are hard and do not move.

There is a tedious little stretch of street: on the pavement at the right a gaseous mass, grey with streams of smoke, makes a noise like rattling shells: the old railway station. Its presence has fertilized the first hundred yards of the Boulevard Noir—from the Boulevard de la Redoute to the Rue Paradis—has given birth there to a dozen streetlights and, side by side, four cafés, the "Railwaymen's Rendezvous" and three others which languish all through the day but which light up in the evening and cast luminous rectangles on the street.

I take three more baths of yellow light, see an old woman come out of the épicerie-mercerie Rabache, drawing her shawl over her head and starting to run: now it's finished. I am on the kerb of the Rue Paradis, beside the last lamp-post. The asphalt ribbon breaks off sharply. Darkness and mud are on the other side of the street. I cross the Rue Paradis. I put my right foot in a puddle of water, my sock is soaked through; my walk begins.

No one lives in this section of the Boulevard Noir. The climate is too harsh there, the soil too barren for life to be established there and grow. The three *Scieries des Frères Soleil* (the

Frères Soleil furnished the panelled arch of the Eglise Saint-Cécile de la Mer, which cost a hundred thousand francs) open on the West with all their doors and windows, on the quiet Rue Jeanne-Berthe-Coeuroy which they fill with purring sounds. They turn their backs of triple adjoining walls on the Boulevard Victor-Noir. These buildings border the left-hand pavement for 400 yards: without the smallest window, not even a skylight.

This time I walked with both feet in the gutter. I cross the street: on the opposite sidewalk, a single gaslight, like a beacon at the extreme end of the earth, lights up a dilapidated fence, broken down in places.

Bits of old posters still clung to the boards. A fine face full of hatred, grimacing against a green background torn into the shape of a star; just below the nose someone had pencilled in a curling moustache. On another strip I could still decipher the word "purâtre" from which red drops fall, drops of blood perhaps. The face and the word might have been part of the same poster. Now the poster is lacerated, the simple, necessary lines which united them have disappeared, but another unity has established itself between the twisted mouth, the drops of blood, the white letters, and the termination "âtre": as though a restless and criminal passion were seeking to express itself by these mysterious signs. I can see the lights from the railroad shining between the boards. A long wall follows the fence. A wall without opening, without doors, without windows, a well which stops 200 yards further on, against a house. I have passed out of range of the lamp-post; I enter the black hole. Seeing the shadow at my feet lose itself in the darkness, I have the impression of plunging into icy water. Before me, at the very end, through the layers of black, I can make out a pinkish pallor: it is the Avenue Galvani. I turn back; behind the gaslamp, very far, there is a hint of light: that is the station with the four cafés. Behind me, in front of me, are people drinking and playing cards in pubs. Here there is nothing but blackness. Intermittently, the wind carries a solitary, faraway ringing to my ears. Familiar sounds, the rumble of motor cars, shouts, and the barking of dogs which hardly venture from the lighted streets, they stay within the warmth. But the ringing pierces the shadows and comes thus far: it is harder, less human than the other noises.

I stop to listen. I am cold, my ears hurt; they must be all red. But I no longer feel myself; I am won over by the purity surrounding me; nothing is alive, the wind whistles, the straight

25

lines flee in the night. The Boulevard Noir does not have the indecent look of bourgeois streets, offering their regrets to the passers-by. No one has bothered to adorn it: it is simply the reverse side. The reverse side of the Rue Jeanne-Berthe Coeuroy, of the Avenue Galvani. Around the station, the people of Bouville still look after it a little; they clean it from time to time because of the travellers. But, immediately after that, they abandon it and it rushes straight ahead, blindly, bumping finally into the Avenue Galvani. The town has forgotten it. Sometimes a great mud-coloured truck thunders across it at top speed. No one even commits any murders there; want of assassins and victims. The Boulevard Noir is inhuman. Like a mineral. Like a triangle. It's lucky there's a boulevard like that in Bouville. Ordinarily you find them only in capitals, in Berlin, near Neuköln or Friedrichshain—in London, behind Greenwich. Straight, dirty corridors, full of drafts, with wide, treeless sidewalk. They are almost always outside the town in these strange sections where cities are manufactured near freight stations, car-barns, abattoirs, gas tanks. Two days after a rainstorm, when the whole city is moist beneath the sun and radiates damp heat, they are still cold, they keep their mud and puddles. They even have puddles which never dry up—except one month out of the year, August.

The Nausea has stayed down there, in the yellow light. I am happy: this cold is so pure, this night so pure: am I myself not a wave of icy air? With neither blood, nor lymph, nor flesh. Flowing down this long canal towards the pallor down there. To be nothing but coldness.

Here are some people. Two shadows. What did they need to come here for?

It is a short woman pulling a man by his sleeve. She speaks in a thin, rapid voice. Because of the wind I understand nothing of what she says.

"You're going to shut your trap now, aren't you?" the man says.

She still speaks. He pushes her roughly. They look at each other, uncertain, then the man thrusts his hands in his pockets and leaves without looking back.

The man has disappeared. A scant three yards separate me from this woman now. Suddenly, deep, hoarse sounds come from her, tear at her and fill the whole street with extraordinary violence.

"Charles, I beg you, you know what I told you? Charles, come back, I've had enough, I'm too miserable!"

I pass so close to her that I could touch her. It's . . . but how can I believe that this burning flesh, this face shining with sorrow? . . . and yet I recognize the scarf, the coat and the large wine-coloured birthmark on the right hand; it is Lucie, the charwoman. I dare not offer her my support, but she must be able to call for it if need be: I pass before her slowly, looking at her. Her eyes stare at me but she seems not to see me; she looks as though she were lost in her suffering. I take a few steps, turn back. . . .

Yes, it's Lucie. But transfigured, beside herself, suffering with a frenzied generosity. I envy her. There she is, standing straight, holding out her arms as if awaiting the stigmata; she opens her mouth, she is suffocating. I feel as though the walls have grown higher, on each side of the street, that they have come closer together, that she is at the bottom of a well. I wait a few moments: I am afraid she will fall: she is too sickly to stand this unwonted sorrow. But she does not move, she seems turned to stone, like everything around her. One moment I wonder if I have not been mistaken about her, if this is not her true nature which has suddenly been revealed to me.

Lucie gives a little groan. Her hand goes to her throat and she opens wide, astonished eyes. No, it is not from herself that she draws strength to suffer. It comes to her from the outside . . . from the boulevard. She should be taken by the arm, led back to the lights, in the midst of people, into quiet, pink streets: down there one cannot suffer so acutely; she would be mollified, she would find her positive look again and the usual level of her sufferings.

I turn my back on her. After all, she is lucky. I have been much too calm these past three years. I can receive nothing more from these tragic solitudes than a little empty purity. I leave.

Thursday, 11.30

I have worked two hours in the reading-room. I went down to the Cour des Hypothèques to smoke a pipe. A square paved with pinkish bricks. The people of Bouville are proud of it because it dates from the eighteenth century. At the entrance to the Rue Chamade and the Rue Suspedard, old chains bar the way to vehicles. Women in black who come to exercise their dogs glide beneath the arcades, along the walls. They rarely come out into the full light, but they cast ingénue glances from the corner of

27

their eyes, on the statue of Gustave Impétraz. They don't know the name of this bronze giant but they see clearly from his frock coat and top hat that he was someone from the beau-monde. He holds his hat in his left hand, placing his right on a stack of papers: it is a little as though their grandfather were there on the pedestal, cast in bronze. They do not need to look at him very long to understand that he thought as they do, exactly as they do, on all subjects. At the service of their obstinately narrow, small ideas he has placed the authority and immense erudition drawn from the papers crushed in his hand. The women in black feel soothed, they can go peacefully minding their own business, running their households, walking their dogs out: they no longer have the responsibility of standing up, for their Christian ideals the high ideals which they get from their fathers; a man of bronze has made himself their guardian.

The encyclopedia devotes a few lines to this personage; I read them last year. I had set the volume on the window ledge; I could see Impétraz' green skull through the pane. I discovered that he flourished around 1890. He was a school inspector. He painted and drew charming sketches and wrote three books: *Popularity and the Ancient Greeks* (1887), *Rollin's Pedagogy* (1891) and a poetic Testament in 1899. He died in 1902, to the deep regret of his dependents and people of good taste.

I lean against the front of the library. I suck out my pipe which threatens to go out. I see an old lady fearfully leaving the gallery of arcades, looking slyly and obstinately at Impétraz. She suddenly grows bolder, she crosses the courtyard as fast as her legs can carry her, stops for a moment in front of the statue, her jaws trembling. Then she leaves, black against the pink pavement, and disappears into a chink in the wall.

This place might have been gay, around 1800, with its pink bricks and houses. Now there is something dry and evil about it, a delicate touch of horror. It comes from that fellow up there on his pedestal. When they cast this scholar in bronze they also turned out a sorcerer.

I look at Impétraz full in the face. He has no eyes, hardly any nose, and beard eaten away by that strange leprosy which sometimes descends, like an epidemic, on all the statues in one neighbourhood. He bows; on the left hand side near his heart his waistcoat is soiled with a light green stain. He looks. He does not live, but neither is he inanimate. A mute power emanates from him: like a wind driving me backwards: Impétraz would like to chase me out of the Cour des Hypothèques. But I shall not leave before I finish this pipe.

A great, gaunt shadow suddenly springs up behind me. I jump.

"Excuse me, Monsieur, I didn't mean to disturb you. I saw your lips moving. You were undoubtedly repeating passages from your book." He laughs. "You were hunting Alexandrines."

I look at the Self-Taught Man with stupor. But he seems surprised at my surprise:

"Should we not, Monsieur, carefully avoid Alexandrines in prose?"

I have been slightly lowered in his estimation. I ask him what he's doing here at this hour. He explains that his boss has given him the day off and he came straight to the library; that he is not going to eat lunch, that he is going to read till closing time. I am not listening to him any more, but he must have strayed from his original subject because I suddenly hear:

". . . to have, as you, the good fortune of writing a book."

I have to say something.

"Good fortune," I say, dubiously.

He mistakes the sense of my answer and rapidly corrects himself:

"Monsieur, I should have said: 'merit.'"

We go up the steps. I don't feel like working. Someone has left *Eugénie Grandet* on the table, the book is open at page 27. I pick it up, mechanically, and begin to read page 27, then page 28: I haven't the courage to begin at the beginning. The Self-Taught Man has gone quickly to the shelves along the wall; he brings back two books which he places on the table, looking like a dog who has found a bone.

"What are you reading?"

He seems reluctant to tell me: he hesitates, rolls his great, roving eyes, then stiffly holds out the books. *Peat-Mosses and Where to Find Them* by Larbalétrier, and *Hitopadesa, or, Useful Instruction* by Lastex. So? I don't know what's bothering him: the books are definitely decent. Out of conscience I thumb through *Hitopadesa* and see nothing but the highest types of sentiment.

3.00 *p.m.*

I have given up *Eugénie Grandet* and begun work without any heart in it. The Self-Taught Man, seeing that I am writing, observes me with respectful lust. From time to time I raise my head a little and see the immense, stiff collar and the chicken-like neck coming out of it. His clothes are shabby but his shirt is dazzling white. He has just taken another book from the same shelf, I can make out the title upside-down: *The Arrow of Caudebec, A Norman Chronicle* by Mlle Julie Lavergne. The Self-Taught Man's choice of reading always disconcerts me.

Suddenly the names of the authors he last read come back to my mind: Lambert, Langlois, Larbalétrier, Lastex, Lavergne. It is a revelation; I have understood the Self-Taught Man's method; he teaches himself alphabetically.

I study him with a sort of admiration. What will-power he must have to carry through, slowly, obstinately, a plan on such a vast scale. One day, seven years ago (he told me he had been a student for seven years) he came pompously into this reading-room. He scanned the innumerable books which lined the walls and he must have said, something like Rastignac, "Science! It is up to us." Then he went and took the first book from the first shelf on the far right; he opened to the first page, with a feeling of respect and fear mixed with an unshakable decision. Today he has reached "L"—"K" after "J," "L" after "K." He has passed brutally from the study of coleopterae to the quantum theory, from a work on Tamerlaine to a Catholic pamphlet against Darwinism, he has never been disconcerted for an instant. He has read everything; he has stored up in his head most of what anyone knows about parthenogenesis, and half the arguments against vivisection. There is a universe behind and before him. And the day is approaching when closing the last book on the last shelf on the far left: he will say to himself, "Now what?"

This is his lunch time; innocently he eats a slice of bread and a bar of Gala Peter. His eyes are lowered and I can study at leisure his fine, curved lashes, like a woman's. When he breathes he gives off an aroma of old tobacco mixed with the sweet scent of chocolate.

Friday, 3.00 p.m.

A little more and I would have fallen into the lure of the mirror. I avoid it only to fall into that of the window: indolent, arms dangling, I go to the window. The Building Yard, the Fence, the Old Station—the Old Station, the Fence, the Building Yard. I give such a big yawn that tears come into my eyes. I hold my pipe in my right hand and my tobacco in my left. I should fill this pipe. But I don't have the heart to do it. My arms hang loosely, I lean my forehead against the windowpane. That old woman annoys me. She trots along obstinately, with unseeing eyes. Sometimes she stops, frightened, as if an invisible fear had brushed against her. There she is under my window, the wind blows her skirts against her knees. She stops, straightens her kerchief. Her hands tremble. She is off again: now I can see her from the back. Old wood louse! I suppose she's going to turn right, into the Boulevard Victor-Noir. That gives her a hundred yards to go: it will take her ten minutes at the rate she's going, ten minutes during which time I shall stay like this, watching her, my forehead glued against the window. She is going to stop twenty times, start again, stop again . . .

I *see* the future. It is there, poised over the street, hardly more dim than the present. What advantage will accrue from its realisation? The old woman stumps further and further away, she stops, pulls at a grey lock of hair which escapes from her kerchief. She walks, she was there, now she is here . . . I don't know where I am any more: do I *see* her motions, or do I *foresee* them? I can no longer distinguish present from future and yet it lasts, it happens little by little; the old woman advances in the deserted street, shuffling her heavy, mannish brogues. This is time, time laid bare, coming slowly into existence, keeping us waiting, and when it does come making us sick because we realise it's been there for a long time. The old woman reaches the corner of the street, no more than a bundle of black clothes. All right then, it's new, she wasn't there a little while ago. But it's a tarnished deflowered newness, which can never surprise. She is going to turn the corner, she turns—during an eternity.

I tear myself from the window and stumble across the room; I glue myself against the looking glass. I stare at myself, I disgust myself: one more eternity. Finally I flee from my image and fall on the bed. I watch the ceiling, I'd like to sleep.

Calm. Calm. In can no longer feel the slipping, the rustling of time. I see pictures on the ceiling. First rings of light, then crosses. They flutter. And now another picture is forming, at the bottom of my eyes this time. It is a great, kneeling animal. I see its front paws and pack saddle. The rest is in fog. But I recognize it: it is a camel I saw at Marrakesh, tethered to a stone. He knelt and stood up six times running; the urchins laughed and shouted at him.

It was wonderful two years ago: all I had to do was close to my eyes and my head would start buzzing like a bee-hive: I could conjure faces, trees, houses, a Japanese girl in Kamaishiki washing herself naked in a wooden tub, a dead Russian, emptied of blood by a great, gaping wound, all his blood in a pool beside him. I could recapture the taste of kouskouss, the smell of olive oil which fills the streets of Burgos at noon, the scent of fennel floating through the Tetuan streets, the piping of Greek shepherds; I was touched. This joy was used up a long time ago. Will it be reborn today?

A torrid sun moves stiffly in my head like a magic lantern slide. A fragment of blue sky follows; after a few jolts it becomes motionless. I am all golden within. From what Moroccan (or Algerian or Syrian) day did this flash suddenly detach itself? I let myself flow into the past.

Meknes. What was that man from the hills like—the one who frightened us in the narrow street between the Berdaine mosque and that charming square shaded by a mulberry tree? He came towards us, Anny was on my right. Or on my left?

This sun and blue sky were only a snare. This is the hundredth time I've let myself be caught. My memories are like coins in the devil's purse: when you open it you find only dead leaves.

Now I can only see the great, empty eye socket of the hill tribesman. Is this eye really his? The doctor at Baku who explained the principle of state abortions to me was also blind of one eye, and the white empty socket appears every time I want to remember his face. Like the Norns these two men have only one eye between them with which they take turns.

As for the square at Meknes, where I used to go every day, it's even simpler: I do not see it at all any more. All that remains is the vague feeling that it was charming, and these five words are indivisibly bound together: a charming square at Meknes. Undoubtedly, if I close my eyes or stare vaguely at the ceiling I can re-create the scene: a tree in the distance, a short dingy figure run towards me. But I am inventing all this to make out a case. That Moroccan was big and weather-beaten, besides, I only saw him after he had touched me. So I *still* know he was big and weather-beaten: certain details, somewhat curtailed, live in my memory. But I don't *see* anything any more: I can search the past in vain, I can only find these scraps of images and I am not sure what they represent, whether they are memories or just fiction.

There are many cases where even these scraps have disappeared: nothing is left but words: I could still tell stories, tell them too well (as far as anecdotes are concerned, I can stand up to anyone except ship's officers and professional people) but these are only the skeletons. There's the story of a person who does this, does that, but it isn't I, I have nothing in common with him. He travels through countries I know no more about than if I had never been there. Sometimes, in my story, it happens that I pronounce these fine names you read in atlases, Aranjuez or Canterbury. New images are born in me, images such as people create from books who have never travelled. My words are dreams, that is all.

For a hundred dead stories there still remain one or two living ones. I evoke these with caution, occasionally, not too often, for fear of wearing them out, I fish one out, again I see the scenery, the characters, the attitudes. I stop suddenly: there is a flaw, I have seen a word pierce through the web of sensations. I suppose that this word will soon take the place of several images I love. I must stop quickly and think of something else; I don't want to tire my memories. In vain; the next time I evoke them a good part will be congealed.

I make a pretence of getting up, going to look for my photos of Meknes in the chest I pushed under my table. What good would it do? These aphrodisiacs scarcely affect my memory any more. I found a faded little photo under my blotter the other day. A woman was smiling, near a tank. I studied this person for a moment without recognizing her. Then on the other side I read, "Anny, Portsmouth, April 7, '27."

I have never before had such a strong feeling that I was devoid of secret dimensions, confined within the limits of my body, from which airy thoughts float up like bubbles. I build memories with my present self. I am cast out, forsaken in the present: I vainly try to rejoin the past: I cannot escape.

Someone knocks. It's the Self-Taught Man: I had forgotten him. I had promised to show him the photographs of my travels. He can go to Hell.

He sits down on a chair; his extended buttocks touch the back of it and his stiff torso leans forward. I jump from the end of my bed and turn on the light.

"Oh, do we really need that? We were quite comfortable."

"Not for looking at pictures. . . ."

I relieve him of his hat.

"True, Monsieur? Do you really want to show me your pictures?"

"Of course."

This is a plot: I hope he will keep quiet while he looks at them. I dive under the table and push the chest against his patent leather shoes, I put an armload of post cards and photos on his lap: Spain and Spanish Morocco.

But I see by his laughing, open look that I have been singularly mistaken in hoping to reduce him to silence. He glances over a view of San Sebastian from Monte Igueldo, sets it cautiously on the table and remains silent for an instant. Then he sighs:

"Ah, Monsieur, you're lucky . . . if what they say is true—travel is the best school. Is that your opinion, Monsieur?"

I make a vague gesture. Luckily he has not finished.

"It must be such an upheaval. If I were ever to go on a trip, I think I should make written notes of the slightest traits of my character before leaving, so that when I returned I would be able to compare what I was and what I had become. I've read that there are travellers who have changed physically and morally to such an extent that even their closest relatives did not recognize them when they came back."

He handles a thick packet of photographs, abstractedly. He takes one and puts it on the table without looking at it; then he stares intently at the next picture showing Saint Jerome sculptured on a pulpit in the Burgos cathedral.

"Have you seen the Christ made of animal skins at Burgos? There is a very strange book, Monsieur, on these statues made of animal skin and even human skin. And the Black Virgin? She isn't at Burgos but at Saragossa, I think? Yet there may possibly be one at Burgos. The Pilgrims kiss her, don't they?—the one at Saragossa, I mean. And isn't there the print of her foot on a stone?—in a hole—where the mothers push their children?"

Stiffly he pushes an imaginary child with his hands. You'd think he was refusing the gifts of Artaxerxes.

"Ah, manners and customs, Monsieur, they are . . . they are curious."

A little breathless, he points his great ass's jawbone at me. He smells of tobacco and stagnant water. His fine, roving eyes shine like globes of fire and his sparse hair forms a steaming halo on his skull. Under this skull, Samoyeds, Nyam-Nyams,

Malgaches and Fuegians celebrate their strangest solemnities, eat their old fathers, their children, spin to the sound of tom-toms until they faint, run amok, burn their dead, exhibit them on the roofs, leave them to the river current in a boat, lighted by a torch, copulate at random, mother with son, father with daughter, brother with sister, mutilate themselves, castrate themselves, distend their lips with plates, have monstrous animals sculptured on their backs.

"Can one say, with Pascal, that custom is second nature?"

He has fixed his black eyes on mine, he begs for an answer.

"That depends," I say.

He draws a deep breath.

"That's just what I was saying to myself, Monsieur. But I distrust myself so much; one should have read everything."

He almost goes mad over the next photo and shouts joyfully:

"Segovia! Segovia! I've read a book about Segovia!"

Then he adds with a certain nobility:

"Monsieur, I don't remember the name any more. I sometimes have spells of absent-mindedness . . . Na . . . No . . . Nod . . ."

"Impossible," I tell him quickly, "you were only up to Lavergne."

I regret my words immediately: after all, he had never told me about his reading methods, it must have been a precious secret. And in fact, his face falls and his thick lips jut out as if he were going to cry. Then he bows his head and looks at a dozen more post cards without a word.

But after thirty seconds I can see that a powerful enthusiasm is mounting in him and that he will burst if he doesn't speak:

"When I've finished my instruction (I allow six more years for that) I shall join, if I am permitted, the group of students and professors who take an annual cruise to the Near East. I should like to make some new acquaintances," he says unctuously. "To speak frankly, I would also like something unexpected to happen to me, something new, adventures."

He has lowered his voice and his face has taken on a roguish look.

"What sort of adventures?" I ask him, astonished.

"All sorts, Monsieur. Getting on the wrong train. Stopping in an unknown city. Losing your briefcase, being arrested by mistake, spending the night in prison. Monsieur, I believed the word adventure could be defined: an event out of the ordinary without being necessarily extraordinary. People speak of the magic of adventures. Does this expression seem correct to you? I would like to ask you a question, Monsieur."

"What is it?"

He blushes and smiles.

"Possibly it is indiscreet!"

"Ask me, anyway."

He leans towards me, his eyes half-closed, and asks:

"Have you had many adventures, Monsieur?"

"A few," I answer mechanically, throwing myself back to avoid his tainted breath. Yes. I said that mechanically, without thinking. In fact, I am generally proud of having had so many adventures. But today, I had barely pronounced the words than I was seized with contrition; it seems as though I am lying, that I have never had the slightest adventure in my life, or rather, that I don't even know what the word means any more. At the same time, I am weighed down by the same discouragement I had in Hanoi—four years ago when Mercier pressed me to join him and I stared at a Khmer statuette without answering. And the IDEA is there, this great white mass which so disgusted me then: I hadn't seen it for four years.

"Could I ask you . . ." the Self-Taught Man begins . . .

By Jove! To tell him one of those famous tales. But I won't say another word on the subject.

"There," I say, bending down over his narrow shoulders, putting my finger on a photograph, "there, that's Santillana, the prettiest town in Spain."

"The Santillana of Gil Blas? I didn't believe it existed. Ah, Monsieur, how profitable your conversation is. One can tell you've travelled."

I put out the Self-Taught Man after filling his pockets with post cards, prints and photos. He left enchanted and I switched off the light. I am alone now. Not quite alone. Hovering in front of me is still this idea. It has rolled itself into a ball, it stays there like a large cat; it explains nothing, it does not move, and contents itself with saying no. No, I haven't had any adventures.

I fill my pipe, light it and stretch out on the bed, throwing a coat over my legs. What astonishes me is to feel so sad and exhausted. Even if it were true—that I never had any adventures —what difference would that make to me? First, it seems to be a pure question of words. This business at Meknes, for example, I was thinking about a little while ago: a Moroccan jumped on me and wanted to stab me with an enormous knife. But I hit him just below the temple . . . then he began shouting in Arabic and a swarm of lousy beggars came up and chased us all the way to Souk Attarin. Well, you can call that by any name you like, in any case, it was an event which *happened to* ME.

It is completely dark and I can't tell whether my pipe is lit. A trolley passes: red light on the ceiling. Then a heavy truck which makes the house tremble. It must be six o'clock.

I have never had adventures. Things have happened to me, events, incidents, anything you like. But no adventures. It isn't a question of words; I am beginning to understand. There is something to which I clung more than all the rest—without completely realizing it. It wasn't love. Heaven forbid, not glory, not money. It was . . . I had imagined that at certain times my life could take on a rare and precious quality. There was no need for extraordinary circumstances: all I asked for was a little precision. There is nothing brilliant about my life now: but from time to time, for example, when they play music in the cafés, I look back and tell myself: in old days, in London, Meknes, Tokyo, I have known great moments, I have had adventures. Now I am deprived of this. I have suddenly learned, without any apparent reason, that I have been lying to myself for ten years. And naturally, everything they tell about in books can happen in real life, but not in the same way. It is to this way of happening that I clung so tightly.

The beginnings would have had to be real beginnings. Alas! Now I see so clearly what I wanted. Real beginnings are like a fanfare of trumpets, like the first notes of a jazz tune, cutting short tedium, making for continuity: then you say about these evenings within evenings: "I was out for a walk, it was an evening in May." You walk, the moon has just risen, you feel lazy, vacant, a little empty. And then suddenly you think: "Something has happened." No matter what: a slight rustling in the shadow, a thin silhouette crossing the street. But this paltry event is not like the others: suddenly you see that it is the beginning of a great shape whose outlines are lost in mist and you tell yourself, "Something is beginning."

Something is beginning in order to end: adventure does not let itself be drawn out; it only makes sense when dead. I am drawn, irrevocably, towards this death which is perhaps mine as well. Each instant appears only as part of a sequence. I cling to each instant with all my heart: I know that it is unique, irreplaceable—and yet I would not raise a finger to stop it from being annihilated. This last moment I am spending—in Berlin, in London—in the arms of a woman casually met two days ago—moment I love passionately, woman I may adore—all is going to end, I know it. Soon I shall leave for another country. I shall never rediscover either this woman or this night. I grasp at each second, trying to suck it dry: nothing happens which I do not seize, which I do not fix forever in myself, nothing, neither the fugitive tenderness of those lovely eyes, nor the noises of the street, nor the false dawn of early morning: and even so the minute passes and I do not hold it back, I like to see it pass.

All of a sudden something breaks off sharply. The adventure is over, time resumes its daily routine. I turn; behind me, this beautiful melodious form sinks entirely into the past. It grows smaller, contracts as it declines, and now the end makes one with the beginning. Following this gold spot with my eyes I think I would accept—even if I had to risk death, lose a fortune, a friend—to live it all over again, in the same circumstances, from end to end. But an adventure never returns nor is prolonged.

Yes, it's what I wanted—what I still want. I am so happy when a Negress sings: what summits would I not reach if *my own life* made the subject of the melody.

The idea is still there, unnameable. It waits, peacefully. Now it seems to say:

"Yes? Is *that* what you wanted? Well, that's exactly what you've never had (remember you fooled yourself with words, you called the glitter of travel, the love of women, quarrels, and trinkets adventure) and this is what you'll never have—and no one other than yourself."

But Why? WHY?

Saturday noon:

The Self-Taught Man did not see me come into the reading-room. He was sitting at the end of a table in the back; he had set his book down in front of him but he was not reading. He was smiling at a seedy-looking student who often comes to the library. The student allowed himself to be looked at for a moment, then suddenly stuck his tongue out and made a horrible face. The Self-Taught Man blushed, hurriedly plunged his nose into his book and became absorbed by his reading.

I have reconsidered my thoughts of yesterday. I was completely dry: it made no difference to me whether there had been no adventures. I was only curious to know whether there could *never be any*.

This is what I thought: for the most banal even to become an adventure, you must (and this is enough) begin to recount it. This is what fools people: a man is always a teller of tales, he lives surrounded by his stories and the stories of others, he sees everything that happens to him through them; and he tries to live his own life as if he were telling a story.

But you have to choose: live or tell. For example, when I was in Hamburg, with that Erna girl I didn't trust and who was afraid of me, I led a funny sort of life. But I was in the middle of it, I didn't think about it. And then one evening, in a little café in San Pauli, she left me to go to the ladies' room. I stayed alone, there was a phonograph playing "Blue Skies." I began to tell myself what had happened since I landed. I told myself, "The third evening, as I was going into a dance hall called *La Grotte Bleue*, I noticed a large woman, half seas over. And that woman is the one I am waiting for now, listening to 'Blue Skies,' the woman who is going to come back and sit down at my right and put her arms around my neck." Then I felt violently that I was having an adventure. But Erna came back and sat down beside me, she wound her arms around my neck and I hated her without knowing why. I understand now: one had to begin living again and the adventure was fading out.

Nothing happens while you live. The scenery changes, people come in and go out, that's all. There are no beginnings. Days are tacked on to days without rhyme or reason, an interminable, monotonous addition. From time to time you make a semi-total: you say: I've been travelling for three years, I've been in Bouville for three years. Neither is there any end: you never leave a woman, a friend, a city in one go. And then everything looks alike: Shanghai, Moscow, Algiers, everything is the same after two weeks. There are moments—rarely—when you make a landmark, you realize that you're going with a woman, in some messy business. The time of a flash. After that, the procession starts again, you begin to add up hours and days: Monday, Tuesday, Wednesday. April, May, June. 1924, 1925, 1926.

That's living. But everything changes when you tell about life; it's a change no one notices: the proof is that people talk about true stories. As if there could possibly be true stories; things happen one way and we tell about them in the opposite sense. You seem to start at the beginning: "It was a fine autumn evening in 1922. I was a notary's clerk in Marommes." And in reality you have started at the end. It was there, invisible and present, it is the one which gives to words the pomp and value of a beginning. "I was out walking, I had left the town without realizing it, I was thinking about my money troubles." This sentence, taken simply for what it is, means that the man was absorbed, morose, a hundred leagues from an adventure, exactly in the mood to let things happen without noticing them. But the end is there, transforming everything. For us, the man is already the hero of the story. His moroseness, his money troubles are much more precious than ours, they are all gilded by the light of future passions. And the story goes on in the reverse: instants have stopped piling themselves in a lighthearted way one on top of the other, they are snapped up by the end of the story which draws them and each one of them in turn, draws out the preceding instant: "It was night, the street was deserted." The phrase is cast out negligently, it seems superfluous; but we do not let ourselves be caught and we put it aside: this is a piece of information whose value we shall subsequently appreciate. And we feel that the hero has lived all the details of this night like annunciations, promises, or even that he lived only those that were promises, blind and deaf to all that did not herald adventure. We forget that the future was not yet there; the man was walking in a night without forethought, a night which offered him a choice of dull rich prizes, and he did not make his choice.

I wanted the moments of my life to follow and order themselves like those of a life remembered. You might as well try and catch time by the tail.

Sunday:

I had forgotten that this morning was Sunday. I went out and walked along the streets as usual. I had taken along *Eugénie Grandet*. Then, suddenly, when opening the gate of the public park I got the impression that something was signalling to me. The park was bare and deserted. But . . . how can I explain?

It didn't have its usual look, it smiled at me. I leaned against the railing for a moment then suddenly realized it was Sunday. It was there—on the trees, on the grass, like a faint smile. It couldn't be described, you would have had to repeat very quickly: "This is a public park, this is winter, this is Sunday morning."

I let go of the railing, turned back towards the houses and streets of the town and half-aloud I murmured, "It's Sunday."

It's Sunday: behind the docks, along the seacoast, near the freight station, all around the city there are empty warehouses and motionless machines in the darkness. In all the houses, men are shaving behind their windows; their heads are thrown back, sometimes they stare at the looking glass, sometimes at the sky to see whether it's going to be a fine day. The brothels are opening to their first customers, rustics and soldiers. In the churches, in the light of candles, a man is drinking wine in the sight of kneeling women. In all the suburbs, between the interminable walls of factories, long black processions have started walking, they are slowly advancing towards the centre of the town. To receive them, the streets have taken on the look they have when disturbance is expected, all the stores, except the ones on the Rue Tournebride, have lowered their iron shutters. Soon, silently, these black columns are going to invade the death-shamming streets: first the railroad workers from Tourville and their wives who work in the Saint-Symphorin soap factories, then the little bourgeois from Jouxtebouville, then the workers from the Pinot weaving mills, then all the odd jobbers from the Saint-Maxence quarter; the men from Thierache will arrive last on the eleven o'clock trolley. Soon the Sunday crowd will be born, between bolted shops and closed doors.

A clock strikes half-past ten and I start on my way: Sundays, at this hour, you can see a fine show in Bouville, but you must not come too late after High Mass.

The little Rue Joséphin-Soulary is dead, it smells of a cellar. But, as on every Sunday, it is filled with a sumptuous noise, a noise like a tide. I turn into the Rue de Président-Chamart where the houses have four storeys with long white venetian blinds. This street of notaries is entirely filled by the voluminous clamour of Sunday. The noise increases in the Passage Gillet and I recognize it: it is a noise which men make. Then suddenly, on the left, comes an explosion, of light and sound: here is the Rue Tournebride, all I have to do is take my place among my fellows and watch them raising their hats to each other.

Sixty years ago no one could have forseen the miraculous destiny of the Rue Tournebride, which the inhabitants of Bouville today call the Little Prado. I saw a map dated 1847 on which the street was not even mentioned. At that time it must have been a dark, stinking bowel, with a trench between the paving stones in which fishes' heads and entrails were stacked. But, at the end of 1873, the Assemblée Nationale declared the construction of a church on the slope of Montmartre to be of public utility. A few months later, the mayor's wife had a vision: Sainte Cécile, her patron saint, came to remonstrate with her. Was it tolerable for the élite to soil themselves every Sunday going to Saint-René or Saint-Claudien to hear mass with shopkeepers? Hadn't the Assemblée Nationale set an example? Bouville now had, thanks to the protection of Heaven, a first-class financial position; wouldn't it be fitting to build a church wherein to give thanks to the Lord?

These visions were accepted: the city council held a historic meeting and the bishop agreed to organize a subscription. All that was left was the choice of locality. The old families of businessmen and shipowners were of the opinion that the building should be constructed on the summit of the Coteau Vert where they lived, "so that Saint Cécile could watch over Bouville as the Sacré-Coeur-de-Jésus over Paris." The *nouveau-riche* gentlemen of the Boulevard Maritime, of which there were only a few, shook their heads: they would give all that was needed but the church would have to be built on the Place Marignan; if they were going to pay for a church they expected to be able to use it; they were not reluctant to make their power felt by the higher bourgeoisie who considered them parvenus. The bishop suggested a compromise: the church was built halfway between the Coteau Vert and the Boulevard Maritime, on the Place de la Halle-aux-Morues which was baptised Place Sainte-Cécile-de-la-Mer. This monstrous edifice, completed in 1887, cost no less than fourteen million francs.

The Rue Tournebride, wide but dirty and of ill-repute, had to be entirely rebuilt and its inhabitants firmly pushed behind the Place Saint-Cécile; the Little Prado became—especially on Sunday mornings—the meeting place of elegant and distinguished people. Fine shops opened one by one on the passage of the élite. They stayed open Easter Monday, all Christmas Night, and every Sunday until noon. Next to Julien, the pork butcher, renowned for his *pâtés chauds,* Foulon, the pastry cook exhibits his famous specialties, conical petits-fours made of mauve butter, topped by a sugar violet. In the window of Dupaty's library you can see the latest books published by Plon, a few technical works such as a theory of navigation or a treatise on sails and sailing, an enormous illustrated history of Bouville and elegantly appointed editions de luxe: *Koenigsmark* bound in blue leather, the *Livre de mes Fils* by Paul Doumer, bound in tan leather with purple flowers. Ghislaine (Haute Couture, Parisian Models) separates Piégeois the florist from Paquin, the antique dealer. Gustave, the hair dresser, who employs four manicurists, occupies the second floor of an entirely new yellow painted building.

Two years ago, at the corner of the Impasse des Moulins-Gémeaux and the Rue Tournebride, an impudent little shop still advertised for the Tu-Pu-Nez insecticide. It had flourished in the time when codfish were hawked in the Place Sainte-Cécile; it was a hundred years old. The windows were rarely washed: it required a great effort to distinguish, through dust and mist, a crowd of tiny wax figures decked out in orange doublets, representing rats and mice. These animals were disembarking from a high-decked ship, leaning on sticks; barely had they touched the ground when a peasant girl, attractively dressed but filthy and black with dirt, put them all to flight by sprinkling them with Tu-Pu-Nez. I liked this shop very much, it had a cynical and obstinate look, it insolently recalled the rights of dirt and vermin, only two paces from the most costly church in France.

The old herborist died last year and her nephew sold the house. It was enough to tear down a few walls: it is now a small lecture hall, "La Bonbonnière." Last year Henry Bordeaux gave a talk on Alpinism there.

You must not be in a hurry in the Rue Tournebride: the families walk slowly. Sometimes you move up a step because one family has turned into Foulon's or Piégeois'. But, at other times, you must stop and mark time because two families, one going up the street, the other coming down, have met and have solidly clasped hands. I go forward slowly. I stand a whole head above both columns and I see hats, a sea of hats. Most of them are black and hard. From time to time you see one fly off at the end of an arm and you catch the soft glint of a skull; then, after a few instants of heavy flight, it returns. At 16 Rue Tournebride, Urbain, the hatter, specializing in forage caps, has hung up as a symbol, an immense, red archbishop's hat whose gold tassels hang six feet from the ground.

A halt: a group has collected just under the tassels. My neighbour waits impatiently, his arms dangling: this little old man, pale and fragile as porcelain—I think he must be Coffier—president of the Chamber of Commerce. It seems he is intimidating because he never speaks. He lives on the summit of the Coteau Vert, in a great brick house whose windows are always wide open. It's over: the group has broken up. Another group starts forming but it takes up less space: barely formed, it is pushed against Ghislaine's window front. The column does not even stop: it hardly makes a move to step aside; we are walking in front of six people who hold hands: "Bonjour, Monsieur, bonjour cher Monsieur, comment allez-vous? Do put your hat on again, you'll catch cold; Thank you, Madame, it isn't very warm out, is it? My dear, let me present Doctor Lefrançois; Doctor, I am very glad to make your acquaintance, my husband always speaks of Doctor Lefrançois who took such care of him, but do put your hat on, Doctor, you'll catch cold. But a doctor would get well quickly; Alas! Madame, doctors are the least well looked after; the Doctor is a remarkable musician. Really, Doctor? But I never knew, you play the violin? The Doctor is very gifted."

The little old man next to me is surely Coffier; one of the women of the group, the brunette, is devouring him with her eyes, all the while smiling at the Doctor. She seems to be thinking, "There's Monsieur Coffier, president of the Chamber of Commerce; how intimidating he looks, they say he's so frigid." But M. Coffier deigns to see nothing: these people are from the Boulevard Maritime, they do not belong to his world. Since I have been coming to this street to see the Sunday hat-raising, I have learned to distinguish people from the Boulevard and people from the Coteau. When a man wears a new overcoat, a soft felt hat, a dazzling shirt, when he creates a vacuum in passing, there's no mistaking it: he is someone from the Boulevard Maritime. You know people from the Coteau Vert by some kind of shabby, sunken look. They have narrow shoulders and an air of insolence on their worn faces. This fat gentleman holding a child by the hand—I'd swear he comes from the Coteau: his face is all grey and his tie knotted like a string.

The fat man comes near us: he stares at M. Coffier. But, just before he crosses his path, he turns his head away and begins joking in a fatherly way with his little boy. He takes a few more steps, bent over his son, his eyes gazing in the child's eyes, nothing but a father; then suddenly he turns quickly towards us, throws a quick glance at the little old man and makes an ample, quick salute with a sweep of his arm. Disconcerted, the little boy has not taken off his hat: this is an affair between grown-ups.

At the corner of the Rue Basse-de-Vieille our column abuts into a column of the faithful coming out of Mass: a dozen persons rush forward, shaking each other's hand and whirling round, but the hat-raising is over too quickly for me to catch the details; the Eglise Sainte-Cécile stands a monstrous mass above the fat, pale crowd: chalk white against a sombre sky; its sides hold a little of the night's darkness behind these shining walls. We are off again in a slightly modified order. M. Coffier has been pushed behind me. A lady dressed in navy blue is glued to my left side. She has come from Mass. She blinks her eyes, a little dazzled at coming into the light of morning. The gentleman walking in front of her, who has such a thin neck, is her husband.

On the other side of the street a gentleman, holding his wife by the arm, has just whispered a few words in her ear and has started to smile. She immediately wipes all expression from her chalky, cream coloured face and blindly takes a few steps. There is no mistaking these signs: they are going to greet somebody. Indeed, after a moment, the gentleman throws his hands up. When his fingers reach his felt hat, they hesitate a second before coming down delicately on the crown. While he slowly raises his hat, bowing his head a little to help its removal, his wife gives a little start and forces a young smile on her face. A bowing shadow passes them: but their twin smiles do not disappear immediately: they stay on their lips a few instants by a sort of magnetism. The lady and gentleman have regained their impassibility by the time they pass me, but a certain air of gaiety still lingers around their mouths.

It's finished: the crowd is less congested, the hat-raisings less frequent, the shop windows have something less exquisite about them: I am at the end of the Rue Tournebride. Shall I cross and go up the street on the other side? I think I have had enough: I have seen enough pink skulls, thin, distinguished and faded countenances. I am going to cross the Place Marignan. As I cautiously extricate myself from the column, the face of a real gentleman in a black hat springs up near me. The husband of the lady in navy blue. Ah, the fine, long dolichocephalic skull planted with short, wiry hair, the handsome American moustache sown with silver threads. And the smile, above all, the admirable, cultivated smile. There is also an eyeglass, somewhere on a nose.

Turning to his wife he says:

"He's a new factory designer. I wonder what he can be doing here. He's a good boy, he's timid and he amuses me."

Standing against the window of Julien, the pork butcher's shop, the young designer who has just done his hair, still pink, his eyes lowered, an obstinate look on his face, has all the appearance of a voluptuary. This is undoubtedly the first Sunday he has dared cross the Rue Tournebride. He looks like a lad who has been to his First Communion. He has crossed his hands behind his back and turned his face towards the window with an air of exciting modesty; without appearing to see, he looks at four small sausages shining in gelatine, spread out on a bed of parsley.

A woman comes out of the shop and takes his arm. His wife. She is quite young, despite her pocked skin. She can stroll along the Rue Tournebride as much as she likes, no one will mistake her for a lady; she is betrayed by the cynical sparkle of her eyes, by her sophisticated look. Real ladies do not know the price of things, they like adorable follies; their eyes are like beautiful, hothouse flowers.

I reach the Brasserie Vézelise on the stroke of one. The old men are there as usual. Two of them have already started to eat. Four are playing cards and drinking apéritifs. The others are standing, watching them play while their table is being laid. The biggest, the one with a flowing beard, is a stockbroker. Another is a retired commissioner from the Inscription Maritime. They eat and drink like men of twenty. They eat sauerkraut on Sunday. The late arrivals question the others who are already eating:

"The usual Sunday sauerkraut?"

They sit down and breathe sighs of relaxation:

"Mariette, dear, a beer without a head and a sauerkraut."

This Mariette is a buxom wench. As I sit down at a table in the back a red-faced old man begins coughing furiously while being served with a vermouth.

"Come on, pour me out a little more," he says, coughing. But she grows angry herself: she hadn't finished pouring:

"Well, let me pour, will you? Who said anything to you? You holler before you're hurt."

The others begin to laugh.

"*Touché!*"

The stockbroker, going to his seat, takes Mariette by the shoulders:

"It's Sunday, Mariette. I guess we have our boyfriend to take us to the movies?"

"Oh sure! This is Antoinette's day off. I've got a date in here all day."

The stockbroker has taken a chair opposite the clean-shaven, lugubrious-looking old man. The clean-shaven old man immediately begins an animated story. The stockbroker does not listen to him: he makes faces and pulls at his beard. They never listen to each other.

I recognize my neighbours: small businessmen in the neighbourhood. Sunday is their maids' day off. So they come here, always sitting at the same table. The husband eats a fine rib of underdone beef. He looks at it closely and smells it from time to time. The wife picks at her plate. A heavy blonde woman of forty with red, downy cheeks. She has fine, hard breasts under her satin blouse. Like a man, she polishes off a bottle of Bordeaux at every meal.

I am going to read *Eugénie Grandet*. It isn't that I get any great pleasure out of it: but I have to do something. I open the book at random: the mother and daughter are speaking of Eugénie's growing love:

Eugénie kissed her hand saying:

"How good you are, dear Mama!"

At these words, the maternal old face, worn with long suffering, lights up.

"Don't you think he's nice?" Eugénie asked.

Mme Grandet answered only by a smile; then, after a moment of silence, she lowered her voice and said:

"Could you love him already? It would be wrong."

"Wrong?" Eugénie repeated. "Why? You like him, Nanon likes him, why shouldn't I like him? Now, Mama, let's set the table for his luncheon."

She dropped her work, her mother did likewise, saying:

"You are mad."

But she wanted to justify her daughter's madness by sharing it.

Eugénie called Nanon:

"What do you want, Mam'selle?"

"You'll have cream for noon, Nanon?"

"Ah, for noon—yes," the old servant answered.

"Well, give him his coffee very strong. I heard M. des Grassins say that they make coffee very strong in Paris. Put in a lot."

"Where do you want me to get it?"

"Buy some."

"And if Monsieur sees me?"

"He's out in the fields."

My neighbours had been silent ever since I had come, but, suddenly, the husband's voice distracted me from my reading.

The husband, amused and mysterious:

"Say, did you see that?"

The woman gives a start and looks, coming out of a dream. He eats and drinks, then starts again, with the same malicious air:

"Ha ha!"

A moment of silence, the woman has fallen back into her dream.

Suddenly she shudders and asks:

"What did you say?"

"Suzanne, yesterday."

"Ah, yes," the woman says, "she went to see Victor."

"What did I tell you?"

The woman pushes her plate aside impatiently.

"It's no good."

The side of her plate is adorned with lumps of gristle she spits out. The husband follows his idea.

"That little woman there . . ."

He stops and smiles vaguely. Across from us, the old stock-broker is stroking Mariette's arm and breathing heavily. After a moment:

"I told you so, the other day."

"What did you tell me?"

"Victor—that she'd go and see him. What's the matter?" he asks brusquely with a frightened look, "don't you like that?"

"It's no good."

"It isn't the same any more," he says with importance, "it isn't the way it was in Hécart's time. Do you know where he is, Hécart?"

"Domremy, isn't he?"

"Yes, who told you?"

"You did. You told me Sunday."

She eats a morsel of crumb which is scattered on the paper tablecloth. Then, her hand smoothing the paper on the edge of the table, with hesitation:

"You know, you're mistaken, Suzanne is more . . ."

"That may well be, my dear, that may well be," he answers, distractedly. He tries to catch Mariette's eyes, makes a sign to her.

"It's hot."

Mariette leans familiarly on the edge of the table.

"Yes, it is hot," the woman says, sighing deeply, "it's stifling here and besides the beef's no good, I'm going to tell the manager,

48

it's not the way it used to be, do open the window a little,
Mariette."

Amused, the husband continues:

"Say, didn't you see her eyes?"

"When, darling?"

He apes her impatiently:

"When, darling! That's you all over: in summer, when it
snows."

"Ah! you mean yesterday?"

He laughs, looks into the distance, and recites quickly, with
a certain application:

"The eyes of a cat on live coals."

He is so pleased that he seems to have forgotten what he
wanted to say.

She laughs in her turn, without malice:

"Ha ha, old devil!"

She taps on his shoulder.

"Old devil, old devil!"

He repeats, with assurance:

"The eyes of a cat on live coals!"

But she stops laughing:

"No, seriously, you know, she's really respectable."

He leans over, whispers a long story in her ear. Her mouth
hangs open for a moment, the face a little drawn like someone
who is going to burst out laughing, then suddenly she throws
herself back and claws at his hands.

"It isn't true, it isn't true."

He says, in a considered way:

"Listen to me, my pet, will you; since he said so himself.
If it weren't true why should he have said it?"

"No, no."

"But he said so: listen, suppose . . ."

She began to laugh:

"I'm laughing because I'm thinking about René."

"Yes."

He laughs too. She goes on in a low, earnest voice:

"So he noticed it Tuesday."

"Thursday."

"No, Tuesday, you know because of the . . ."

She sketches a sort of ellipsis in the air.

A long silence. The husband dips his bread in the gravy,
Mariette changes the plates and brings them tart. I too shall

want a tart. Suddenly the woman, a little dreamy, with a proud and somewhat shocked smile on her lips, says in a slow, dragging voice:

"Oh no, now come."

There is so much sensuality in her voice that it stirs him: he strokes the back of her neck with his fat hand.

"Charles, stop, you're getting me excited, darling," she murmurs, smiling, her mouth full.

I try to go back to my reading:

"Where do you want me to get it?"

"Buy some."

"And if Monsieur sees me?"

But I still hear the woman, she says:

"Say, I'm going to make Marthe laugh, I'm going to tell her . . ."

My neighbours are silent. After the tart, Mariette serves them prunes and the woman is busy, gracefully laying stones in her spoon. The husband staring at the ceiling, taps out a rhythm on the table. You might think that silence was their normal state and speech a fever that sometimes takes them.

"Where do you want me to get it?"

"Buy some."

I close the book. I'm going out for a walk.

It was almost three o'clock when I came out of the Brasserie vézelise; I felt the afternoon all through my heavy body. Not my afternoon, but theirs, the one a hundred thousand Bouvillois were going to live in common. At this same time, after the long and copious Sunday meal, they were getting up from the table, for them something had died. Sunday had spent its fleeting youth. You had to digest the chicken and the tart, get dressed to go out.

The bell of the Ciné-Eldorado resounded in the clear air. This is a familiar Sunday noise, this ringing in broad daylight. More than a hundred people were lined up along the green wall. They were greedily awaiting the hour of soft shadows, of relaxation, abandon, the hour when the screen, glowing like a white stone under water, would speak and dream for them. Vain desire: something would stay, taut in them: they were too afraid someone would spoil their lovely Sunday. Soon, as every Sunday, they would be disappointed: the film would be ridiculous, their neighbour would be smoking a pipe and spitting between his knees or else Lucien would be disagreeable, he wouldn't have a decent word to say, or else, as if on purpose, just for today, for the one time they went to the movies their intercostal neuralgia would start up again. Soon, as on every Sunday, small, mute rages would grow in the darkened hall.

I followed the calm Rue Bressan. The sun had broken through the clouds, it was a fine day. A family had just come out of a villa called "The Wave." The daughter was buttoning her gloves, standing on the pavement. She could have been about thirty. The mother, planted on the first step, was looking straight ahead with an assured air, breathing heavily. I could only see the enormous back of the father. Bent over the keyhole, he was closing the door and locking it. The house would remain black and empty till they got back. In the neighbouring houses, already bolted and deserted, the floor and furniture creaked gently. Before going out they had put out the fire in the dining-room fireplace. The father rejoins the two women, and the family walks away without a word. Where were they going? On Sunday you go to the memorial cemetery or you visit your parents, or, if you're completely free, you go for a walk along the jetty. I was free: I followed the Rue Bressan which leads to the Jetty Promenade.

The sky was pale blue: a few wisps of smoke, and from time to time, a fleeting cloud passed in front of the sun. In the distance I could see the white cement balustrade which runs along the Jetty Promenade; the sea glittered through the interstices. The family turns right on the Rue de l'Aumônier-Hilaire which climbs up the Coteau Vert. I saw them mount slowly, making three black stains against the sparkling asphalt. I turned left and joined the crowd streaming towards the sea.

There was more of a mixture than in the morning. It seemed as though all these men no longer had strength to sustain this fine social hierarchy they were so proud of before luncheon. Businessmen and officials walked side by side; they let themselves be elbowed, even jostled out of the way by shabby employees. Aristocrats, élite, and professional groups had melted into the warm crowd. Only scattered men were left who were not representative.

A puddle of light in the distance—the sea at low tide. Only a few reefs broke the clear surface. Fishing smacks lay on the sand not far from sticky blocks of stone which had been thrown pell-mell at the foot of the jetty to protect it from the waves, and through the interstices the sea rumbled. At the entrance to the outer harbour, against the sun-bleached sky, a dredge defined its shadow. Every evening until midnight it howls and groans and makes the devil of a noise. But on Sunday the workers are strolling over the land, there is only a watchman on board: there is silence.

The sun was clear and diaphanous like white wine. Its light barely touched the moving figures, gave them no shadow, no relief: faces and hands made spots of pale gold. All these men in topcoats seemed to float idly a few inches above the ground. From time to time the wind cast shadows against us which trembled like water; faces were blotted out for an instant, chalky white.

It was Sunday; massed between the balustrade and the gates of residents' chalets, the crowd dispersed slowly, forming itself into a thousand rivulets behind the "Grand Hôtel de la Compagnie Transatlantique." And children! Children in carriages, children in arms, held by the hand, or walking by twos and threes, in front of their parents, with a stiff and formal look. I had seen all these faces a little while before, almost triumphant in the youth of a Sunday morning. Now, dripping with sunlight, they expressed nothing more than calm, relaxation and a sort of obstinacy.

Little movement: there was still a little hat-raising here and there, but without the expansiveness, the nervous gaiety of the morning. The people all let themselves lean back a little, head high, looking into the distance, abandoned to the wind which swept them and swelled out their coats. From time to time, a short laugh, quickly stifled, the call of a mother, *Jeannot, Jeannot, come here.* And then silence. A faint aroma of pale tobacco: the commercial travellers are smoking it. Salammbô, Aicha; Sunday cigarettes. I thought I could detect sadness on some of the more relaxed faces: but no, these people were neither sad nor gay: they were at rest. Their wide-open, staring eyes passively reflected sea and sky. They would soon go back, drink a cup of family tea together round the dining-room table. For the moment they wanted to live with the least expenditure, economize words, gestures, thoughts, float: they had only one day in which to smooth out their wrinkles, their crow's feet, the bitter lines made by a hard week's work. One day only. They felt the minutes flowing between their fingers; would they have time to store up enough youth to start anew on Monday morning? They filled their lungs because sea air vivifies: only their breathing, deep and regular as that of sleepers, still testified that they were alive. I walked stealthily, I didn't know what to do with my hard, vigorous body in the midst of this tragic, relaxed crowd.

The sea was now the colour of slate; it was rising slowly. By night it would be high; tonight the Jetty Promenade would be more deserted than the Boulevard Victor-Noir. In front and on the left, a red fire would burn in the channel.

The sun went down slowly over the sea. In passing, it lit up the window a Norman chalet. A woman, dazzled by it, wearily brought her hand to her eyes, and shook her head.

"Gaston, it's blinding me," she says with a little laugh.

"Hey, that sun's all right," her husband says, "it doesn't keep you warm but it's a pleasure to watch it."

Turning to the sea, she spoke again:

"I thought we might have seen it."

"Not a chance," the man says, "it's in the sun."

They must have been talking about the Ile Caillebotte whose southern tip could sometimes be seen between the dredge and the quay of the outer-harbour.

The light grows softer. At this uncertain hour one felt evening drawing in. Sunday was already past. The villas and grey balustrade seemed only yesterday. One by one the faces lost their leisured look, several became almost tender.

A pregnant woman leaned against a fair, brutal-looking young man.

"There, there . . . there, look," she said.

"What?"

"There . . . there . . . the seagulls."

He shrugged: there were no seagulls. The sky had become almost pure, a little blush on the horizon.

"I heard them. Listen, they're crying. . . ."

He answered:

"Something's creaking, that's all."

A gas lamp glowed. I thought the lamplighter had already passed. The children watch for him because he gives the signal for them to go home. But it was only a last ray of the setting sun. The sky was still clear, but the earth was bathed in shadow. The crowd was dispersing, you could distinctly hear the death rattle of the sea. A young woman, leaning with both hands on the balustrade, raised her blue face towards the sky, barred in black by lip-stick. For a moment I wondered if I were not going to love humanity. But, after all, it was their Sunday, not mine.

The first light to go on was that of the lighthouse on the Ile

53

Caillebotte; a little boy stopped near me and murmured in ecstasy, "Oh, the lighthouse!"

Then I felt my heart swell with a great feeling of adventure.

*   *   *   *   *

I turn left and, through the Rue des Voiliers, rejoin the Little Prado. The iron shutters have been lowered on all the shop windows. The Rue Tournebride is light but deserted, it has lost its brief glory of the morning; nothing distinguishes it any longer from the neighbouring streets. A fairly strong wind has come up. I hear the archbishop's metal hat creaking.

I am alone, most of the people have gone back home, they are reading the evening paper, listening to the radio. Sunday has left them with a taste of ashes and their thoughts are already turning towards Monday. But for me there is neither Monday nor Sunday: there are days which pass in disorder, and then, sudden lightning like this one.

Nothing has changed and yet everything is different. I can't describe it; it's like the Nausea and yet it's just the opposite: at last an adventure happens to me and when I question myself I see that it happens *that I am myself and that I am here;* I am the one who splits the night, I am as happy as the hero of a novel.

Something is going to happen: something is waiting for me in the shadow of the Rue Basse-de-Vieille, it is over there, just at the corner of this calm street that my life is going to begin. I see myself advancing with a sense of fatality. There is a sort of white milestone at the corner of the street. From far away, it seemed black and, at each stride, it takes on a whiter colour. This dark body which grows lighter little by little makes an extraordinary impression on me: when it becomes entirely clear, entirely white, I shall stop just beside it and the adventure will begin. It is so close now, this white beacon which comes out of the shadows, that I am almost afraid: for a moment I think of turning back. But it is impossible to break the spell. I advance, I stretch out my hand and touch the stone.

Here is the Rue Basse-de-Vieille and the enormous mass of Sainte-Cécile crouching in the shadow, its windows glowing. The metal hat creaks. I do not know whether the whole world has suddenly shrunk or whether I am the one who unifies all sounds and shapes: I cannot even conceive of anything around me being other than what it is.

I stop for a moment, I wait, I feel my heart beating; my

eyes search the empty square. I see nothing. A fairly strong wind has risen. I am mistaken. The Rue Basse-de-Vieille was only a stage: the *thing* is waiting for me at the end of the Place Ducoton.

I am in no hurry to start walking again. It seems as if I had touched the goal of my happiness. In Marseilles, in Shanghai, Meknes, what wouldn't I have done to achieve such satisfaction? I expect nothing more today, I'm going home at the end of an empty Sunday: it is there.

I leave again. The wail of a siren comes to me on the wind. I am all alone, but I march like a regiment descending on a city. At this very moment there are ships on the sea resounding with music; lights are turned on in all the cities of Europe; Communists and Nazis shooting it out in the streets of Berlin, unemployed pounding the pavements of New York, women at their dressing-tables in a warm room putting mascara on their eyelashes. And I am here, in this deserted street and each shot from a window in Neukölln, each hiccough of the wounded being carried away, each precise gesture of women at their toilet answers to my every step, my every heartbeat.

I don't know what to do in front of the Passage Gillet. Isn't anyone waiting for me at the end of the passage? But there is also at the Place Ducoton at the end of the Rue Tournebride something which needs me in order to come to life. I am full of anguish: the slightest movement irks me. I can't imagine what they want with me. Yet I must choose: I surrender the Passage Gillet, I shall never know what had been reserved for me.

The Place Ducoton is empty. Am I mistaken? I don't think I could stand it. Will nothing really happen? I go towards the lights of the Café Mably. I am lost, I don't know whether I'm going in: I glance through the large, steamed windows.

The place is full. The air is blue with cigarette smoke and steam rising from damp clothing. The cashier is at her counter. I know her well: she's red haired, as I am; she has some sort of stomach trouble. She is rotting quietly under her skirts with a melancholy smile, like the odour of violets given off by a decomposing body. A shudder goes through me: she . . . she is the one who was waiting for me. She was there, standing erect above the counter, smiling. From the far end of the café something returns which helps to link the scattered moments of that Sunday and solder them together and which gives them a meaning. I have spent the whole day only to end there, with my nose glued against the window, to gaze at this delicate face blossoming against the red curtain. All has stopped; my life has stopped: this wide window, this heavy air, blue as water, this fleshy white plant at the bottom of the water, and I myself, we form a complete and static whole: I am happy.

When I found myself on the Boulevard de la Redoute again nothing was left but bitter regret. I said to myself: Perhaps there is nothing in the world I cling to as much as this feeling of adventure; but it comes when it pleases; it is gone so quickly and how empty I am once it has left. Does it, ironically, pay me these short visits in order to show me that I have wasted my life?

Behind me, in the town, along the great, straight streets lit up by the cold reflection from the lamp posts, a formidable social event was dissolving. Sunday was at an end.

Monday:

How could I have written that pompous, absurd sentence yesterday:

"I was alone but I marched like a regiment descending on a city."

I do not need to make phrases. I write to bring certain circumstances to light. Beware of literature. I must follow the pen, without looking for words.

At heart, what disgusts me is having been so sublime last evening. When I was twenty I used to get drunk and then explain that I was a fellow in the style of Descartes. I knew I was inflating myself with heroism, but I let myself go, it pleased me. After that, the next morning I felt as sick as if I had awakened in a bed full of vomit. I never vomit when I'm drunk but that would really be better. Yesterday I didn't even have the excuse of drunkenness. I got excited like an imbecile. I must wash myself clean with abstract thoughts, transparent as water.

This feeling of adventure definitely does not come from events: I have proved it. It's rather the way in which the moments are linked together. I think this is what happens: you suddenly feel that time is passing, that each instant leads to another, this one to another one, and so on; that each instant is annihilated, and that it isn't worth while to hold it back, etc., etc. And then you attribute this property to events which appear to you *in* the instants; what belongs to the form you carry over to the content. You talk a lot about this amazing flow of time but you hardly see it. You see a woman, you think that one day she'll be

56

old, only you don't see her grow old. But there are moments when you think you *see* her grow old and feel yourself growing old with her: this is the feeling of adventure.

If I remember correctly, they call that the irreversibility of time. The feeling of adventure would simply be that of the irreversibility of time. But why don't we always have it? Is it that time is not always irreversible? There are moments when you have the impression that you can do what you want, go forward or backward, that it has no importance; and then other times when you might say that the links have been tightened and, in that case, it's not a question of missing your turn because you could never start again.

Anny made the most of time. When she was in Djibouti and I was in Aden, and I used to go and see her for twenty-four hours, she managed to multiply the misunderstandings between us until there were only exactly sixty minutes before I had to leave; sixty minutes, just long enough to make you feel the seconds passing one by one. I remember one of those terrible evenings. I was supposed to leave at midnight. We went to an open-air movie; we were desperate, she as much as I. Only she led the game. At eleven o'clock, at the beginning of the main picture, she took my hand and held it in hers without a word. I was flooded with a bitter joy and I understood, without having to look at my watch, that it was eleven o'clock. From that time on we began to feel the minutes passing. That time we were leaving each other for three months. At one moment they threw a completely blank image on the screen, the darkness lifted, and I saw Anny was crying. Then, at midnight, she let go of my hand, after pressing it violently; I got up and left without saying a word to her. That was a good job.

7.00 *p.m.*

Work today. It didn't go too badly; I wrote six pages with a certain amount of pleasure. The more so since it was a question of abstract considerations on the reign of Paul I. After last evening's orgy I stayed tightly buttoned up all day. It would not do to appeal to my heart! But I felt quite at ease unwinding the mainsprings of the Russian autocracy.

But this Rollebon annoys me. He is mysterious in the smallest things. What could he have been doing in the Ukraine in 1804? He tells of his trip in veiled words:

"Posterity will judge whether my efforts, which no success

could recompense, did not merit something better than a brutal denial and all the humiliations which had to be borne in silence, when I had locked in my breast the wherewithal to silence the scoffers once and for all."

I let myself be caught once: he showed himself full of pompous reticence on the subject of a short trip he took to Bouville in 1790. I lost a month verifying his assertions. Finally, it came out that he had made the daughter of one of his tenant farmers pregnant. Can it be that he is nothing more than a low comedian?

I feel full of ill-will towards this lying little fop; perhaps it is spite: I was quite pleased that he lied to others but I would have liked him to make an exception of me; I thought we were thick as thieves and that he would finally tell me the truth. He told me nothing, nothing at all; nothing more than he told Alexander or Louis XVIII whom he duped. It matters a lot to me that Rollebon should have been a good fellow. Undoubtedly a rascal: who isn't? But a big or little rascal? I don't have a high enough opinion of historical research to lose my time over a dead man whose hand, if he were alive, I would not deign to touch. What do I know about him? You couldn't dream of a better life than his: but did he live it? If only his letters weren't so formal. . . . Ah, I wish I had known his look, perhaps he had a charming way of leaning his head on his shoulder or mischievously placing his long index on his nose, or sometimes, between two polished lies, having a sudden fit of violence which he stifled immediately. But he is dead: all that is left of him is "A Treatise on Strategy" and "Reflexions on Virtue."

I could imagine him so well if I let myself go: beneath his brilliant irony which made so many victims, he was simple, almost naïve. He thinks little, but at all times, by a profound intuition, he does exactly what should be done. His rascality is candid, spontaneous, generous, as sincere as his love of virtue. And when he betrays his benefactors and friends, he turns back gravely to the events, and draws a moral from them. He never thought he had the slightest right over others, any more than others over him: he considered as unjustified and gratuitous the gifts life gave him. He attached himself strongly to everything but detaches himself easily. He never wrote his own letters or his works himself: but had them composed by the public scribe.

But if this is where it all leads me, I'd be better off writing a novel on the Marquis de Rollebon.

11.00 *p.m.*

I dined at the *Rendezvous des Cheminots*. The patronne was there and I had to kiss her, but it was mainly out of politeness. She disgusts me a little, she is too white and besides, she smells like a newborn child. She pressed my head against her breast in a burst of passion: she thinks it is the right thing. I played distractedly with her sex under the cover; then my arm went to sleep. I thought about de Rollebon: after all, why shouldn't I write a novel on his life? I let my arm run along the woman's thigh and suddenly saw a small garden with low, wide trees on which immense hairy leaves were hanging. Ants were running everywhere, centipedes and ringworm. There were even more horrible animals: their bodies were made from a slice of toast, the kind you put under roast pigeons; they walked sideways with legs like a crab. The larger leaves were black with beasts. Behind the cactus and the Barbary fig trees, the Velleda of the public park pointed a finger at her sex. "This park smells of vomit," I shouted.

"I didn't want to wake you up," the woman said, "but the sheet got folded under my back and besides I have to go down and look after the customers from the Paris train."

Shrove Tuesday:

I gave Maurice Barrès a spanking. We were three soldiers and one of us had a hole in the middle of his face. Maurice Barrès came up to us and said, "That's fine!" and he gave each of us a small bouquet of violets. "I don't know where to put them," said the soldier with the hole in his head. Then Maurice Barrès said, "Put them in the hole you have in your head." The soldier answered, "I'm going to stick them up your ass." And we turned over Maurice Barrès and took his pants off. He had a cardinal's red robe on under his trousers. We lifted up the robe and Maurice Barrès began to shout: "Look out! I've got on trousers with foot-straps." But we spanked him until he bled and then we took the petals of violets and drew the face of Déroulède on his backside.

For some time now I have been remembering my dreams much too often. Moreover, I must toss quite a bit because every morning I find the blankets on the floor. Today is Shrove Tuesday but that means very little in Bouville; in the whole town there are hardly a hundred people to dress up.

As I was going down the stairs the landlady called me:

"There's a letter for you."

A letter: the last one I got was from the curator of the Rouen public library, last May. The landlady leads me to her office and holds out a long thick yellow envelope: Anny had written to me. I hadn't heard from her for five years. The letter had been sent to my old Paris address, it was postmarked the first of February.

I go out; I hold the envelope between my fingers, I dare not open it: Anny hasn't changed her letter paper, I wonder if she still buys it at the little stationer's in Piccadilly. I think that she has also kept her coiffure, her heavy blonde locks she didn't want to cut. She must struggle patiently in front of mirrors to save her face: it isn't vanity or fear of growing old; she wants to stay as she is, just as she is. Perhaps this is what I liked best in her, this austere loyalty to her most insignificant features.

The firm letters of the address, written in violet ink (she hasn't changed her ink, either) still shine a little:

"Monsieur Antoine Roquentin"

How I love to read my name on envelopes. In a mist I have recaptured one of her smiles, I can see her eyes, her inclined head: whenever I sat down she would come and plant herself in front of me, smiling. She stood half a head higher than I, she grasped my shoulders and shook me with outstretched arms.

The envelope is heavy, it must have at least six pages in it. My old concierge has scrawled hieroglyphics over this lovely writing:

"Hotel Printania—Bouville"

These small letters do not shine.

When I open the letter my disillusion makes me six years younger:

I don't know how Anny manages to fill up her envelopes: there's never anything inside.

That sentence—I said it a hundred times during the spring of 1924, struggling, as today, to extract a piece of paper, folded in four, from its lining. The lining is a splendour: dark green with gold stars; you'd think it was a heavy piece of starched cloth. It alone makes three-quarters of the envelope's weight.

Anny had written in pencil:

"I am passing through Paris in a few days. Come and see me at the Hotel d'Espagne, on February 20. Please! (she had added 'I beg you' above the line and joined it to 'to see me' in a curious spiral). I *must* see you. Anny."

In Meknes, in Tangiers, when I went back, in the evening, I sometimes used to find a note on my bed: "I want to see you right away." I used to run, Anny would open the door for me, her eyebrows raised, looking surprised. She had nothing more to tell me; she was even a little irritated that I had come. I'll go; she may refuse to see me. Or they may tell me at the desk: "No one by that name is stopping here." I don't believe she'd do that. Only she could write me, a week from now and tell me she's changed her mind and to make it some other time.

People are at work. This is a flat and stale Shrove Tuesday. The Rue des Mutilés smells strongly of damp wood, as it does every time it's going to rain. I don't like these queer days: the movies have matinées, the school children have a vacation; there is a vague feeling of holiday in the air which never ceases to attract attention but disappears as soon as you notice it.

I am undoubtedly going to see Anny but I can't say that the idea makes me exactly joyous. I have felt *désoeuvré* ever since I got her letter. Luckily it is noon; I'm not hungry but I'm going to eat to pass the time. I go to Camille's, in the Rue des Horlogers.

It's a quiet place; they serve sauerkraut or cassoulet all night. People go there for supper after the theatre; policemen send travellers there who arrive late at night and are hungry. Eight marble tables. A leather bench runs along the walls. Two mirrors eaten away by rust spots. The panes of the two windows and the door are frosted glass. The counter is in a recess in the back. There is also a room on the side. But I have never been in it; it is reserved for couples.

"Give me a ham omelet."

The waitress, an enormous girl with red cheeks, can never keep herself from giggling when she speaks to a man.

"I'm afraid I can't. Do you want a potato omelet? The ham's locked up: the patron is the only one who cuts it."

I order a cassoulet. The patron's name is Camille, a hard man.

The waitress goes off. I am alone in this dark old room. There is a letter from Anny in my despatch case. A false shame keeps me from reading it again. I try to remember the phrases one by one.

"My Dear Antoine——"

I smile: certainly not, Anny certainly did not write "My Dear Antoine."

Six years ago—we had just separated by mutual agreement—I decided to leave for Tokyo. I wrote her a few words. I could no longer call her "my dear love"; in all innocence I began, "My Dear Anny."

"I admire your cheek," she answered, "I have never been and am not your dear Anny. And I must ask you to believe that you are not my dear Antoine. If you don't know what to call me, don't call me anything, it's better that way."

I take her letter from my despatch case. She did not write "My Dear Antoine." Nor was there anything further at the end of the letter: "I must see you. Anny." Nothing that could give me any indication of her feelings. I can't complain: I recognize her love of perfection there. She always wanted to have "perfect moments." If the time was not convenient, she took no more interest in anything, her eyes became lifeless, she dragged along lazily like a great awkward girl. Or else she would pick a quarrel with me:

"You blow your nose solemnly like a bourgeois, and you cough very carefully in your handkerchief."

It was better not to answer, just wait: suddenly, at some signal which escapes me now, she shuddered, her fine languishing features hardened and she began her ant's work. She had an imperious and charming magic; she hummed between her teeth, looking all around, then straightened herself up smiling, came to shake me by the shoulders, and, for a few instants, seemed to give orders to the objects that surrounded her. She explained to me, in a low rapid voice, what she expected of me.

"Listen, do you want to make an effort or don't you? You were so stupid the last time. Don't you see how beautiful this moment could be? Look at the sky, look at the colour of the sun on the carpet. I've got my green dress on and my face isn't made up, I'm quite pale. Go back, go and sit in the shadow; you understand what you have to do? Come on! How stupid you are! Speak to me!"

I felt that the success of the enterprise was in my hands: the moment had an obscure meaning which had to be trimmed and perfected; certain motions had to be made, certain words spoken: I staggered under the weight of my responsibility. I stared and saw nothing, I struggled in the midst of rites which

Anny invented on the spot and tore them to shreds with my strong arms. At those times she hated me.

Certainly, I would go to see her. I still respect and love her with all my heart. I hope that someone else has had better luck and skill in the game of perfect moments.

"Your damned hair spoils everything," she said. "What can you do with a red-head?"

She smiled. First I lost the memory of her eyes, then the memory of her long body. I kept her smile as long as possible and then, finally lost that three years ago. Just now, brusquely, as I was taking the letter from the landlady's hands, it came back to me; I thought I saw Anny smiling. I try to refresh my memory: I need to feel all the tendernes that Anny inspires; it is there, this tenderness, it is near me, only asking to be born. But the smile does not return: it is finished. I remain dry and empty.

A man comes in, shivering.

"Messieurs, dames, bonjour."

He sits down without taking off his greenish overcoat. He rubs his long hands, clasping and unclasping his fingers.

"What will you have?"

He gives a start, his eyes look worried:

"Eh? give me a Byrrh and water."

The waitress does not move. In the glass her face seems to sleep. Her eyes are indeed open but they are only slits. That's the way she is, she is never in a hurry to wait on customers, she always takes a moment to dream over their orders. She must allow herself the pleasure of imagining: I believe she's thinking about the bottle she's going to take from above the counter, the white label and red letters, the thick black syrup she is going to pour out: it's a little as though she were drinking it herself.

I slip Anny's letter back into my despatch case: she has done what she could; I cannot reach the woman who took it in her hands, folded and put it in the envelope. Is it possible even to think of someone in the past? As long as we loved each other, we never allowed the meanest of our instants, the smallest grief, to be detached and forgotten, left behind. Sounds, smells, nuances of light, even the thoughts we never told each other; we carried them all away and they remained alive: even now they have the power to give us joy and pain. Not a memory: an implacable, torrid love, without shadow, without escape, without shelter. Three years rolled into one. That is why we parted: we did not have enough strength to bear this burden. And then, when Anny left me, all of a sudden, all at once, the three years crumbled into the past. I didn't even suffer, I felt emptied out. Then time began to flow again and the emptiness grew larger. Then, in Saïgon when I decided to go back to France, all that was still left—strange faces, places, quays on the banks of long rivers—all was wiped out. Now my past is nothing more than an enormous vacuum. My present: this waitress in the black blouse dreaming near the counter, this man. It seems as though I have learned all I know of life in books. The palaces of Benares, the terrace of the Leper King, the temples of Java with their great broken steps, are reflected in my eyes for an instant, but they have remained there, on the spot. The tramway that passes in front of the Hotel Printania in the evening does not catch the reflection of the neon sign-board; it flames up for an instant, then goes on with black windows.

This little man has not stopped looking at me: he bothers me. He tries to give himself importance. The waitress has finally decided to serve him. She raises her great black arm lazily, reaches the bottle, and brings it to him with a glass.

"Here you are, Monsieur."

"Monsieur Achille," he says with urbanity.

She pours without answering; all of a sudden he takes his finger from his nose, places both hands flat on the table. He throws his head back and his eyes shine. He says in a cold voice:

"Poor girl."

The waitress gives a start and I start too: he has an indefinable expression, perhaps one of amazement, as if it were someone else who had spoken. All three of us are uncomfortable.

The fat waitress recovers first: she has no imagination. She measures M. Achille with dignity: she knows quite well that one hand alone would be enough to tear him from his seat and throw him out.

"And what makes you think I'm a poor girl?"

He hesitates. He looks taken aback, then he laughs. His face crumples up into a thousand wrinkles, he makes vague gestures with his wrist.

"She's annoyed. It was just to say something: I didn't mean to offend."

But she turns her back on him and goes behind the counter: she is really offended. He laughs again:

"Ha ha! You know that just slipped out. Are you cross? She's cross with me," he says, addressing himself vaguely to me.

I turn my head away. He raises his glass a little but he is not thinking about drinking: he blinks his eyes, looking surprised and intimidated; he looks as if he were trying to remember something. The waitress is sitting at the counter; she picks up her sewing. Everything is silent again: but it isn't the same silence. It's raining: tapping lightly against the frosted glass windows; if there are any more masked children in the street, the rain is going to spoil their cardboard masks.

The waitress turns on the lights: it is hardly two o'clock but the sky is all black, she can't see to sew. Soft glow: people are in their houses, they have undoubtedly turned on the lights too. They read, they watch the sky from the window. For them it means something different. They have aged differently. They live in the midst of legacies, gifts, each piece of furniture holds a memory. Clocks, medallions, portraits, shells, paperweights, screens, shawls. They have closets full of bottles, stuffs, old clothes, newspapers; they have kept everything. The past is a landlord's luxury.

Where shall I keep mine? You don't put your past in your pocket; you have to have a house. I have only my body: a man entirely alone, with his lonely body, cannot indulge in memories; they pass through him. I shouldn't complain: all I wanted was to be free.

The little man stirs and sighs. He is all wrapped in his overcoat but from time to time he straightens up and puts on a haughty look. He has no past either. Looking closely, you would undoubtedly find in a cousin's house a photograph showing him at a wedding, with a wing collar, stiff shirt and a slight, young man's moustache. Of myself I don't think that even that is left.

Here he is looking at me again. This time he's going to speak to me, and I feel all taut inside. There is no sympathy between us: we are alike, that's all. He is alone, as I am, but more sunken into solitude than I. He must be waiting for his own Nausea or something of that sort. Now there are still people who *recognize* me, who see me and think: "He's one of us." So? What does he want? He must know that we can do nothing for one another. The families are in their houses, in the midst of their memories. And here we are, two wanderers, without memory. If he were suddenly to stand up and speak to me, I'd jump into the air.

The door opens with a great to-do: it is Doctor Rogé. "Good day everybody."

He comes in, ferocious and suspicious, swaying, swaying a little on his long legs which can barely support his body. I see him often, on Sundays, at the Brasserie Vézelise, but he doesn't know me. He is built like the old monitors at Joinville, arms like thighs, a chest measurement of 110, and he can't stand up straight.

"Jeanne, my little Jeanne."

He trots over to the coat rack to hang up his wide felt hat on the peg. The waitress has put away her sewing and comes without hurrying, sleep walking, to help the doctor out of his raincoat.

"What will you have, Doctor?"

He studies her gravely. That's what I call a handsome, masculine face. Worn, furrowed by life and passions. But the doctor has understood life, mastered his passions.

"I really don't know what I want," he says in a deep voice.

He has dropped onto the bench opposite me; he wipes his forehead. He feels at ease as soon as he gets off his feet. His great eyes, black and imperious, are intimidating.

"I'll have . . . I'll have . . . Oh, calvados. . . ."

The waitress, without making a move, studies this enormous, pitted face. She is dreamy. The little man raises his head with a smile of relief. And it is true: this colossus has freed us. Something horrible was going to catch us. I breathe freely: we are among men now.

"Well, is that calvados coming?"

The waitress gives a start and leaves. He has stretched out his stout arms and grasped the table at both ends. M. Achille is joyful; he would like to catch the doctor's eye. But he swings his legs and shifts about on the bench in vain, he is so thin that he makes no noise.

The waitress brings the calvados. With a nod of her head she points out the little man to the doctor. Doctor Rogé slowly turns: he can't move his neck.

"So it's you, you old swine," he shouts, "aren't you dead yet?"

He addresses the waitress:

"You let people like that in here?"

He stares at the little man ferociously. A direct look which puts everything in place. He explains:

"He's crazy as a loon, that's that."

He doesn't even take the trouble to let on that he's joking. He knows that the loony won't be angry, that he's going to smile.

And there it is: the man smiles with humility. A crazy loon: he relaxes, he feels protected against himself: nothing will happen to him today. I am reassured too. A crazy old loon: so that was it, so that was all.

The doctor laughs, he gives me an engaging, conspiratorial glance: because of my size, undoubtedly—and besides, I have a clean shirt on—he wants to let me in on his joke.

I do not laugh, I do not respond to his advances: then, without stopping to laugh, he turns the terrible fire of his eyes on me. We look at each other in silence for several seconds: he sizes me up, looking at me with half-closed eyes, up and down he places me. In the crazy loon category? In the tramp category?

Still, he is the one who turns his face away: allows himself to deflate before one lone wretch, without social importance, it isn't worth talking about—you can forget it right away. He rolls a cigarette and lights it, then stays motionless with his eyes hard and staring like an old man's.

The fine wrinkles; he has all of them: horizontal ones running across his forehead, crow's feet, bitter lines at each corner of the mouth, without counting the yellow cords depending from his chin. There's a lucky man: as soon as you perceive him, you can tell he must have suffered, that he is someone who has lived. He deserves his face for he has never, for one instant, lost an occasion of utilizing his past to the best of his ability: he has stuffed it full, used his experience on women and children, exploited them.

M. Achille is probably happier than he has ever been. He is agape with admiration; he drinks his Byrrh in small mouthfuls and swells his cheeks out with it. The doctor knew how to take him! The doctor wasn't the one to let himself be hypnotized by an old madman on the verge of having his fit; one good blow, a few rough, lashing words, that's what they need. The doctor has experience. He is a professional in experience: doctors, priests, magistrates and army officers know men through and through as if they had made them.

I am ashamed for M. Achille. We are on the same side, we should have stood up against them. But he left me, he went over to theirs: he honestly believes in experience. Not in his, not in mine. In Doctor Rogé's. A little while ago M. Achille felt queer, he felt lonely: now he knows that there are others like him, many others: Doctor Rogé has met them, he could tell M. Achille the case history of each one of them and tell him how they ended up.

M. Achille is simply a case and lets himself be brought back easily to the accepted ideas.

How I would like to tell him he's being deceived, that he is the butt of the important. Experienced professionals? They have dragged out their life in stupor and semi-sleep, they have married hastily, out of impatience, they have made children at random. They have met other men in cafés, at weddings and funerals. Sometimes, caught in the tide, they have struggled against it without understanding what was happening to them. All that has happened around them has eluded them; long, obscure shapes, events from afar, brushed by them rapidly and when they turned to look all had vanished. And then, around forty, they christen their small obstinacies and a few proverbs with the name of experience, they begin to simulate slot machines: put a coin in the left hand slot and you get tales wrapped in silver paper, put a coin in the slot on the right and you get precious bits of advice that stick to your teeth like caramels. As far as that goes, I too could have myself invited to people's houses and they'd say among themselves that I was a *"grand voyageur devant l'Eternel."* Yes: the Mohamedans squat to pass water; instead of ergot, Hindu midwives use ground glass in cow dung; in Borneo when a woman has her period she spends three days and nights on the roof of her house. In Venice I saw burials in gondolas, Holy Week festivals in Seville, I saw the Passion Play at Oberammergau. Naturally, that's just a small sample of all I know: I could lean back in a chair and begin amusement:

"Do you know Jihlava, Madame? It's a curious little town in Moravia where I stayed in 1924."

And the judge who has seen so many cases would add at the end of my story:

"How true it is, Monsieur, how human it is. I had a case just like that at the beginning of my career. It was in 1902. I was deputy judge in Limoges . . ."

But I was bothered too much by that when I was young. Yet I didn't belong to a professional family. There are also amateurs. These are secretaries, office workers, shopkeepers, people who listen to others in cafés: around forty they feel swollen, with an experience they can't get rid of. Luckily they've made children on whom they can pass it off. They would like to make us believe that their past is not lost, that their memories are condensed, gently transformed into Wisdom. Convenient past! Past handed out of a pocket! little gilt books full of fine sayings. "Believe me,

I'm telling you from experience, all I know I've learned from life." Has life taken charge of their thoughts? They explain the new by the old—and the old they explain by the older still, like those historians who turn a Lenin into a Russian Robespierre, and a Robespierre into a French Cromwell: when all is said and done, they have never understood anything at all. . . . You can imagine a morose idleness behind their importance: they see the long parade of pretences, they yawn, they think there's nothing new under the sun. "Crazy as a loon"—and Doctor Rogé vaguely recalls other crazy loons, not remembering any one of them in particular. Now, nothing M. Achille can do will surprise us: *because* he's a crazy loon!

He is not one: he is afraid. What is he afraid of? When you want to understand something you stand in front of it, alone, without help: all the past in the world is of no use. Then it disappears and what you wanted to understand disappears with it.

General ideas are more flattering. And then professionals and even amateurs always end up by being right. Their wisdom prompts them to make the least possible noise, to live as little as possible, to let themselves be forgotten. Their best stories are about the rash and the original, who were chastised. Yes, that's how it happens and no one will say the contrary. Perhaps M. Achille's conscience is not easy. Perhaps he tells himself he wouldn't be there if he had heeded his father's advice or his elder sister's. The doctor has the right to speak: he has not wasted his life; he has known how to make himself useful. He rises calm and powerful, above this flotsam and jetsam; he is a rock.

Doctor Rogé has finished his calvados. His great body relaxes and his eyelids droop heavily. For the first time I see his face without the eyes: like a cardboard mask, the kind they're selling in the shops today. His cheeks have a horrid pink colour. . . . The truth stares me in the face: this man is going to die soon. He surely knows; he need only look in the glass: each day he looks a little more like the corpse he will become. That's what their experience leads to, that's why I tell myself so often that they smell of death: it is their last defence. The doctor would like to believe, he would like to hide out the stark reality; that he is alone, without gain, without a past, with an intelligence which is clouded, a body which is disintegrating. For this reason he has carefully built up, furnished, and padded his nightmare compensation: he says he is making progress. Has he vacuums in his thoughts, moments when everything spins round in his head?

It's because his judgment no longer has the impulse of youth. He no longer understands what he reads in books? It's because he's so far away from books now. He can't make love any more? But he has made love in the past. Having made love is much better than still making it: looking back, he compares, ponders. And this terrible corpse's face! To be able to stand the sight of it in the glass he makes himself believe that the lessons of experience are graven on it.

The doctor turns his head a little. His eyelids are half-open and he watches me with the red eyes of sleep. I smile at him. I would like this smile to reveal all that he is trying to hide from himself. That would give him a jolt if he could say to himself: "There's someone who *knows* I'm going to die!" But his eyelids droop: he sleeps. I leave, letting M. Achille watch over his slumber.

The rain has stopped, the air is mild, the sky slowly rolls up fine black images: it is more than enough to frame a perfect moment; to reflect these images, Anny would cause dark little tides to be born in our hearts. I don't know how to take advantage of the occasion: I walk at random, calm and empty, under this wasted sky.

Wednesday:

I must not be afraid.

Thursday:

Four pages written. Then a long moment of happiness. Must not think too much about the value of History. You run the risk of being disgusted with it. Must not forget that de Rollebon now represents the only justification for my existence.

A week from today I'm going to see Anny.

Friday:

The fog was so thick on the Boulevard de la Redoute that I thought it wise to stick close to the walls of the Caserne; on my right, the headlights of cars chased a misty light before them and it was impossible to see the end of the pavement. There were people around me; I sometimes heard the sound of their steps or the low hum of their voices: but I saw no one. Once, a woman's face took shape somewhere at the height of my shoulder, but the fog engulfed it immediately; another time someone brushed by me breathing very heavily. I didn't know where I was going, I was too absorbed: you had to go ahead with caution, feel the ground with the end of your foot and even stretch your hands ahead of you. I got no pleasure from this exercise. Yet I wasn't thinking about going back, I was caught. Finally, after half an hour, I noticed a bluish vapour in the distance. Using this as a guide, I soon arrived at the edge of a great glow; in the centre, piercing the fog with its lights, I recognized the Café Mably.

The Café Mably has twelve electric lights, but only two of them were on, one above the counter, the other on the ceiling. The only waiter there pushed me forcibly into a dark corner.

"This way, Monsieur, I'm cleaning up."

He had on a jacket, without vest or collar, with a white and violet striped shirt. He was yawning, looking at me sourly, running his fingers through his hair.

"Black coffee and rolls."

He rubbed his eyes without answering and went away. I was up to my eyes in shadow, an icy, dirty shadow. The radiator was surely not working.

I was not alone. A woman with a waxy complexion was sitting opposite me and her hands trembled unceasingly, sometimes smoothing her blouse, sometimes straightening her black hat. She was with a big blond man eating a brioche without saying a word. The silence weighed on me, I wanted to light my pipe but I would have felt uncomfortable attracting their attention by striking the match.

The telephone bell rings. The hands stopped: they stayed clutching at the blouse. The waiter took his time. He calmly finished sweeping before going to take off the receiver. "Hello, is that Monsieur Georges? Good morning, Monsieur Georges . . . Yes, Monsieur Georges . . . The patron isn't here . . . Yes, he should be down . . . Yes, but with a fog like this . . . He generally comes down about eight . . . Yes, Monsieur Georges, I'll tell him. Good-bye, Monsieur Georges."

Fog weighed on the windows like a heavy curtain of grey velvet. A face pressed against the pane for an instant, disappeared.

The woman said plaintively:

"Tie up my shoe for me."

"It isn't untied," the man said without looking.

She grew agitated. Her hands moved along her blouse and over her neck like large spiders.

"Yes, yes, do up my shoe."

He bent down, looking cross, and lightly touched her foot under the table.

"It's done."

She smiled with satisfaction. The man called the waiter.

"How much do I owe you?"

"How many brioches?" the waiter asked.

I had lowered my eyes so as not to seem to stare at them. After a few instants I heard a creaking and saw the hem of a skirt and two shoes stained with dry mud appear. The man's shoes followed, polished and pointed. They came towards me, stopped and turned sideways: he was putting on his coat. At that moment a hand at the end of a stiff arm moved downwards; hesitated a moment, then scratched at the skirt.

"Ready?" the man asked.

The hand opened and touched a large splash of mud on the right shoe, then disappeared.

He had picked up a suitcase near the coat rack. They went out, I saw them swallowed up in the fog.

"They're on the stage," the waiter told me as he brought me coffee.

"They play the *entr'acte* at the Ciné-Palace. The woman blindfolds herself and tells the name and age of people in the audience. They're leaving today because it's Friday and the programme changes."

He went to get a plate of rolls from the table the people had just left.

"Don't bother."

I didn't feel inclined to eat those rolls.

"I have to turn off the light. Two lights for one customer at nine in the morning: the patron would give me hell."

Shadow floods the café. A feeble illumination, spattered with grey and brown, falls on the upper windows.

"I'd like to see M. Fasquelle."

I hadn't seen the old woman come in. A gust of cold air made me shiver.

"M. Fasquelle hasn't come down yet."

"Mme Florent sent me," she went on, "she isn't well. She won't be in today."

Mme Florent is the cashier, the red-haired girl.

"This weather," the old woman said, "is bad for her stomach."

The waiter put on an important air:

"It's the fog," he answered, "M. Fasquelle has the same trouble; I'm surprised he isn't down yet. Somebody telephoned for him. Usually he's down at eight."

Mechanically the old woman looked at the ceiling.

"Is he up there?"

"Yes, that's his room."

In a dragging voice, as if she were talking to herself, the old woman said:

"Suppose he's dead. . . ."

"Well! . . ." The waiter's face showed lively indignation. "Well I never!"

Suppose he were dead. . . . This thought brushed by me. Just the kind of idea you get on foggy days.

The old woman left. I should have done the same: it was cold and dark. The fog filtered in under the door, it was going to rise slowly and penetrate everything. I could have found light and warmth at the library.

Again a face came and pressed against the window; it grimaced.

"You just wait," the waiter said angrily and ran out.

The face disappeared, I was alone. I reproached myself bitterly for leaving my room. The fog would have filled it by this time; I would be afraid to go back.

Behind the cashier's table, in the shadow, something cracked. It came from the private staircase: was the manager coming down at last? No: there was no one; the steps were cracking by themselves. M. Fasquelle was still sleeping. Or else he was dead, up there above my head. Found dead in bed one foggy morning sub heading. in the café, customers went on eating without suspecting.

But was he still in bed? Hadn't he fallen out, dragging the sheets with him, bumping his head against the floor?

I know M. Fasquelle very well; he sometimes asks after my health. A big, jolly fellow with a carefully combed beard: if he is dead it's from a stroke. He will be the colour of eggplant with his tongue hanging out of his mouth. The beard in the air, the neck violet under the frizzle of hair.

The private stairway is lost in darkness. I can hardly make out the newel post. This shadow would have to be crossed. The stairs would creak. Above, I would find the door of the room . . .

The body is there over my head. I would turn the switch: I would touch his warm skin to see . . . I can't stand any more,

I get up. If the waiter catches me on the stairs I'll tell him I heard a noise.

The waiter came in suddenly, breathless.

"*Oui*, Monsieur!" he shouted.

Imbecile! He advanced towards me.

"That's two francs."

"I heard a noise up there," I told him.

"It's about time!"

"Yes, but I think something's wrong: it sounded like choking, and then there was a thud."

It sounded quite natural in the dark café with the fog behind the windows. I shall never forget his eyes.

"You ought to go up and see," I added slyly.

"Oh, no!" he said; then: "I'm afraid he'd give me hell. What time is it?"

"Ten."

"If he isn't down here by ten-thirty I'll go up."

I took a step towards the door.

"You're going? You aren't going to stay?"

"No."

"Did it sound like a death rattle?"

"I don't know," I told him as I walked out, "maybe just because I was thinking about it."

The fog had lifted a little. I hurried towards the Rue Tournebride: I longed for its lights. It was a disappointment: there was light, certainly, dripping down the store windows. But it wasn't a gay light: it was all white because of the fog and rained down on your shoulders.

A lot of people about, especially women, maids, charwomen, ladies as well, the kind who say, "I do my own buying, it's safer." They sniffed at the window displays and finally went in.

I stopped in front of Julien's pork-butcher shop. Through the glass, from time to time, I could see a hand designing the truffled pigs' feet and the sausages. Then a fat blonde girl bent over, her bosom showing, and picked up a piece of dead flesh between her fingers. In his room five minutes from there, M. Fasquelle was dead.

I looked around me for support, a refuge from my thoughts. There was none: little by little the fog lifted, but some disquieting thing stayed behind in the streets. Perhaps not a real menace: it was pale, transparent. But it was that which finally frightened me. I leaned my forehead against the window. I noticed a dark red drop on the mayonnaise of a stuffed egg: it was blood. This red on the yellow made me sick at my stomach.

Suddenly I had a vision: someone had fallen face down and was bleeding in the dishes. The egg had rolled in blood; the slice of tomato which crowned it had come off and fallen flat, red on red. The mayonnaise had run a little: a pool of yellow cream which divided the trickle of blood into two arms.

"This is really too silly, I must pull myself together. I'm going to work in the library."

Work? I knew perfectly well I shouldn't write a line. Another day wasted. Crossing the park, I saw a great blue cape, motionless on the bench where I usually sit. There's someone at least who isn't cold.

When I entered the reading-room, the Self-Taught Man was just coming out. He threw himself on me:

"I have to thank you, Monsieur. Your photographs have allowed me to spend many unforgettable hours."

I had a ray of hope when I saw him; it might be easier to get through this day together. But, with the Self-Taught Man, you only appear to be two.

He rapped on an in-quarto volume. It was a History of Religion.

"Monsieur, no one was better qualified than Nouçapié to attempt this vast synthesis. Isn't that true?"

He seemed weary and his hands were trembling.

"You look ill," I said.

"Ah, Monsieur, I should think so! Something abominable has happened to me."

The guardian came towards us: a peevish little Corsican with moustaches like a drum major. He walks for whole hours among the tables, clacking his heels. In winter he spits in his handkerchiefs then dries them on the stove.

The Self-Taught Man came close enough to breathe in my face.

"I won't tell you anything in front of this man," he said in confidence. "If you would, Monsieur . . ."

"Would what?"

He blushed and his lips swayed gracefully.

"Monsieur, ah, Monsieur: all right, I'll lay my cards on the table. Will you do me the honour of lunching with me on Wednesday?"

"With pleasure."

I had as much desire to eat with him as I had to hang myself.

"I'm so glad," the Self-Taught Man said. He added rapidly, "I'll pick you up at your hotel, if you like," then disappeared, afraid, undoubtedly, that I would change my mind if he gave me time.

It was eleven-thirty. I worked until quarter of two. Poor work: I had a book in my hands but my thoughts returned incessantly to the Café Mably. Had M. Fasquelle come down by now? At heart, I didn't believe he was dead and this was precisely what irritated me: it was a floating idea which I could neither persuade myself to believe or disbelieve. The Corsican's shoes creaked on the floor. Several times he came and stood in front of me as though he wanted to talk to me. But he changed his mind and went away.

The last readers left around one o'clock. I wasn't hungry; above all I didn't want to leave. I worked a moment more then started up; I felt shrouded in silence.

I raised my head: I was alone. The Corsican must have gone down to his wife who is the concierge of the library; I wanted to hear the sound of his footsteps. Just then I heard a piece of coal fall in the stove. Fog had filled the room: not the real fog, that had gone a long time ago—but the other, the one the streets were still full of, which came out of the walls and pavements. The inconsistency of inanimate objects! The books were still there, arranged in alphabetical order on the shelves with their brown and black backs and their labels *up 1f* 7.996 (For Public Use—French Literature—) or *up sn* (For Public Use—Natural Science). But . . . how can I explain it? Usually, powerful and squat, along with the stove, the green lamps, the wide windows, the ladders, they dam up the future. As long as you stay between these walls, whatever happens must happen on the right or the left of the stove. Saint Denis himself could come in carrying his head in his hands and he would still have to enter on the right, walk between the shelves devoted to French Literature and the table reserved for women readers. And if he doesn't touch the ground, if he floats ten inches above the floor, his bleeding neck will be just at the level of the third shelf of books. Thus these objects serve at least to fix the limits of probability.

Today they fixed nothing at all: it seemed that their very existence was subject to doubt, that they had the greatest difficulty in passing from one instant to the next. I held the book I was reading tightly in my hands: but the most violent sensations went dead. Nothing seemed true; I felt surrounded by cardboard scenery which could quickly be removed. The world was waiting, holding its breath, making itself small—it was waiting for its convulsion, its Nausea, just like M. Achille the other day.

I got up. I could no longer keep my place in the midst of these unnatural objects. I went to the window and glanced out at the skull of Impétraz. I murmured: *Anything* can happen, *anything*. But evidently, it would be nothing horrible, such as humans might invent. Impétraz was not going to start dancing on his pedestal: it would be something else entirely.

Frightened, I looked at these unstable beings which, in an hour, in a minute, were perhaps going to crumble: yes, I was there, living in the midst of these books full of knowledge describing the immutable forms of the animal species, explaining that the right quantity of energy is kept integral in the universe; I was there, standing in front of a window whose panes had a definite refraction index. But what feeble barriers! I suppose it is out of laziness that the world is the same day after day. Today it seemed to want to change. And then, *anything, anything* could happen.

I had no time to lose: the Café Mably affair was at the root of this uneasiness. I must go back there, see M. Fasquelle alive, touch his beard or his hands if need be. Then, perhaps, I would be free.

I seized my overcoat and threw it round my shoulders; I fled. Crossing the Public Gardens I saw once more the man in the blue cape. He had the same ghastly white face with two scarlet ears sticking out on either side.

The Café Mably sparkled in the distance: this time the twelve lights must have been lit. I hurried: I had to get it over. First I glanced in through the big window, the place was deserted. The cashier was not there, nor the waiter—nor M. Fasquelle.

I had to make a great effort to go in; I did not sit down. I shouted "Waiter!" No one answered. An empty cup on a table. A lump of sugar on the saucer.

"Anyone here?"

An overcoat hung from a peg. Magazines were piled up in black cardboard boxes on a low table. I was on the alert for the slightest sound, holding my breath. The private stairway creaked slightly. I heard a foghorn outside. I walked out backwards, my eyes never leaving the stairway.

I know: customers are rare at two in the afternoon. M. Fasquelle had influenza; he must have sent the waiter out on an errand—maybe to get a doctor. Yes, but I needed to see M. Fasquelle. At the Rue Tournebride I turned back, I studied the garish, deserted café with disgust. The blinds on the second floor were drawn.

A real panic took hold of me. I didn't know where I was going. I ran along the docks, turned into the deserted streets in the Beauvoisis district; the houses watched my flight with their mournful eyes. I repeated with anguish: Where shall I go? where shall I go? *Anything* can happen. Sometimes, my heart pounding, I made a sudden right-about-turn: what was happening behind my back? Maybe it would start behind me and when I would turn around, suddenly, it would be too late. As long as I could stare at things nothing would happen: I looked at them as much as I could, pavements, houses, gaslights; my eyes went rapidly from one to the other, to catch them unawares, stop them in the midst of their metamorphosis. They didn't look too natural, but I told myself forcibly: this is a gaslight, this is a drinking fountain, and I tried to reduce them to their everyday aspect by the power of my gaze. Several times I came across barriers in my path: the Café des Bretons, the Bar de la Marine. I stopped, hesitated in front of their pink net curtains: perhaps these snug places had been spared, perhaps they still held a bit of yesterday's world, isolated, forgotten. But I would have to push the door open and enter. I didn't dare; I went on. Doors of houses frightened me especially. I was afraid they would open of themselves. I ended by walking in the middle of the street.

I suddenly came out on the Quai des Bassins du Nord. Fishing smacks and small yachts. I put my foot on a ring set in the stone. Here, far from houses, far from doors, I would have a moment of respite. A cork was floating on the calm, black-speckled water.

"And *under* the water? You haven't thought what could be *under* the water."

A monster? A giant carapace? sunk in the mud? A dozen pairs of claws or fins labouring slowly in the slime. The monster rises. At the bottom of the water. I went nearer, watching every eddy and undulation. The cork stayed immobile among the black spots.

Then I heard voices. It was time. I turned and began my race again.

I caught up with two men who were talking in the Rue Castiglione. At the sound of footsteps they started violently and both turned round. I saw their worried eyes upon me, then behind me to see if something else was coming. Were they like me? were they, too, afraid? We looked at each other in passing: a little more and we would have spoken. But the looks suddenly expressed defiance: on a day like this you don't speak to just anyone.

I found myself breathless on the Rue Boulibet. The die was cast: I was going back to the library, take a novel and try to read. Going along the park railing I noticed the man in the cape. He was still there in the deserted park; his nose had grown as red as his ears.

I was going to push open the gate but the expression on his face stopped me: he wrinkled his eyes and half-grinned, stupidly and affectedly. But at the same time he stared straight ahead at something I could not see with a look so hard and with such intensity that I suddenly turned back.

Opposite to him, one foot raised, her mouth half-opened, a little girl of about ten, fascinated, was watching him, pulling nervously at her scarf, her pointed face thrusting forward.

The man was smiling to himself, like someone about to play a good joke. Suddenly he stood up, his hands in the pockets of his cloak which fell to his feet. He took two steps forward, his eyes rolling. I thought he was going to fall. But he kept on smiling sleepily.

I suddenly understood: the cloak! I wanted to stop it. It would have been enough to cough or open the gate. But in my turn I was fascinated by the little girl's face. Her features were drawn with fear and her heart must have been beating horribly: yet I could also read something powerful and wicked on that rat-like face. It was not curiosity but rather a sort of assured expectation. I felt impotent: I was outside, on the edge of the park, on the edge of their little drama: but they were riveted one to the other by the obscure power of their desires, they made a pair together. I held my breath, I wanted to see what expression would come on that elfish face when the man, behind my back, would spread out the folds of his cloak.

But suddenly freed, the little girl shook her head and began to run. The man in the cloak had seen me: that was what stopped him. For a second he stayed motionless in the middle of the path, then went off, his back hunched. The cloak flapped against his calves.

I pushed open the gate and was next to him in one bound.

"Hey!" I shouted.

He began to tremble.

"A great menace weighs over the city," I said politely, and went on.

I went into the reading-room and took the *Chartreuse de Parme* from a table. I tried to absorb myself in reading, to find a refuge in the lucid Italy of Stendhal. Sometimes I succeeded, in spurts, in short hallucinations, then fell back again into this day of menace; opposite an old man who was clearing his throat, a young man, dreaming, leaning back in his chair.

Hours passed, the windows had turned black. There were four of us, not counting the Corsican who was in the office, stamping the latest acquisitions of the library. There was the little old man, the blond young man, a girl working for her degree—and I. From time to time one of us would look up, glance rapidly and scornfully at the other three as if he were afraid of them. Once the old man started to laugh: I saw the girl tremble from head to foot. But I had deciphered from upside down the title of the book she was reading: it was a light novel.

Ten minutes to seven. I suddenly realized that the library closed at seven. Once again I was going to be cast out into the town. Where would I go? What would I do?

The old man had finished his book. But he did not leave. He tapped his finger on the table with sharp, regular beats.

"Closing time soon," the Corsican said.

The young man gave a start and shot me a quick glance. The girl turned towards the Corsican, then picked up her book again and seemed to dive into it.

"Closing time," said the Corsican five minutes later.

The old man shook his head undecidedly. The girl pushed her book away without getting up.

The Corsican looked baffled. He took a few hesitating steps, then turned out the switch. The lamps went out at the reading tables. Only the centre bulb stayed lighted.

"Do we have to leave?" the old man asked quietly.

The young man got up slowly and regretfully. It was a question of who was going to take the longer time putting on his coat. When I left the girl was still seated, one hand flat on her book.

Below, the door gaped into the night. The young man, who was walking ahead, turned, slowly went down the stairs, and crossed the vestibule; he stopped for an instant on the threshold, then threw himself into the night and disappeared.

At the bottom of the stairs I looked up. After a moment the old man left the reading-room, buttoning his overcoat. By the time he had gone down three steps I took strength, closed my eyes and dived out.

I felt a cool little caress on my face. Someone was whistling in the distance. I raised my eyes: it was raining. A soft, calm rain. The square was lighted peacefully by four lamp-posts. A provincial square in the rain. The young man was going further away, taking great strides, and whistling. I wanted to shout to the others who did not yet know that they could leave without fear, that the menace had passed.

The old man appeared at the door. He scratched his cheek, embarrassed, then smiled broadly and opened his umbrella.

Saturday morning:

A charming sun with a light mist which promises a clear day. I had breakfast at the Café Mably.

Mme Florent, the cashier, smiled graciously at me. I called to her from my table:

"Is M. Fasquelle sick?"

"Yes; a bad go of flu: he'll have to stay in bed a few days. His daughter came from Dunkirk this morning. She's going to stay here and take care of him."

For the first time since I got her letter I am definitely happy at the idea of seeing Anny again. What has she been doing for six years? Shall we feel strange when we see each other? Anny doesn't know what it is to feel awkward. She'll greet me as if I had left her yesterday. I hope I shan't make a fool of myself, and put her off at the beginning. I must remember not to offer her my hand when I get there: she hates that.

How many days shall we stay together? Perhaps I could bring her back to Bouville. It would be enough if she would live here only for a few hours; if she would sleep at the Hotel Printania for one night. It would never be the same after that; I shouldn't be afraid any more.

Afternoon:

When I paid my first visit to the Bouville museum last year I was struck by the portrait of Olivier Blévigne. Faulty proportion? Perspective? I couldn't tell, but something bothered me: this deputy didn't seem plumb on his canvas.

I have gone back several times since then. But my worry persisted. I didn't want to admit that Bordurin, Prix de Rome, had made a mistake in his drawing.

But this afternoon, turning the pages of an old collection of the *Satirique Bouvillois,* a blackmail-sheet whose owner was accused of high treason during the war, I caught a glimpse of the truth. I went to the museum as soon as I left the library.

I crossed the shadow of the vestibule quickly. My steps made no sound on the black and white tiles. A whole race of plaster folk twisted their arms. In passing I glanced, through two great openings, and saw cracked vases, plates, and a blue and yellow satyr on a pedestal. It was the Bernard Palissy Room, devoted to ceramics and minor arts. But ceramics do not amuse me. A lady and gentleman in mourning were respectfully contemplating the baked objects.

Above the entrance to the main hall—the Salon Bordurin-Renaudas—someone had hung, undoubtedly only a little while ago, a large canvas which I did not recognize. It was signed by Richard Séverand and entitled "The Bachelor's Death." It was a gift of the State.

Naked to the waist, his body a little green, like that of a dead man, the bachelor was lying on an unmade bed. The disorder of sheets and blankets attested to a long death agony. I smiled, thinking about M. Fasquelle. But he wasn't alone: his daughter was taking care of him. On the canvas, the maid, his mistress, her features marked by vice, had already opened a bureau drawer and was counting the money. An open door disclosed a man in a cap, a cigarette stuck to his lower lip, waiting in the shadows. Near the wall a cat lapped milk indifferently.

This man had lived only for himself. By a harsh and well-deserved punishment, no one had come to his bedside to close his eyes. This painting gave me a last warning: there was still time, I could retrace my steps. But if I were to turn a deaf ear, I had been forewarned: more than a hundred and fifty portraits were hanging on the wall of the room I was about to enter;

with the exception of a few young people, prematurely taken from their families, and the mother superior of a boarding school, none of those painted had died a bachelor, none of them had died childless or intestate, none without the last rites. Their souls at peace that day as on other days, with God and the world, these men had slipped quietly into death, to claim their share of eternal life to which they had a right.

For they had a right to everything: to life, to work, to wealth, to command, to respect, and, finally, to immortality.

I took a moment to compose myself and entered. A guardian was sleeping near the window. A pale light, falling from the windows, made flecks on the paintings. Nothing alive in this great rectangular room, except a cat who was frightened at my approach and fled. But I felt the looks of a hundred and fifty pairs of eyes on me.

All who belonged to the Bouville élite between 1875 and 1910 were there, men and women, scrupulously painted by Renaudas and Bordurin.

The men had built Sainte-Cécile-de-la-Mer. In 1882, they founded the Federation of Shipowners and Merchants of Bouville "to group in one powerful entity all men of good will, to co-operate in national recovery and to hold in check the parties of disorder. . . ." They made Bouville the best equipped port in France for unloading coal and wood. The lengthening and widening of the quays were their work. They extended the Marine Terminal and, by constant dredging, brought the low-tide depth of anchorage to 10.7 meters. In twenty years, the catch of the fishing fleet which was 5,000 barrels in 1869, rose, thanks to them, to 18,000 barrels. Stopping at no sacrifice to assist the improvement of the best elements in the working-class, they created, on their own initiative, various centres for technical and professional study which prospered under their lofty protection. They broke the famous shipping strike in 1898 and gave their sons to their country in 1914.

The women, worthy helpmates of these strugglers, founded most of the town's charitable and philanthropic organizations. But above all, they were wives and mothers. They raised fine children, taught them rights and duties, religion, and a respect for the traditions which made France great.

The general complexion of these portraits bordered on dark brown. Lively colours had been banished, out of decency. However, in the portraits of Renaudas, who showed a partiality towards old men, the snowy hair and sidewhiskers showed up well against deep black backgrounds; he excelled in painting hands. Bordurin, who was a little weak on theory, sacrificed the hands somewhat but the collars shone like white marble.

It was very hot; the guardian was snoring gently. I glanced around the walls: I saw hands and eyes; here and there a spot of light obliterated a face. As I began walking towards the portrait of Olivier Blévigne, something held me back: from the moulding, Pacôme, the merchant, cast a bright look down on me.

He was standing there, his head thrown slightly back; in one hand he held a top hat and gloves against his pearl-grey trousers. I could not keep myself from a certain admiration: I saw nothing mediocre in him, nothing which allowed of criticism: small feet, slender hands, wide wrestler's shoulders, a hint of whimsy. He courteously offered visitors the unwrinkled purity of his face; the shadow of a smile played on the lips. But his grey eyes were not smiling. He must have been about fifty: but he was as young and fresh as a man of thirty. He was beautiful.

I gave up finding fault with him. But he did not let go of me. I read a calm and implacable judgment in his eyes.

Then I realized what separated us: what I thought about him could not reach him; it was psychology, the kind they write about in books. But his judgment went through me like a sword and questioned my very right to exist. And it was true, I had always realized it; I hadn't the right to exist. I had appeared by chance, I existed like a stone, a plant or a microbe. My life put out feelers towards small pleasures in every direction. Sometimes it sent out vague signals; at other times I felt nothing more than a harmless buzzing.

But for this handsome, faultless man, now dead, for Jean Pacôme, son of the Pacôme of the Défence Nationale, it had been an entirely different matter: the beating of his heart and the mute rumblings of his organs, in his case, assumed the form of rights to be instantly obeyed. For sixty years, without a halt, he had used his right to live. The slightest doubt had never crossed those magnificent grey eyes. Pacôme had never made a mistake. He had always done his duty, all his duty, his duty as son, husband, father, leader. He had never weakened in his demands for his due: as a child, the right to be well brought up, in a united family, the right to inherit a spotless name, a prosperous business; as a husband, the right to be cared for, surrounded with tender affection; as a father, the right to be venerated; as a leader, the right to be obeyed without a murmur. For a right is nothing more than the other aspect of duty. His extraordinary success (today the Pacômes are the richest family in Bouville) could never have surprised him. He never told himself he was happy, and while he was enjoying himself he must have done so with moderation, saying: "This is my refreshment." Thus pleasure itself, also becoming a right, lost its aggressive futility. On the left, a little above his bluish-grey hair, I noticed a shelf of books. The bindings were handsome; they were surely classics. Every evening before going to sleep, Pacôme undoubtedly read over a few pages of "his old Montaigne" or one of Horace's odes in the Latin text. Sometimes, too, he must have read a contemporary work to keep up to date. Thus he knew Barrès and Bourget. He would put his book down after a moment. He would smile. His look, losing its admirable circumspection, became almost dreamy. He would say: "How easy and how difficult it is to do one's duty."

He had never looked any further into himself: he was a leader.

There were other leaders on the walls: nothing but leaders. He was a leader—this tall, *ver-de-gris* man in his armchair. His white waistcoat was a happy reminder of his silver hair. (Attention to artistry was not excluded from these portraits, which were above all painted for moral edification, and exactitude was pushed to the furthest limit of scruple.) His long, slender hand was placed on the head of a small boy. An open book rested on his knees which were covered by a rug. But his look had strayed into the distance. He was seeing all those things which are invisible to young people. His name was written on a plaque of gilded wood below his portrait: his name must have been Pacôme or Parrottin, or Chaigneau. I had not thought of looking: for his close relatives, for this child, for himself, he was simply the grandfather; soon, if he deemed the time fitting to instruct his grandson about the scope of his future duties, he would speak of himself in the third person:

"You're going to promise your grandfather to be good, my boy, to work hard next year. Perhaps Grandfather won't be here any more next year."

In the evening of his life, he scattered his indulgent goodness over everyone. Even if he were to see me—though to him I was transparent—I would find grace in his eyes: he would think that I, too, had grandparents once. He demanded nothing: one has no more desires at that age. Nothing except for people to lower their voices slightly when he entered, nothing except a touch of tenderness and smiling respect when he passed, nothing except for his daughter-in-law to say sometimes: "Father is amazing; he's younger than all of us"; nothing except to be the only one able to calm the temper of his grandson by putting his hands on the boy's head and saying: "Grandfather knows how to take care of all those troubles"; nothing except for his son, several times a year, to come asking his advice on delicate matters; finally, nothing more than to feel himself serene, appeased, and infinitely wise. The old gentleman's hand barely weighed on his grandson's curls: it was almost a benediction. What could he be thinking of? Of his honourable past which conferred on him the right to speak on everything and to have the last word on everything. I had not gone far enough the other day: experience was much more than a defence against death; it was a right; the right of old men.

General Aubry, hanging against the moulding, with his great sabre, was a leader. Another leader: President Hébert, well read, friend of Impétraz. His face was long and symmetrical with an interminable chin, punctuated, just under the lip, by a goatee: he thrust out his jaw slightly, with the amused air of being distinguished, of rolling out an objection on principles like a faint belch. He dreamed, he held a quill pen: he was taking his relaxation too, by Heaven, and it was writing verses. But he had the eagle eye of a leader.

And soldiers? I was in the centre of the room, the cynosure of all these grave eyes. I was neither father nor grandfather, not even a husband. I did not have a vote, I hardly paid any taxes: I could not boast of being a taxpayer, an elector, nor even of having the humble right to honour which twenty years of obedience confers on an employee. My existence began to worry me seriously. Was I not a simple spectre? "Hey!" I suddenly told myself, "I am the soldier!" It really made me laugh.

A portly quinquagenarian politely returned a handsome smile. Renaudas had painted him with loving care, no touch was too tender for those fleshy, finely-chiselled little ears, especially for the hands, long, nervous, with loose fingers: the hands of a real savant or artist. His face was unknown to me: I must have passed before the canvas often without noticing it. I went up to it and read: *Rémy Parrottin, born in Bouville in* 1849, *Professor at the Ecole de Médecine, Paris.*

Parrottin: Doctor Wakefield had spoken to me of him: "Once in my life I met a great man, Rémy Parrottin. I took courses under him during the winter of 1904 (you know I spent two years in Paris studying obstetrics). He made me realize what it was to be a leader. He had it in him, I swear he did. He electrified us, he could have led us to the ends of the earth. And with all that he was a gentleman: he had an immense fortune— gave a good part of it to help poor students."

This is how this prince of science, the first time I heard him spoken of, inspired strong feelings in me. Now I stood before him and he was smiling at me. What intelligence and affability in his smile! His plump body rested leisurely in the hollow of a great leather armchair. This unpretentious wise man put people at their ease immediately. If it hadn't been for the spirit in his look you would have taken him for just anybody.

It did not take long to guess the reason for his prestige: he was loved because he understood everything; you could tell him anything. He looked a little like Renan, all in all, with more distinction. He was one of those who say:

"Socialists? Well, I go further than they do!" When you followed him down this perilous road you were soon to leave behind, not without a shiver, family, country, private property rights, and the most sacred values. You even doubted for a second the right of the bourgeois élite to command. Another step and suddenly everything was re-established, miraculously founded on solid reason, good old reasons. You turned around and saw the Socialists, already far behind you, all tiny, waving their handkerchiefs and shouting: "Wait for us!"

Through Wakefield I knew that the Master liked, as he himself said with a smile, "to deliver souls." To prolong his own, he surrounded himself with youth: he often received young men of good family who were studying medicine. Wakefield had often been to his house for luncheon. After the meal they retired to the smoking-room. The Master treated these students who were at their first cigarettes like men: he offered them cigars. He stretched out on a divan and discoursed at great length, his eyes half-closed, surrounded by an eager crowd of disciples. He evoked memories, told stories, drawing a sharp and profound moral from each. And if there were among those well-bred young men one who seemed especially headstrong, Parrottin would take a special interest in him. He made him speak, listened to him attentively, gave him ideas and subjects for meditation. It usually happened that one day the young man, full of generous ideas, excited by the hostility of his parents, weary of thinking alone, his hand against every man, asked to visit the Master privately, and, stammering with shyness, confided in him his most intimate thoughts, his indignations, his hopes. Parrottin embraced him. He said: "I understand you. I understood you from the first day." They talked on. Parrottin went far, still farther, so far that the young man followed him with great difficulty. After a few conversations of this sort one could detect a favourable change in the young rebel. He saw clearly within himself, he learned to know the deep bonds which attached him to his family, to his environment; at last he understood the admirable role of the élite. And finally, as if by magic, found himself once again, enlightened, repentant. "He cured more souls," concluded Wakefield, "than I've cured bodies."

Rémy Parrottin smiled affably at me. He hesitated, tried to understand my position, to turn gently and lead me back to the fold. But I wasn't afraid of him: I was no lamb. I looked at his fine forehead, calm and unwrinkled, his small belly, his hand set flat against his knee. I returned his smile and left.

Jean Parrottin, his brother, president of the S.A.B., leaned both hands on the edge of a table loaded with papers; his whole attitude signified to the visitor that the audience was over. His look was extraordinary; although abstracted yet shining with high endeavour. His dazzling eyes devoured his whole face. Behind this glow I noticed the thin, tight lips of a mystic. "It's odd," I said, "he looks like Rémy Parrottin." I turned to the Great Master: examining him in the light of this resemblance, a sense of aridity and desolation, a family resemblance took possession of his face. I went back to Jean Parrottin.

This man was one-ideaed. Nothing more was left in him but bones, dead flesh and Pure Right. A real case of possession, I thought. Once Right has taken hold of a man exorcism cannot drive it out; Jean Parrottin had consecrated his whole life to thinking about his Right: nothing else. Instead of the slight headache I feel coming on each time I visit a museum, he would have felt the painful right of having his temples cared for. It never did to make him think too much, or attract his attention to unpleasant realities, to his possible death, to the sufferings of others. Undoubtedly, on his death bed, at that moment when, ever since Socrates, it has been proper to pronounce certain elevated words, he told his wife, as one of my uncles told his, who had watched beside him for twelve nights, "I do not thank you, Thérèse; you have only done your duty." When a man gets that far, you have to take your hat off to him.

His eyes, which I stared at in wonderment, indicated that I must leave. I did not leave. I was resolutely indiscreet. I knew, as a result of studying at great length a certain portrait of Philip II in the library of the Escurial, that when one is confronted with a face sparkling with righteousness, after a moment this sparkle dies away, and only an ashy residue remains: this residue interested me.

Parrottin put up a good fight. But suddenly his look burned out, the picture grew dim. What was left? Blind eyes, the thin mouth of a dead snake, and cheeks. The pale, round cheeks of a child: they spread over the canvas. The employees of the S.A.B. never suspected it: they never stayed in Parrottin's office long enough. When they went in, they came up against that terrible look like a wall. From behind it, the cheeks were in shelter, white and flabby. How long did it take his wife to notice them? Two years? Five years? One day, I imagine, as her husband was sleeping, on his side with a ray of light caressing his nose, or else on a hot day, while he was having trouble with his digestion, sunk into an armchair, his eyes half-closed, with a splash of sunlight on his chin, she dared to look him in the face: all this flesh appeared to her defenceless, bloated, slobbering, vaguely obscene. From that day on, Mme Parrottin undoubtedly took command.

I took a few steps backward and in one glance covered all these great personages: Pacôme, President Hébert, both Parrottins, and General Aubry. They had worn top hats; every Sunday on the Rue Tournebride they met Mme Gratien, the mayor's wife, who saw Sainte Cécile in a dream. They greeted her with great ceremonious salutes, the secret of which is now lost.

They had been painted very minutely; yet, under the brush, their countenances had been stripped of the mysterious weakness of men's faces. Their faces, even the last powerful, were clear as porcelain: in vain I looked for some relation they could bear to trees and animals, to thoughts of earth or water. In life they evidently did not require it. But, at the moment of passing on to posterity, they had confided themselves to a renowned painter in order that he should discreetly carry out on their faces the system of dredgings, drillings, and irrigations by which, all around Bouville, they had transformed the sea and the land.

Thus, with the help of Renaudas and Bordurin, they had enslaved Nature: without themselves and within themselves. What these sombre canvases offered to me was man reconsidered by man, with, as sole adornment, the finest conquest of man: a bouquet of the Rights of Man and Citizen. Without mental reservation, I admired the reign of man.

A woman and a man came in. They were dressed in black and tried to make themselves inconspicuous. They stopped, enchanted, on the doorstep and the man automatically took off his hat.

"Ah!" the lady said, deeply touched.

The gentleman quickly regained his sang-froid. He said respectfully:

"It's a whole era!"

"Yes," the lady said, "this is in the time of my grandmother."

They took a few steps and met the look of Jean Parrottin. The woman stood gaping, but the man was not proud: he looked humble, he must have known intimidating looks and brief interviews well. He tugged gently at the woman's arm.

"Look at that one," he said.

Rémy Parrottin's smile had always put the humble at ease. The woman went forward and read studiously:

"Portrait of Rémy Parrottin, born in Bouville in 1849. Professor of the Ecole de Médecine, Paris, by Renaudas."

"Parrottin, of the Academy of Science," her husband said, "by Renaudas of the Institute. That's History!"

The lady nodded, then looked at the Great Master.

"How handsome he is," she said, "how intelligent he looks!"

The husband made an expansive gesture.

"They're the ones who made Bouville what it is," he said with simplicity.

"It's right to have had them put here, all together," the woman said tenderly.

We were three soldiers manœuvring in this immense hall. The husband who laughed with respect, silently, shot me a troubled glance and suddenly stopped laughing. A sweet joy flooded over me: well, I was right! It was really too funny.

The woman came near me.

"Gaston," she said, suddenly bold, "come here!"

The husband came towards us.

"Look," she went on, "he has a street named after him:

Olivier Blévigne. You know, the little street that goes up the Coteau Vert just before you get to Jouxtebouville."

After an instant, she added:

"He doesn't look exactly easy."

"No. Some people must have found him a pretty awkward customer."

These words were addressed to me. The man, watching me out of the corner of his eye, began to laugh softly, this time with a conceited air, a busy-body, as if he were Olivier Blévigne himself.

Olivier Blévigne did not laugh. He thrust his compact jaw towards us and his Adam's apple jutted out.

There was a moment of ecstatic silence.

"You'd think he was going to move," the lady said.

The husband explained obligingly:

"He was a great cotton merchant. Then he went into politics; he was a deputy."

I knew it. Two years ago I had looked him up in the *Petit Dictionnaire des Grands Hommes de Bouville* by Abbé Morellet. I copied the article.

"*Blévigne, Olivier-Martial, son of the late Olivier-Martial Blévigne, born and died in Bouville (1849–1908), studied law in Paris, passed Bar examinations in 1872. Deeply impressed by the Commune insurrection, which forced him, as it did so many other Parisians, to take refuge in Versailles under the protection of the National Assembly, he swore, at an age when young men think only of pleasure, 'to consecrate his life to the re-establishment of order.' He kept his word: immediately after his return to our city, he founded the famous Club de l'Ordre which every evening for many years united the principal businessmen and shipowners of Bouville. This aristocratic circle, which one might jokingly describe as being more restricted than the Jockey Club, exerted, until 1908, a salutary influence on the destiny of our great commercial port. In 1880, Olivier Blévigne married Marie-Louise Pacôme, younger daughter of Charles Pacôme, businessman (see Pacôme), and at the death of the latter, founded the company of Pacôme-Blévigne & Son. Shortly thereafter he entered actively into politics and placed his candidature before the deputation.*

"*'The country,' he said in a celebrated speech, 'is suffering from a most serious malady: the ruling class no longer wants to rule. And who then shall rule, gentlemen, if those who, by their* heredity, their education, their experience, have been rendered most fit for the exercising of power, turn from it in resignation or weariness? I have often said: to rule is not a right of the élite; it is a primary duty of the élite. Gentlemen, I beg of you: let us restore the principle of authority!'

"Elected first on October 4, 1885, he was constantly re-elected thereafter. Of an energetic and virile eloquence, he delivered many brilliant speeches. He was in Paris in 1898 when the terrible strike broke out. He returned to Bouville immediately and became the guiding spirit of the resistance. He took the initiative of negotiating with the strikers. These negotiations, inspired by an open-minded attempt at conciliation, were interrupted by the small uprising in Jouxtebouville. We know that the timely intervention of the military restored calm to our minds.

"The premature death of his son Octave, who had entered the Ecole Polytechnique at a very early age and of whom he wanted to 'make a leader' was a terrible blow to Olivier Blévigne. He was never to recover from it and died two years later, in February, 1908.

"Collected speeches: Moral Forces (1894: out of print), The Duty to Punish (1900: all speeches in this collection were given à propos of the Dreyfus Case: out of print), Will-power (1902: out of print). After his death, his last speeches and a few letters to intimate friends were collected under the title Labour Improbus (Plon, 1910). Iconography: there is an excellent portrait of him, by Bordurin, at the Bouville museum."

An excellent portrait, granted. Olivier Blévigne had a small black moustache, and his olive-tinted face somewhat resembled Maurice Barrès. The two men had surely met each other: they used to sit on the same benches. But the deputy from Bouville did not have the nonchalance of the President of the League of Patriots. He was stiff as a poker and sprang at you from his canvas like a jack-in-the-box. His eyes sparkled: the pupil was black, the cornea reddish. He pursed up his fleshy little mouth and held his right hand against his breast.

How this portrait annoyed me! Sometimes Blévigne seemed too large or too small to me. But today I knew what to look for.

I had learned the truth turning over the pages of the Satirique Bouvillois. The issue of 6 November, 1905 was devoted entirely to Blévigne. He was pictured on the cover, tiny, hanging on to the mane of old Combes, and the caption read: "The

Lion's Louse." Everything was explained from the first page on: Olivier Blévigne was only five feet tall. They mocked his small stature and squeaking voice which more than once threw the whole Chamber into hysterics. They accused him of putting rubber lifts in his shoes. On the other hand, Mme Blévigne, née Pacôme, was a horse. "Here we can well say," the paper added, "that his other half is his double."

Five feet tall! Yes, Bordurin, with jealous care, had surrounded him with objects which ran no risk of diminishing him; a hassock, a low armchair, a shelf with a few little books, a small Persian table. Only he had given him the same stature as his neighbour Jean Parrottin and both canvases had the same dimensions. The result was that the small table, in one picture, was almost as large as the immense table in the other, and that the hassock would have almost reached Parrottin's shoulder. The eye instinctively made a comparison between the two: my discomfort had come from that.

Now I wanted to laugh. Five feet tall! If I had wanted to talk to Blévigne I would have had to lean over or bend my knees. I was no longer surprised that he held up his nose so impetuously: the destiny of these small men is always working itself out a few inches above their head.

Admirable power of art. From this shrill-voiced mannikin, nothing would pass on to posterity save a threatening face, a superb gesture and the bloodshot eyes of a bull. The student terrorised by the Commune, the deputy, a bad-tempered midget; that was what death had taken. But, thanks to Bordurin, the President of the Club de l'Ordre, the orator of "Moral Forces," was immortal.

"Oh, poor little Pipo!"

The woman gave a stifled cry: under the portrait of Octave Blévigne "son of the late . . ." a pious hand had traced these words:

"Died at the Ecole Polytechnique in 1904."

"He's dead! Just like the Arondel boy. He looked intelligent. How hard it must have been for his poor mother! They make them work too hard in those big schools. The brain works, while you're asleep. I like those two-cornered hats, it looks so stylish. Is that what you call a 'cassowary?'"

"No. They have cassowaries at Saint-Cyr."

In my turn I studied the prematurely dead polytechnician. His wax complexion and well-groomed moustache would have been enough to turn one's idea to approaching death. He had foreseen his fate as well: a certain resignation could be read in his clear, far-seeing eyes. But at the same time he carried his head high; in this uniform he represented the French Army.

Tu Marcellus eris! Manibus date lilia plenis . . .

A cut rose, a dead polytechnician: what could be sadder?

I quietly followed the long gallery, greeting in passing, without stopping, the distinguished faces which peered from the shadows: M. Bossoire, President of the Board of Trade; M. Faby, President of the Board of Directors of the Autonomous Port of Bouville; M. Boulange, businessman, with his family; M. Rannequin, Mayor of Bouville; M. de Lucien, born in Bouville, French Ambassador to the United States and a poet as well; an unknown dressed like a prefect; Mother Sainte-Marie-Louise, Mother Superior of the Orphan Asylum; M. and Mme Théréson; M. Thiboust-Gouron, General President of the Trades Council; M. Bobot, principle administrator of the Inscription Maritime; Messrs. Brion, Minette, Grelot, Lefèbvre, Dr. and Mme Pain, Bordurin himself, painted by his son, Pierre Bordurin. Clear, cold looks, fine features, thin lips, M. Boulange was economical and patient, Mother Sainte-Marie-Louise of an industrious piety, M. Thiboust-Gouron was as hard on himself as on others. Mme Théréson struggled without weakening against deep illness. Her infinitely weary mouth told unceasingly of her suffering. But this pious woman had never said: "It hurts." She took the upper hand: she made up bills of fare and presided over welfare societies. Sometimes, she would slowly close her eyes in the middle of a sentence and all traces of life would leave her face. This fainting spell lasted hardly more than a second; shortly afterward, Mme Théréson would re-open her eyes and finish her sentence. And in the work room they whispered: "Poor Mme Théréson! She never complains."

I had crossed the whole length of the salon Bordurin-Renaudas. I turned back. Farewell, beautiful lilies, elegant in your painted little sanctuaries, good-bye, lovely lilies, our pride and reason for existing, good-bye you bastards!

Monday:

I'm not writing my book on Rollebon any more; it's finished, I *can't* write any more of it. What am I going to do with my life?

It was three o'clock. I was sitting at my table; I had set beside me the file of letters I stole in Moscow; I was writing:

"Care had been taken to spread the most sinister rumours. M. de Rollebon must have let himself be taken in by this manœuvre since he wrote to his nephew on the 13th of September that he had just made his will."

The Marquis was there: waiting for the moment when I should have definitively installed him in a niche in history, I had loaned him my life. I felt him like a glow in the pit of my stomach.

I studdenly realized an objection someone might raise: Rollebon was far from being frank with his nephew, whom he wanted to use, if the plot failed, as his defence witness with Paul I. It was only too possible that he had made up the story of the will to make himself appear completely innocent.

This was a minor objection; it wouldn't hold water. But it was enough to plunge me into a brown study. Suddenly I saw the fat waitress at "Camille's" again, the haggard face of M. Achille, the room in which I had so clearly felt I was forgotten, forsaken in the present. Wearily I told myself:

How can I, who have not the strength to hold to my own past, hope to save the past of someone else?

I picked up my pen and tried to get back to work; I was up to my neck in these reflections on the past, the present, the world. I asked only one thing: to be allowed to finish my book in peace.

But as my eyes fell on the pad of white sheets, I was struck by its look and I stayed, pen raised, studying this dazzling paper: so hard and far seeing, so present. The letters I had just inscribed on it were not even dry yet and already they belonged to the past.

"Care had been taken to spread the most sinister rumours . . ."

I had thought out this sentence, at first it had been a small part of myself. Now it was inscribed on the paper, it took sides against me. I didn't recognize it any more. I couldn't conceive it again. It was there, in front of me; in vain for me to trace some sign of its origin. Anyone could have written it. But I . . . I wasn't sure I wrote it. The letters glistened no longer, they were dry. That had disappeared too; nothing was left but their ephemeral spark.

I looked anxiously around me: the present, nothing but the present. Furniture light and solid, rooted in its present, a table, a bed, a closet with a mirror—and me. The true nature of the present revealed itself: it was what exists, and all that was not present did not exist. The past did not exist. Not at all. Not in things, not even in my thoughts. It is true that I had realized a long time ago that mine had escaped me. But until then I believed that it had simply gone out of my range. For me the past was only a pensioning off: it was another way of existing, a state of vacation and inaction; each event, when it had played its part, put itself politely into a box and became an honorary event: we have so much difficulty imagining nothingness. Now I knew: things are entirely what they appear to be—and behind them . . . there is nothing.

This thought absorbed me a few minutes longer. Then I violently moved my shoulders to free myself and pulled the pad of paper towards me.

". . . that he had just made his will."

An immense sickness flooded over me suddenly and the pen fell from my hand, spluttering ink. What happened? Did I have the Nausea? No, it wasn't that, the room had its paternal, everyday look. The table hardly seemed heavier and more solid to me, nor my pen more compact. Only M. de Rollebon had just died for the second time.

He was still there inside me a little while ago, quiet and warm, and I could feel him stir from time to time. He was quite alive, more alive to me than the Self-Taught Man or the woman at the "Railwaymen's Rendezvous." He undoubtedly had his whims, he could stay several days without showing himself; but often, on a mysteriously fine day, like a weather prophet, he put his nose out and I could see his pale face and bluish cheeks. And even when he didn't show himself, he was a weight on my heart and I felt full up.

Nothing more was left now. No more than, on these traces of dry ink, is left the memory of their freshness. It was my fault: I had spoken the only words I should not have said: I had said that the past did not exist. And suddenly, noiseless, M. de Rollebon had returned to his nothingness.

I held his letters in my hands, felt them with a kind of despair:

He is the one, I said, he is the one who made these marks, one by one. He leaned on this paper, he put his hand against the sheets to prevent them from turning under his pen.

Too late: these words had no more sense. Nothing existed but a bundle of yellow pages which I clasped in my hands. It is true there was that complicated affair. Rollebon's nephew assassinated by the Czar's police in 1810, his papers confiscated and taken to the Secret Archives, then, a hundred and ten years later, deposited by the Soviets who acted for him, in the State Library where I stole them in 1923. But that didn't seem true, and I had no real memory of a theft I had committed myself. It would not have been difficult to find a hundred more credible stories to explain the presence of these papers in my room: all would seem hollow and ephemeral in face of these scored sheets. Rather than count on them to put me in communication with Rollebon, I would do better to take up spirit rapping. Rollebon was no more. No more at all. If there were still a few bones left of him, they existed for themselves, independently, they were nothing more than a little phosphate and calcium carbonate with salts and water.

I made one last attempt; I repeated the words of Mme de Genlis by which I usually evoked the Marquis: "His small, wrinkled countenance, clean and sharp, all pitted with smallpox, in which there was a singular malice which struck the eye, no matter what effort he made to dissemble it."

His face appeared to me with docility, his pointed nose, his bluish cheeks, his smile. I could shape his features at will, perhaps with even greater ease than before. Only it was nothing more than an image in me, a fiction. I sighed, let myself lean back against the chair, with an intolerable sense of loss.

Four o'clock strikes. I've been sitting here an hour, my arms hanging. It's beginning to get dark. Apart from that, nothing in this room has changed: the white paper is still on the table, next to the pen and inkwell. But I shall never write again on this page already started. Never again, following the Rue des Mutilés and the Boulevard de la Redoute, shall I turn into the library to look through their archives.

I want to get up and go out, do anything—no matter what—to stupefy myself. But if I move one finger, if I don't stay absolutely still, I know what will happen. I don't *want* that to happen to me yet. It will happen too soon as it is. I don't move; mechanically I read the paragraph I left unfinished on the pad of paper:

"Care had been taken to spread the most sinister rumours. M. de Rollebon must have let himself be caught by this manœuvre since he wrote to his nephew on the 13th of September that he had just made his will."

The great Rollebon affair was over, like a great passion. I must find something else. A few years ago, in Shanghai, in

Mercier's office, I suddenly woke from a dream. Then I had another dream, I lived in the Czar's court, in old palaces so cold that the icicles formed above the doors in winter. Today I wake up in front of a pad of white paper. The torches, the ice carnivals, the uniforms, the lovely cool shoulders have disappeared. *Something* has stayed behind in this warm room, something I don't want to see.

M. de Rollebon was my partner; he needed me in order to exist and I needed him so as not to feel my existence. I furnished the raw material, the material I had to re-sell, which I didn't know what to do with: existence, *my* existence. His part was to have an imposing appearance. He stood in front of me, took up my life to *lay bare* his own to me. I did not notice that I existed any more, I no longer existed in myself, but in him; I ate for him, breathed for him, each of my movements had its sense outside, there, just in front of me, in him; I no longer saw my hand writing letters on the paper, not even the sentence I had written—but behind, beyond the paper, I saw the Marquis who had claimed the gesture as his own, the gesture which prolonged, consolidated his existence. I was only a means of making him live, he was my reason for living, he had delivered me from myself. What shall I do now?

Above all, not move, *not move* . . . Ah!

I could not prevent this movement of the shoulders . . .

The thing which was waiting was on the alert, it has pounced on me, it flows through me, I am filled with it. It's nothing: I am the Thing. Existence, liberated, detached, floods over me. I exist.

I exist. It's sweet, so sweet, so slow. And light: you'd think it floated all by itself. It stirs. It brushes by me, melts and vanishes. Gently, gently. There is bubbling water in my mouth. I swallow. It slides down my throat, it caresses me—and now it comes up again into my mouth. For ever I shall have a little pool of whitish water in my mouth—lying low—grazing my tongue. And this pool is still me. And the tongue. And the throat is me.

I see my hand spread out on the table. It lives—it is me. It opens, the fingers open and point. It is lying on its back. It shows me its fat belly. It looks like an animal turned upside down. The fingers are the paws. I amuse myself by moving them very rapidly, like the claws of a crab which has fallen on its back.

The crab is dead: the claws draw up and close over the belly of my hand. I see the nails—the only part of me that doesn't live. And once more. My hand turns over, spreads out flat on its stomach, offers me the sight of its back. A silvery back, shining a little—like a fish except for the red hairs on the knuckles. I feel my hand. I am these two beasts struggling at the end of my arms. My hand scratches one of its paws with the nail of the other paw; I feel its weight on the table which is not me. It's long, long, this impression of weight, it doesn't pass. There is no reason for it to pass. It becomes intolerable . . . I draw back my hand and put it in my pocket; but immediately I feel the warmth of my thigh through the stuff. I pull my hand out of my pocket and let it hang against the back of the chair. Now I feel a weight at the end of my arm. It pulls a little, softly, insinuatingly it exists. I don't insist: no matter where I put it it will go on existing; I can't suppress it, nor can I suppress the rest of my body, the sweaty warmth which soils my shirt, nor all this warm obesity which turns lazily, as if someone were stirring it with a spoon, nor all the sensations going on inside, going, coming, mounting from my side to my armpit or quietly vegetating from morning to night, in their usual corner.

I jump up: it would be much better if I could only stop thinking. Thoughts are the dullest things. Duller than flesh. They stretch out and there's no end to them and they leave a funny taste in the mouth. Then there are words, inside the thoughts, unfinished words, a sketchy sentence which constantly returns: "I have to fi. . . I ex. . . Dead . . . M. de Roll is dead . . . I am not . . . I ex. . ." It goes, it goes . . . and there's no end to it. It's worse than the rest because I feel responsible and have complicity in it. For example, this sort of painful rumination: *I exist*, I am the one who keeps it up. I. The body lives by itself once it has begun. But thought—*I* am the one who continues it, unrolls it. I exist. How serpentine is this feeling of existing—I unwind it, slowly. . . . If I could keep myself from thinking! I try, and succeed: my head seems to fill with smoke . . . and then it starts again: "Smoke . . . not to think . . . don't want to think . . . I think I don't want to think. I mustn't think that I don't want to think. Because that's still a thought." Will there never be an end to it?

My thought is *me*: that's why I can't stop. I exist because I think . . . and I can't stop myself from thinking. At this very moment—it's frightful—if I exist, it is because I am horrified at existing. *I am the one* who pulls myself from the nothingness to which I aspire: the hatred, the disgust of existing, there are as many ways to *make* myself exist, to thrust myself into existence. Thoughts are born at the back of me, like sudden giddiness, I feel them being born behind my head . . . if I yield, they're going to come round in front of me, between my eyes—and I always yield, the thought grows and grows and there it is, immense, filling me completely and renewing my existence.

My saliva is sugary, my body warm: I feel neutral. My knife is on the table. I open it. Why not? It would be a change in any case. I put my left hand on the pad and stab the knife into the palm. The movement was too nervous; the blade slipped, the wound is superficial. It bleeds. Then what? What has changed? Still, I watch with satisfaction, on the white paper, across the lines I wrote a little while ago, this tiny pool of blood which has at last stopped being me. Four lines on a white paper, a spot of blood, that makes a beautiful memory. I must write beneath it: "Today I gave up writing my book on the Marquis de Rollebon."

Am I going to take care of my hand? I wonder. I watch the small, monotonous trickle of blood. Now it is coagulating. It's over. My skin looks rusty around the cut. Under the skin, the only thing left is a small sensation exactly like the others, perhaps even more insipid.

Half-past five strikes. I get up, my cold shirt sticks to my flesh. I go out. Why? Well, because I have no reason not to. Even if I stay, even if I crouch silently in a corner, I shall not forget myself. I will be there, my weight on the floor. I am.

I buy a newspaper along my way. Sensational news. Little Lucienne's body has been found! Smell of ink, the paper crumples between my fingers. The criminal has fled. The child was raped. They found her body, the fingers clawing at the mud. I roll the paper into a ball, my fingers clutching at the paper; smell of ink; my God how strongly things exist today. Little Lucienne was raped. Strangled. Her body still exists, her flesh bleeding. *She* no longer exists. Her hands. She no longer exists. The houses. I walk between the houses, I am between the houses, on the pavement; the pavement under my feet exists, the houses close around me, as the water closes over me, on the paper the shape of a swan. I am. I am, I exist, I think, therefore I am; I am because I think, why do I think? I don't want to think any more, I am because I think that I don't want to be, I think that

I . . . because . . . ugh! I flee. The criminal has fled, the violated body. She felt this other flesh pushing into her own. I . . . there I . . . Raped. A soft, criminal desire to rape catches me from behind, gently behind the ears, the ears race behind me, the red hair, it is red on my head, the wet grass, red grass, is it still I? Hold the paper, existence against existence, things exist one against the other, I drop the paper. The house springs up, it exists; in front of me, along the wall I am passing, along the wall I exist, in front of the wall, one step, the wall exists in front of me, one, two, behind me, a finger scratching at my pants, scratches, scratches and pulls at the little finger soiled with mud, mud on my finger which came from the muddy gutter and falls back slowly, softly, softening, scratching less strongly than the fingers of the little girl the criminal strangled, scratching the mud, the earth less strong, the finger slides slowly, the head falls first and rolling embraces my thigh; existence is soft, and rolls and tosses, I toss between the houses, I am, I exist, I think therefore I toss, I am, existence is a fallen chute, will not fall, will fall, the finger scratches at the window, existence is an imperfection. The gentleman. The handsome gentleman exists. The gentleman feels that he exists. No, the handsome gentleman who passes, proud and gentle as a convolvulus, does not feel that he exists. To expand; my cut hand hurts, exist, exist, exist. The handsome gentleman exists, the Legion of Honour, the moustache exists, it is all; how happy one must be to be nothing more than a Legion of Honour and a moustache and no one sees the rest, he sees the two pointed ends of his moustache on both sides of the nose; I do not think, therefore I am a moustache. He sees neither his gaunt body nor his big feet, if you looked in the crotch of the trousers you would surely discover a pair of little balls. He has the Legion of Honour, the bastards have the right to exist: "I exist because it is my right," I have the right to exist, therefore I have the right not to think: the finger is raised. Am I going to . . . caress in the opening of white sheets the white ecstatic flesh which falls back gently, touch the blossoming moisture of armpits, the elixis and cordials and florescence of flesh, enter into the existence of another, into the red mucus with the heavy, sweet, sweet odour of existence, feel myself exist between these soft, wet lips, the lips red with pale blood, throbbing lips yawning, all wet with existence, all wet with clear pus, between the wet sugary lips weeping like eyes? My body of living flesh which murmurs and turns gently, liquors which turn to cream, the flesh which turns, turns, the sweet sugary water of my flesh, the blood on my hand. I suffer in my wounded flesh which turns, walks, I walk, I flee, I am a criminal with bleeding flesh, bleeding with existence to these walls. I am cold, I take a step, I am cold, a step, I turn left, he turns left, he thinks he turns left, mad, am I mad? He says he is afraid of going mad, existence, do you see into existence, he stops, the body stops, he thinks he stops, where does he come from? What is he doing? He starts off, he is afraid, terribly afraid, the criminal, desire like a fog, desire, disgust, he says he is disgusted with existence, is he disgusted, weary of being disgusted with existence? He runs. What does he hope for? He runs to flee to throw himself into the lake? He runs, the heart, the heart beats, it's a holiday, the heart exists, the legs exist, the breath exists, they exist running, breathing, beating, all soft, all gently breathless, leaving me breathless, he says he's breathless; existence takes my thoughts from behind and gently expands them *from behind*; someone takes me from behind, they force me to think from behind, therefore to be something, behind me, breathing in light bubbles of existence, he is a bubble of fog and desire, he is pale as death in the glass, Rollebon is dead, Antoine Roquentin is not dead, I'm fainting: he says he would like to faint, he runs, he runs like a ferret, "from behind" from behind *from behind*, little Lucienne assaulted from behind, violated by existence from behind, he begs for mercy, he is ashamed of begging for mercy, pity, help, help therefore I exist, he goes into the Bar de la Marine, the little mirrors of the little brothel, he is pale in the little mirrors of the little brothel the big redhead who drops onto a bench, the gramophone plays, exists, all spins, the gramophone exists, the heart beats: spin, spin, liquors of life, spin, jellies, sweet sirups of my flesh, sweetness, the gramophone:

> *When that yellow moon begins to beam*
> *Every night I dream my little dream.*

The voice, deep and hoarse, suddenly appears and the world vanishes, the world of existence. A woman in the flesh had this voice, she sang in front of a record, in her finest get up, and they recorded her voice. The woman: bah! she existed like me, like Rollebon, I don't want to know her. But there it is. You can't say it exists. The turning record exists, the air struck by the voice which vibrates, exists, the voice which made an impression the record existed. I who listen, I exist. All is full, existence everywhere, dense, heavy and sweet. But, beyond all this sweetness, inaccessible, near and so far, young, merciless and serene, there is this . . . this rigour.

Tuesday:
Nothing. Existed.

Wednesday:
There is a sunbeam on the paper napkin. In the sunbeam there is a fly, dragging himself along, stupefied, sunning himself and rubbing his antennæ one against the other. I am going to do him the favour of squashing him. He does not see this giant finger advancing with the gold hairs shining in the sun.

"Don't kill it, Monsieur!" the Self-Taught Man shouted.

"I did it a favour."

Why am I here?—and why shouldn't I be here? It is noon, I am waiting for it to be time to sleep. (Fortunately sleep has not fled from me.) In four days I shall see Anny again: for the moment, my sole reason for living. And afterwards? When Anny leaves me? I know what I surreptitiously hope for: I hope she will never leave me. Yet I should know that Anny would never agree to grow old in front of me. I am weak and lonely, I need her. I would have liked to see her again in my strength: Anny is without pity for strayed sheep.

"Are you well, Monsieur? Do you feel all right?"

The Self-Taught Man looks at me out of the corner of his eyes, laughing. He pants a little, his mouth open, like a dog. I admit: this morning I was almost glad to see him, I needed to talk.

"How glad I am to have you at my table," he says. "If you're cold, we could go and sit next to the stove. These gentlemen are leaving soon, they've asked for the bill."

Someone is taking care of me, asking if I am cold: I am speaking to another man: that hasn't happened to me for years.

"They're leaving, do you want to change places?"

The two men have lighted cigarettes. They leave, there they are in the pure air, in the sunlight. They pass along the wide windows, holding their hats in both hands. They laugh; the wind bellies out their overcoats. No, I don't want to change places. What for? And then, through the windows, between the white roofs of the bathing-cabins I see the sea, green, compact.

The Self-Taught Man has taken two rectangles of purple cardboard from his wallet. He will soon hand them over the counter. I decipher on the back of one of them:

Maison Bottanet, cuisine bourgeoise
Le déjeuner à prix fixe: 8 francs
Hors d'œuvre au choix
Viande garnie
Fromage ou dessert
140 francs les 20 cachets

The man eating at the round table near the door—I recognize him now: he often stops at the Hotel Printania, he's a commercial traveller. From time to time he looks at me, attentive and smiling; but he doesn't see me; he is too absorbed in his food. On the other side of the counter, two squat, red-faced men are eating mussels and drinking white wine. The smaller, who has a thin yellow moustache is telling a story which makes him laugh. He pauses, laughs, showing sparkling teeth. The other does not laugh; his eyes are hard. But he often nods his head affirmatively. Near the window, a slight, dark-complexioned man with distinguished features and fine white hair, brushed back, reads his paper thoughtfully. A leather despatch case is on the bench beside him. He drinks Vichy water. In a moment all these people are going to leave; weighted down by food, caressed by the breeze, coat wide open, face a little flushed, their heads muzzy, they will walk along by the balustrade, watching the children on the beach and the ships on the sea; they will go to work. I will go nowhere, I have no work.

The Self-Taught Man laughs innocently and the sun plays through his sparse hair:

"Would you like to order?"

He hands me the menu: I am allowed one hors d'œuvre: either five slices of sausage or radishes or shrimps, or a dish of stuffed celery. Snails are extra.

"I'll have sausage," I tell the waitress.

He tears the menu from my hands:

"Isn't there anything better? Here are Bourgogne snails."

"I don't care to much for snails."

"Ah! What about oysters?"

"They're four francs more," the waitress says.

"All right, oysters, Mademoiselle—and radishes for me."

Blushing, he explains to me:

"I like radishes very much."

So do I.

I glance over the list of meats. Spiced beef tempts me. But I know in advance that I shall have chicken, the only extra meat.

"This gentleman will have," he says, "the chicken. Spiced beef for me."

He turns the card. The wine list is on the back:

"We shall have some wine," he says solemnly.

"Well!" the waitress says, "times have changed. You never drank any before."

"I can stand a glass of wine now and then. Will you bring us a carafe of pink Anjou?"

The Self-Taught Man puts down the menu, breaks his bread into small bits and rubs his knife and fork with his napkin. He glances at the white-haired man reading the paper, then smiles at me:

"I usually come here with a book, even though it's against doctor's orders: one eats too quickly and doesn't chew. But I have a stomach like an ostrich, I can swallow anything. During the winter of 1917, when I was a prisoner, the food was so bad that everyone got ill. Naturally, I went on the sick list like everybody else: but nothing was the matter."

He had been a prisoner of war. . . . This is the first time he mentioned it to me; I can't get over it: I can't picture him as anything other than the Self-Taught Man.

"Where were you a prisoner?"

He doesn't answer. He puts down his fork and looks at me with prodigious intensity. He is going to tell me his troubles: now I remember he said something was wrong, in the library. I am all ears: I am only too glad to feel pity for other people's troubles, that will make a change. I have no troubles, I have money like a capitalist, no boss, no wife, no children; I exist, that's all. And that trouble is so vague, so metaphysical that I am ashamed of it.

The Self-Taught Man doesn't seem to want to talk. What a curious look he gives me. It isn't a casual glance, but heart searching. The soul of the Self-Taught Man is in his eyes, his magnificent, blindman's eyes, where it blooms. Let mine do the same, let it come and stick its nose against the windows: they could exchange greetings.

I don't want any communion of souls, I haven't fallen so low. I draw back. But the Self-Taught Man throws his chest

105

out above the table, his eyes never leaving mine. Fortunately the waitress brings him his radishes. He drops back in his chair, his soul leaves his eyes, and he docilely begins to eat.

"Have you straightened out your troubles?"

He gives a start.

"What troubles, Monsieur?" he asks, nervously.

"You know, the other day you told me . . ."

He blushes violently.

"Ha!" he says in a dry voice. "Ha! Yes, the other day. Well, it's that Corsican, Monsieur, that Corsican in the library."

He hesitates a second time, with the obstinate look of a sheep.

"It's really nothing worth bothering you about, Monsieur."

I don't insist. Without seeming to, he eats, with extraordinary speed. He has already finished his radishes when the girl brings me the oysters. Nothing is left on his plate but a heap of radish stalks and a little damp salt.

Outside, a young couple has stopped in front of the menu which a cook in cardboard holds out to them in his left hand (he has a frying pan in his right). They hesitate. The woman is cold, she tucks her chin into her fur collar. The man makes up his mind first, he opens the door and steps inside to let the woman pass.

She enters. She looks around her amiably and shivers a little:

"It's hot," she says gravely.

The young man closes the door.

"Messieurs, dames," he says.

The Self-Taught Man turns round with a pleasant: "Messieurs, dames."

The other customers do not answer, but the distinguished-looking gentleman lowers his paper slightly and scrutinizes the new arrivals with a profound look.

"Don't bother, thank you."

Before the waitress, who had run up to help him, could make a move, the young man had slipped out of his raincoat. In place of a morning coat he wears a leather blouse with a zip. The waitress, a little disappointed, turns to the young woman. But once more he is ahead of her and helps the girl out of her coat with gentle, precise movements. They sit near us, one against the other. They don't look as if they'd known each other very long. The young woman has a weary face, pure and a little sullen. She suddenly takes off her hat, shakes her black hair and smiles.

The Self-Taught Man studies them at great length, with a kindly eye; then he turns to me and winks tenderly as if to say: "How wonderful they are!"

They are not ugly. They are quiet, happy at being together, happy at being seen together. Sometimes when Anny and I went into a restaurant in Piccadilly we felt ourselves the objects of admiring attention. It annoyed Anny, but I must confess that I was somewhat proud. Above all, amazed; I never had the clean-cut look that goes so well with that young man and no one could even say that my ugliness was touching. Only we were young: now, I am at the age to be touched by the youth of others. But I am not touched. The woman has dark, gentle eyes; the young man's skin has an orange hue, a little leathery, and a charming, small, obstinate chin. They are touching, but they also make me a little sick. I feel them so far from me: the warmth makes them languid, they pursue the same dream in their hearts, so low, so feeble. They are comfortable, they look with assurance at the yellow walls, the people, and they find the world pleasant as it is just as it is, and each one of them, temporarily, draws life from the life of the other. Soon the two of them will make a single life, a slow, tepid life which will have no sense at all—but they won't notice it.

They look as though they frighten each other. Finally, the young man, awkward and resolute, takes the girl's hand with the tips of his fingers. She breathes heavily and together they lean over the menu. Yes, they're happy. So what.

The Self-Taught Man puts on an amused, mysterious air: "I saw you the day before yesterday."

"Where?"

"Ha, ha!" he says, respectfully teasing.

He makes me wait for a second, then:

"You were coming out of the museum."

"Oh, yes," I say, "not the day before yesterday: Saturday."

The day before yesterday I certainly had no heart for running around museums.

"Have you seen that famous reproduction in carved wood—Orsini's attempted assassination?"

"I don't recall it."

"Is it possible? It's in a little room on the right, as you go in. It's the work of an insurgent of the Commune who lived in

Bouville until the amnesty, hiding in an attic. He wanted to go to America but the harbour police there were too quick for him. An admirable man. He spent his spare time carving a great oak panel. The only tools he had were a penknife and a nail file. He did the delicate parts with the file: the hands and eyes. The panel is five feet long by three feet wide; there are seventy figures, each one no larger than a hand, without counting the two horses pulling the emperor's carriage. And the faces, Monsieur, the faces made by the file, they have a distinct physiognomy, a human look. Monsieur, if I may allow myself to say so, it is a work worth seeing."

I don't want to be involved:

"I had simply wanted to see Bordurin's paintings again."

The Self-Taught Man suddenly grows sad:

"Those portraits in the main hall, Monsieur?" he asks, with a trembling smile, "I understand nothing about painting. Of course, I realize that Bordurin is a great painter, I can see he has a certain touch, a certain knack as they say. But pleasure, Monsieur, aesthetic pleasure is foreign to me."

I tell him sympathetically:

"I feel the same way about sculpture."

"Ah, Monsieur, I too, alas! And about music and about dancing. Yet I am not without a certain knowledge. Well, it is inconceivable: I have seen young people who don't know half what I know who, standing in front of a painting, seem to take pleasure in it."

"They must be pretending," I said to encourage him.

"Perhaps. . . ."

The Self-Taught Man dreams for a moment:

"What I regret is not so much being deprived of a certain taste, but rather that a whole branch of human activity is foreign to me. . . . Yet I am a man and *men* have painted those pictures. . . ."

Suddenly his tone changes:

"Monsieur, at one time I ventured to think that the beautiful was only a question of taste. Are there not different rules for each epoch? Allow me, Monsieur. . . ."

With surprise I see him draw a black leather notebook from his pocket. He goes through it for an instant: a lot of blank pages, and further on, a few lines written in red ink. He has turned pale. He has set the notebook flat on the tablecloth and spread his huge hand on the open page. He coughs with embarrassment:

"Sometimes things come to my mind—I dare not call them thoughts. It is very curious, I am there, I'm reading when suddenly, I don't know where it comes from, I feel illuminated. First I paid no attention and then I resolved to buy a notebook."

He stops and looks at me: he is waiting.

"Ah," I say.

"Monsieur, these maxims are naturally unpolished: my instruction is not yet completed."

He picks up the notebook with trembling hands, he is deeply moved:

"And there just happens to be something here about painting. I should be very happy if you would allow me to read . . ."

"With pleasure," I say.

He reads:

"No longer do people believe what the eighteenth century held to be true. Why should we still take pleasure in works because they thought them beautiful?"

He looks at me pleadingly.

"What must one think, Monsieur? Perhaps it is a paradox? I thought to endow my idea with the quality of a caprice."

"Well, I . . . I find that very interesting."

"Have you read it anywhere before?"

"No, of course not."

"Really, nowhere? Then, Monsieur," he says, his face growing sad, "it is because it is not true. If it were true, someone would already have thought of it."

"Wait a minute," I tell him, "now that I think about it, I believe I have read something like that."

His eyes are shining; he takes out his pencil.

"Which author?" he asks me, his voice precise.

"Oh . . . Renan."

He is in Paradise.

"Would you be kind enough to quote the exact passage for me?" he asks, sucking the point of his pencil.

"Oh, as a matter of fact, I read that quite a while ago."

"Oh, it doesn't matter, it doesn't matter."

He writes *Renan* in his notebook, just below his maxim.

"I have come upon Renan! I wrote the name in pencil," he explains, delighted, "but this evening I'll go over it in red ink."

He looks ecstatically at his notebook for a moment, and I

expect him to read me other maxims. But he closes it cautiously and stuffs it back in his pocket. He undoubtedly has decided that this is enough happiness for one time.

"How pleasant it is," he says intimately, "to be able to talk sometimes, as now, with abandon."

This, as might be supposed, puts an end to our languishing conversation. A long silence follows.

The atmosphere of the restaurant has changed since the arrival of the young couple. The two red-faced men are silent; they are nonchalantly detailing the young lady's charms. The distinguished-looking gentleman has put down his paper and is watching the couple with kindness, almost complicity. He thinks that old age is wise and youth is beautiful, he nods his head with a certain coquetry: he knows quite well that he is still handsome, well preserved, that with his dark complexion and his slender figure he is still attractive. He plays at feeling paternal. The waitress' feelings appear simpler: she is standing in front of the young people staring at them open-mouthed.

They are speaking quietly. They have been served their hors d'œuvres but they don't touch them. Listening carefully I can make out snatches of their conversation. I understand better what the woman says, her voice is rich and veiled.

"No, Jean, no."

"Why not?" the young man murmurs with passionate vivacity.

"I told you why."

"That's not a reason."

A few words escape me then the young woman makes a charming, lax gesture:

"I've tried too often. I'm past the age when you can start your life again. I'm old, you know."

The young man laughs ironically. She goes on:

"I couldn't stand being deceived."

"You must have confidence in life," the young man says; "the way you are this moment isn't living."

She sighs:

"I know!"

"Look at Jeannette."

"Yes," she says, making a little grimace.

"Well, I think what she did was splendid. She had courage."

"You know," the young woman says, "she rather jumped at

the opportunity. You must know that if I'd wanted, I could have had a hundred opportunities like that. I preferred to wait."

"You were right," he says, tenderly, "you were right in waiting for me."

She laughs in turn:

"Great stupid! I didn't say that."

I don't listen to them any more: they annoy me. They're going to sleep together. They know it. Each one knows that the other knows it. But since they are young, chaste and decent, since each one wants to keep his self-respect and that of the other, since love is a great poetic thing which you must not frighten away, several times a week they go to dances and restaurants, offering the spectacle of their ritual, mechanical dances. . . .

After all, you have to kill time. They are young and well built, they have enough to last them another thirty years. So they're in no hurry, they delay and they are not wrong. Once they have slept together they will have to find something else to veil the enormous absurdity of their existence. Still . . . is it absolutely necessary to lie?

I glance around the room. What a comedy! All these people sitting there, looking serious, eating. No, they aren't eating: they are recuperating in order to successfully finish their tasks. Each one of them has his little personal difficulty which keeps him from noticing that he exists; there isn't one of them who doesn't believe himself indispensable to something or someone. Didn't the Self Taught Man tell me the other day: "No one better qualified than Nouçapié to undertake this vast synthesis?" Each one of them does one small thing and no one is better qualified than he to do it. No one is better qualified than the commercial traveller over there to sell Swan Toothpaste. No one is better qualified than that interesting young man to put his hand under his girl friend's skirts. And I am among them and if they look at me they must think that no one is better qualified than I to do what I'm doing. But I *know*. I don't look like much, but I know I exist and that they exist. And if I knew how to convince people I'd go and sit down next to that handsome white-haired gentleman and explain to him just what existence means. I burst out laughing at the thought of the face he would make. The Self-Taught Man looks at me with surprise. I'd like to stop but I can't; I laugh until I cry.

"You are gay, Monsieur," the Self-Taught Man says to me circumspectly.

"I was just thinking," I tell him, laughing, "that here we sit, all of us, eating and drinking to preserve our precious existence and really there is nothing, nothing, absolutely no reason for existing."

The Self-Taught Man becomes serious, he makes an effort to understand me. I laughed too loud: I saw several faces turn towards me. Then I regretted having said so much. After all, that's nobody's business.

He repeats slowly:

"No reason for existing . . . you undoubtedly mean, Monsieur, that life is without a goal? Isn't that what one might call pessimism?"

He thinks for an instant, then says gently:

"A few years ago I read a book by an American author. It was called *Is Life Worth Living?* Isn't that the question you are asking yourself?"

Certainly not, that is not the question I am asking myself. But I have no desire to explain.

"His conclusion," the Self-Taught Man says, consolingly, "is in favour of voluntary optimism. Life has a meaning if we choose to give it one. One must first act, throw one's self into some enterprise. Then, if one reflects, the die is already cast, one is pledged. I don't know what you think about that, Monsieur?"

"Nothing," I say.

Rather I think that that is precisely the sort of lie that the commercial traveller, the two young people and the man with white hair tell themselves.

The Self-Taught Man smiles with a little malice and much solemnity.

"Neither is it my opinion. I do not think we need look so far to know the direction our life should take."

"Ah?"

"There is a goal, Monsieur, there is a goal . . . there is humanity."

That's right: I forgot he was a humanist. He remains silent for a moment, long enough to make most of his spiced beef and a whole slice of bread disappear cleanly and inexorably. "There are people . . ." He has just painted a whole picture of himself, this philanthropist. Yes, but he doesn't know how to express himself. His soul is in his eyes, unquestionably, but soul is not enough. Before, when I used to hang around some Parisian humanists, I would hear them say a hundred times: "there are people," and it was quite another thing. Virgan was without equal. He would take off his spectacles, as if to show himself naked in his man's flesh, and stare at me with eloquent eyes, with a weary, insistent look which seemed to undress me, and drag out my human essence, then he would murmur melodiously: "There are people, old man, there are people," giving the "there are" a sort of awkward power, as if his love of people, perpetually new and astonished, was caught up in its giant wings.

The Self-Taught Man's mimicry had not acquired this smoothness; his love for people is naïve and barbaric: a provincial humanist.

"People," I told him, "people . . . in any case, you don't seem to worry about them very much: you're always alone, always with your nose in a book."

The Self-Taught Man clapped his hands and began to laugh maliciously:

"You're wrong. Ah, Monsieur, allow me to tell you so: what an error!"

He pulls himself together for an instant, and finishes a discreet gulp. His face is radiant as dawn. Behind him, the young woman breaks out in a light laugh. Her friend bends over her, whispering in her ear.

"Your error is only too natural," the Self-Taught Man says, "I should have told you a long time ago. . . . But I am so timid, Monsieur: I was waiting for the opportunity."

"Here it is," I told him politely.

"I think so too. I think so too! Monsieur, what I am about to tell you . . ." He stops, blushing: "But perhaps I am imposing on you?"

I assure him that he isn't. He breathes a sigh of happiness.

"One does not find men like you every day, Monsieur, men whose breadth of vision is joined to so much penetration. I have been wanting to speak to you for months, explain to you what I have been, what I have become. . . ."

His plate is as empty and clean as if it had just been brought to him. I suddenly discover, next to my plate, a small tin dish where a drum-stick swims in a brown gravy. It has to be eaten.

"A little while ago I spoke of my captivity in Germany. It all started there. Before the War I was lonely and didn't realize it; I lived with my parents, good people, but I didn't get on with them. When I think of those years . . . how could I have lived that way? I was dead, Monsieur, and I didn't know it; I had a collection of postage stamps."

He looks at me and interrupts himself:

"Monsieur, you are pale, you look fatigued. I hope I'm not disturbing you?"

"You interest me greatly."

"Then the War came and I enlisted without knowing why. I spent two years without understanding, because life at the front left little time for thoughts and besides, the soldiers were too common. I was taken prisoner at the end of 1917. Since then I have been told that many soldiers recovered their childhood faith while they were prisoners. Monsieur," the Self-Taught Man says, lowering his eyelids over bloodshot eyes, "I do not believe in God; His existence is belied by science. But, in the internment camp, I learned to believe in men."

"They bore their fate with courage?"

"Yes," he says vaguely, "there was that, too. Besides, we were well treated. But I wanted to speak of something else; the last months of the War, they hardly gave us any work to do. When it rained they made us go into a big wooden shed, about two hundred of us altogether, jammed in tightly. They closed the door and left us there, pressed one against the other, in almost total darkness."

He hesitated an instant.

"I don't know how to explain it, Monsieur. All those men were there, you could hardly see them but you could feel them against you, you could hear the sound of their breathing. . . . One of the first times they locked us in the shed, the crush was so great that at first I thought I was going suffocate, then, suddenly, an overwhelming joy came over me, I almost fainted: then I felt that I loved these men like brothers, I wanted to embrace all of them. Each time I went back there I felt the same joy."

I have to eat my chicken which by now must be cold. The Self-Taught Man has been silent for a long time and the waitress is waiting to change the plates.

"That shed took on a sacred character in my eyes. Sometimes I managed to escape the watchfulness of my guards, I slipped into it all alone and there, in the shadow, the memory of the joys I had known, filled me with a sort of ecstasy. Hours passed and I did not notice them. Sometimes I wept."

I must be sick: there is no other way of explaining this terrible rage which suddenly overwhelms me. Yes, the rage of a sick

114

man: my hands were shaking, the blood had rushed to my face, and finally my lips began to tremble. All this simply because the chicken was cold. I was cold too and that was the worst: I mean that inside me I was cold, freezing, and had been like that for thirty-six hours. Anger passed through me like a whirlwind, my conscience, effort to react, to fight against this lowered temperature caused something like a tremor to pass through me. Vain effort: undoubtedly, for nothing. I would have rained down blows and curses on the Self-Taught Man or the waitress. But I should not have been in the spirit of it. My rage and fury struggled to the surface and, for a moment, I had the terrible impression of being turned into a block of ice enveloped in fire, a kind of "omelette surprise." This momentary agitation vanished and I heard the Self-Taught Man say:

"Every Sunday I used to go to Mass. Monsieur, I have never been a believer. But couldn't one say that the real mystery of the Mass is the communion of souls? A French chaplain, who had only one arm, celebrated the Mass. We had a harmonium. We listened, standing, our heads bare, and as the sounds of the harmonium carried me away, I felt myself at one with all the men surrounding me. Ah, Monsieur, how I loved those Masses. Even now, in memory of them, I sometimes go to church on Sunday morning. We have a remarkable organist at Sainte-Cécile."

"You must have often missed that life?"

"Yes, Monsieur, in 1919, the year of my liberation, I spent many miserable months. I didn't know what to do with myself, I was wasting away. Whenever I saw men together I would insert myself into their group. It has happened to me," he added, smiling, "to follow the funeral procession of a stranger. One day, in despair, I threw my stamp collection in the fire. . . . But I found my vocation."

"Really?"

"Someone advised me . . . Monsieur, I know that I can count on your discretion. I am—perhaps these are not your ideas, but you are so broad-minded—I am a Socialist."

He lowered his eyes and his long lashes trembled:

"I have been a registered member of the Socialist Party, S.F.I.O., since the month of September 1921. That is what I wanted to tell you."

He is radiant with pride. He gazes at me, his head thrown back, his eyes half-closed, mouth open, looking like a martyr.

"That's very fine," I say, "that's very fine."

"Monsieur, I knew that you would commend me. And how could you blame someone who comes and tells you: I have spent my life in such and such a way, I am perfectly happy?"

He spreads his arms and presents his open palms to me, the fingers pointing to the ground, as if he were about to receive the stigmata. His eyes are glassy, I see a dark pink mass rolling in his mouth.

"Ah," I say, "as long as you're happy. . . ."

"Happy?" His look is disconcerting, he has raised his eyelids and stares harshly at me. "You will be able to judge, Monsieur. Before taking this decision I felt myself in a solitude so frightful that I contemplated suicide. What held me back was the idea that no one, absolutely no one, would be moved by my death, that I would be even more alone in death than in life."

He straightens himself, his cheeks swell.

"I am no longer lonely, Monsieur. I shall never be so."

"Ah, you know a lot of people?" I ask.

He smiles and I immediately realize my mistake.

"I mean that I no longer *feel* alone. But naturally, Monsieur, it is not necessary for me to be with anyone."

"But," I say, "what about the Socialist section. . . ."

"Ah! I know everybody there. But most of them only by name. Monsieur," he says mischievously, "is one obliged to choose his friends so narrowly? All men are my friends. When I go to the office in the morning, in front of me, behind me, there are other men going to work. I see them, if I dared I would smile at them, I think that I am a Socialist, that all of them are my life's goal, the goal of my efforts and that they don't know it yet. It's a holiday for me, Monsieur."

His eyes question me; I nod approval, but I feel he is a little disappointed, that he would like more enthusiasm. What can I do? Is it my fault if, in all he tells me, I recognize the lack of the genuine article? Is it my fault if, as he speaks, I see all the humanists I have known rise up? I've known so many of them! The radical humanist is the particular friend of officials. The so-called "left" humanist's main worry is keeping human values; he belongs to no party because he does not want to betray the human, but his sympathies go towards the humble; he consecrates his beautiful classic culture to the humble. He is generally a widower with a fine eye always clouded with tears: he weeps at anniversaries. He also loves cats, dogs, and all the higher mammals. The Communist writer has been loving men since the second Five-Year Plan; he punishes because he loves. Modest as all strong men, he knows how to hide his feelings, but he also knows, by a look, an inflection of his voice, how to recognize, behind his rough and ready justicial utterances, his passion for his brethren. The Catholic humanist, the late-comer, the Benjamin, speaks of men with a marvellous air. What a beautiful fairy tale, says he, is the humble life of a London dockhand, the girl in the shoe factory! He has chosen the humanism of the angels; he writes, for their edification, long, sad and beautiful novels which frequently win the Prix Femina.

Those are the principal rôles. But there are others, a swarm of others: the humanist philosopher who bends over his brothers like a wise elder brother who has a sense of his responsibilities; the humanist who loves men as they are, the humanist who loves men as they ought to be, the one who wants to save them with their consent and the one who will save them in spite of themselves, the one who wants to create new myths, and the one who is satisfied with the old ones, the one who loves death in man, the one who loves life in man, the happy humanist who always has the right word to make people laugh, the sober humanist whom you meet especially at funerals or wakes. They all hate each other: as individuals, naturally not as men. But the Self-Taught Man doesn't know it: he has locked them up inside himself like cats in a bag and they are tearing each other in pieces without his noticing it.

He is already looking at me with less confidence.

"Don't you feel as I do, Monsieur?"

"Gracious . . ."

Under his troubled, somewhat spiteful glance, I regret disappointing him for a second. But he continues amiably:

"I know: you have your research, your books, you serve the same cause in your own way."

My books, *my* research: the imbecile. He couldn't have made a worse howler.

"That's not why I'm writing."

At that instant the face of the Self-Taught Man is transformed: as if he had scented the enemy. I had never seen that expression on his face before. Something has died between us.

Feigning surprise, he asks:

"But . . . if I'm not being indiscreet, why do you write, Monsieur?"

"I don't know: just to write."

He smiles, he thinks he has put me out:

"Would you write on a desert island? Doesn't one always write to be read?"

He gave this sentence his usual interrogative turn. In reality, he is affirming. His veneer of gentleness and timidity has peeled off; I don't recognize him any more. His features assume an air of heavy obstinacy; a wall of sufficiency. I still haven't got over my astonishment when I hear him say:

"If someone tells me: I write for a certain social class, for a group of friends. Good luck to them. Perhaps you write for posterity. . . . But, Monsieur, in spite of yourself, you write for someone."

He waits for an answer. When it doesn't come, he smiles feebly.

"Perhaps you are a misanthrope?"

I know what this fallacious effort at conciliation hides. He asks little from me: simply to accept a label. But it is a trap: if I consent, the Self-Taught Man wins, I am immediately turned round, reconstituted, overtaken, for humanism takes possession and melts all human attitudes into one. If you oppose him head on, you play his game; he lives off his opponents. There is a race of beings, limited and headstrong, who lose to him every time: he digests all their violences and worst excesses; he makes a white, frothy lymph of them. He has digested anti-intellectualism, Manicheism, mysticism, pessimism, anarchy and egotism: they are nothing more than stages, unfinished thoughts which find their justification only in him. Misanthropy also has its place in the concert: it is only a dissonance necessary to the harmony of the whole. The misanthrope is a man: therefore the humanist must be misanthropic to a certain extent. But he must be a scientist as well to have learned how to water down his hatred, and hate men only to love them better afterwards.

I don't want to be integrated, I don't want my good red blood to go and fatten this lymphatic beast: I will not be fool enough to call myself "anti-humanist." I *am not* a humanist, that's all there is to it.

"I believe," I tell the Self-Taught Man, "that one cannot hate a man more than one can love him."

The Self-Taught Man looks at me pityingly and aloof. He murmurs, as though he were paying no attention to his words:

"You must love them, you must love them. . . ."

"Whom must you love? The people here?"

"They too. All."

He turns towards the radiant young couple: that's what you must love. For a moment he contemplates the man with white hair. Then his look returns to me: I read a mute question on his face. I shake my head: "No." He seems to pity me.

"You don't either," I tell him, annoyed, "you don't love them."

"Really, Monsieur? Would you allow me to differ?"

He has become respectful again, respectful to the tip of his toes, but in his eyes he has the ironic look of someone who is amusing himself enormously. He hates me. I should have been wrong to have any feeling for this maniac. I question him in my turn.

"So, those two young people behind you—you love them?"

He looks at them again, ponders:

"You want to make me say," he begins, suspiciously, "that I love them without knowing them. Well, Monsieur, I confess, I don't know them. . . . Unless love is knowing," he adds with a foolish laugh.

"But what do you love?"

"I see they are young and I love the youth in them. Among other things, Monsieur."

He interrupts himself and listens:

"Do you understand what they're saying?"

Do I understand? The young man, emboldened by the sympathy which surrounds him, tells, in a loud voice, about a football game his team won against a club from Le Havre last year.

"He's telling a story," I say to the Self-Taught Man.

"Ah! I can't hear them very well. But I hear the voices, the soft voice, the grave voice: they alternate. It's . . . it's so sympathetic."

"Only I also hear what they're saying, unfortunately."

"Well?"

"They're playing a comedy."

"Really? The comedy of youth, perhaps?" he asks ironically. "Allow me, Monsieur, to find that quite profitable. Is playing it enough to make one young again?"

I stay deaf to his irony; I continue:

"You turn your back on them, what they say escapes you. . . . What colour is the woman's hair?"

He is worried:

"Well, I . . ." He glances quickly at the young couple and regains his assurance. "Black!"

"So you see!"

"See what?"

"You see that you don't love them. You wouldn't recognize them in the street. They're only symbols in your eyes. You are not at all touched by them: you're touched by the Youth of the Man, the Love of Man and Woman, the Human Voice."

"Well? Doesn't that exist?"

"Certainly not, it doesn't exist! Neither Youth nor Maturity nor Old Age nor Death. . . ."

The face of the Self-Taught Man, hard and yellow as a quince, has stiffened into a reproachful lockjaw. Nevertheless, I keep on:

"Just like that old man drinking Vichy water there behind you. I suppose you love the Mature Man in him: Mature Man going courageously towards his decline and who takes care of himself because he doesn't want to let himself go?"

"Exactly," he says definitely.

"And you don't think he's a bastard?"

He laughs, he finds me frivolous, he glances quickly at the handsome face framed in white hair:

"But Monsieur, admitting that he seems to be what you say, how can you judge a man by his face? A face, Monsieur, tells nothing when it is at rest."

Blind humanists! This face is so outspoken, so frank—but their tender, abstract soul will never let itself be touched by the sense of a face.

"How can you," the Self-Taught Man says, "*stop* a man, say he *is* this or that? Who can empty a man! Who can know the resources of a man?"

Empty a man! I salute, in passing, the Catholic humanism from which the Self-Taught Man borrowed this formula without realizing it.

"I know," I tell him, "I know that all men are admirable. You are admirable. I am admirable. In as far as we are creations of God, naturally."

He looks at me without understanding, then with a thin smile:

"You are undoubtedly joking, Monsieur, but it is true that all men deserve our admiration. It is difficult, Monsieur, very difficult to be a man."

Without realizing it, he has abandoned the love of men in Christ; he nods his head, and by a curious phenomenon of mimicry, he resembles this poor man of Gehenna.

"Excuse me," I say, "but I am not quite sure of being a man: I never found it very difficult. It seemed to me that you had only to let yourself alone."

The Self-Taught Man laughs candidly, but his eyes stay wicked:

"You are too modest, Monsieur. In order to tolerate your condition, the human condition, you, as everybody else, need much courage. Monsieur, the next instant may be the moment of your death, you know it and you can smile: isn't that admirable? In your most insignificant actions," he adds sharply, "there is an enormous amount of heroism."

"What will you gentlemen have for dessert?" the waitress says.

The Self-Taught Man is quite white, his eyelids are half-shut over his stony eyes. He makes a feeble motion with his hand, as if inviting me to choose.

"Cheese," I say heroically.

"And you?"

He jumps.

"Eh? Oh, yes: well . . . I don't want anything. I've finished."

"Louise!"

The two stout men pay and leave. One of them limps. The patron shows them to the door: they are important customers, they were served a bottle of wine in a bucket of ice.

I study the Self-Taught Man with a little remorse: he has been happy all the week imagining this luncheon, where he could share his love of men with another man. He has so rarely the opportunity to speak. And now I have spoiled his pleasure. At heart he is as lonely as I am: no one cares about him. Only he doesn't realize his solitude. Well, yes: but it wasn't up to me to open his eyes. I feel very ill at ease: I'm furious, but not against him, against Virgan and the others, all the ones who have poisoned this poor brain. If I could have them here in front of me I would have much to say to them. I shall say nothing to the Self-Taught Man, I have only sympathy for him: he is someone like M. Achille, someone on my side, but who has been betrayed by ignorance and good will!

A burst of laughter from the Self-Taught Man pulls me out of my sad reflections.

"You will excuse me, but when I think of the depth of my love for people, of the force which impels me towards them and when I see us here, reasoning, arguing . . . it makes me want to laugh."

I keep quiet, I smile constrainedly. The waitress puts a plate of chalky Camembert in front of me. I glance around the room and a violent disgust floods me. What am I doing here? Why did I have to get mixed up in a discussion on humanism? Why are these people here? Why are they eating? It's true they don't know they exist. I want to leave, go to some place where I will be really in my own niche, where I will fit in. . . . But my place is nowhere; I am unwanted, *de trop*.

The Self-Taught Man grows softer. He expected more resistance on my part. He is ready to pass a sponge over all I have said. He leans towards me confidentially:

"You love them at heart, Monsieur, you love them as I do: we are separated by words."

I can't speak any more, I bow my head. The Self-Taught Man's face is close to mine. He smiles foolishly, all the while close to my face, like a nightmare. With difficulty I chew a piece of bread which I can't make up my mind to swallow. People. You must love people. Men are admirable. I want to vomit—and suddenly, there it is: the Nausea.

A fine climax: it shakes me from top to bottom. I saw it coming more than an hour ago, only I didn't want to admit it. This taste of cheese in my mouth. . . . The Self-Taught Man is babbling and his voice buzzes gently in my ears. But I don't know what he's talking about. I nod my head mechanically. My hand is clutching the handle of the dessert knife. I *feel* this black wooden handle. My hand holds it. My hand. Personally, I would rather let this knife alone: what good is it to be always touching something? Objects are not made to be touched. It is better to slip between them, avoiding them as much as possible. Sometimes you take one of them in your hand and you have to drop it quickly. The knife falls on the plate. The white-haired man starts and looks at me. I pick up the knife again, I rest the blade against the table and bend it.

So this is Nausea: this blinding evidence? I have scratched my head over it! I've written about it. Now I know: I exist—the world exists—and I know that the world exists. That's all. It makes no difference to me. It's strange that everything makes so little difference to me: it frightens me. Ever since the day I wanted to play ducks and drakes. I was going to throw that pebble, I looked at it and then it all began: I felt that it *existed*. Then after that there were other Nauseas; from time to time objects start existing in your hand. There was the Nausea of the "Railwaymen's Rendezvous" and then another, before that, the night I was looking out the window; then another in the park, one Sunday, then others. But it had never been as strong as today.

"... Of ancient Rome, Monsieur?"

The Self-Taught Man is asking me a question, I think. I turn towards him and smile. Well? What's the matter with him? Why is he shrinking back into his chair? Do I frighten people now? I shall end up that way. But it makes no difference to me. They aren't completely wrong to be afraid: I feel as though I could do anything. For example, stab this cheese knife into the Self-Taught Man's eye. After that, all these people would trample me and kick my teeth out. But that isn't what stops me: a taste of blood in the mouth instead of this taste of cheese makes no difference to me. Only I should make some move, introduce some superfluous event: the Self-Taught Man's cry would be too much—and the blood flowing down the cheek and all the people jumping up. There are quite enough things like that which exist already.

Everyone is watching me; the two representatives of youth have interrupted their gentle chat. The woman's mouth looks like a chicken's backside. And yet they ought to see that I am harmless.

I get up, everything spins around me. The Self-Taught Man stares at me with his great eyes which I shall not gouge out.

"Leaving already?" he murmurs.

"I'm a little tired. It was very nice of you to invite me. Good-bye."

As I am about to leave I notice that I have kept the dessert knife in my left hand. I throw it on my plate which begins to clink. I cross the room in the midst of silence. No one is eating: they are watching me, they have lost their appetite. If I were to go up to the young woman and say "Boo!" she'd begin screaming, that's certain. It isn't worth the trouble.

Still, before going out, I turn back and give them a good look at my face so they can engrave it in their memory.

"Good-bye, ladies and gentlemen."

They don't answer. I leave. Now the colour will come back to their cheeks, they'll begin to jabber.

123

I don't know where to go, I stay planted in front of the cardboard chef. I don't need to turn around to know they are watching me through the windows: they are watching my back with surprise and disgust; they thought I was like them, that I was a man, and I deceived them. I suddenly lost the appearance of a man and they saw a crab running backwards out of this human room. Now the unmasked intruder has fled: the show goes on. It annoys me to feel on my back this stirring of eyes and frightened thoughts. I cross the street. The other pavement runs along the beach and the bath houses.

Many people are walking along the shore, turning poetic springtime faces towards the sea; they're having a holiday because of the sun. There are lightly dressed women who have put on last spring's outfit; they pass, long and white as kid gloves; there are also big boys who go to high school and the School of Commerce, old men with medals. They don't know each other but they look at each other with an air of connivance because it's such a fine day and they are men. Strangers embrace each other when war is declared; they smile at each other every spring. A priest advances slowly, reading his breviary. Now and then he raises his head and looks at the sea approvingly:—the sea is also a breviary, it speaks of God. Delicate colours, delicate perfumes, souls of spring. "What a lovely day, the sea is green, I like this dry cold better than the damp." Poets! If I grabbed one of them by the back of the coat, if I told him: "Come, help me," he'd think, "What's this crab doing here?" and would run off, leaving his coat in my hands.

I turn back, lean both hands on the balustrade. The *true* sea is cold and black, full of animals; it crawls under this thin green film made to deceive human beings. The sylphs all round me have let themselves be taken in: they only see the thin film, which proves the existence of God. I see beneath it! The veneer melts, the shining velvety scales, the scales of God's catch explode everywhere at my look, they split and gape. Here is the Saint-Elémir tramway, I turn round and the objects turn with me, pale and green as oysters.

Useless, it was useless to get in since I don't want to go anywhere.

Bluish objects pass the windows. In jerks all stiff and brittle; people, walls; a house offers me its black heart through open windows; and the windows pale, all that is black becomes blue, blue this great yellow brick house advancing uncertainly, trembling, suddenly stopping and taking a nose dive. A man gets on and sits down opposite to me. The yellow house starts up again, it leaps against the windows, it is so close that you can only see part of it, it is obscured. The windows rattle. It rises, crushing, higher than you can see, with hundreds of windows opened on black hearts; it slides along the car brushing past it; night has come between the rattling windows. It slides interminably, yellow as mud, and the windows are sky blue. Suddenly it is no longer there, it has stayed behind, a sharp, grey illumination fills the car and spreads everywhere with inexorable justice: it is the sky; through the windows you can still see layer on layer of sky because we're going up Eliphar Hill and you can see clearly between the two slopes, on the right as far as the sea, on the left as far as the airfield. No smoking—not even a *gitane.*

I lean my hand on the seat but pull it back hurriedly: it exists. This thing I'm sitting on, leaning my hand on, is called a seat. They made it purposely for people to sit on, they took leather, springs and cloth, they went to work with the idea of making a seat and when they finished, *that* was what they had made. They carried it here, into this car and the car is now rolling and jolting with its rattling windows, carrying this red thing in its bosom. I murmur: "It's a seat," a little like an exorcism. But the word stays on my lips: it refuses to go and put itself on the thing. It stays what it is, with its red plush, thousands of little red paws in the air, all still, little dead paws. This enormous belly turned upward, bleeding, inflated—bloated with all its dead paws, this belly floating in this car, in this grey sky, is not a seat. It could just as well be a dead donkey tossed about in the water, floating with the current, belly in the air in a great grey river, a river of floods; and I could be sitting on the donkey's belly, my feet dangling in the clear water. Things are divorced from their names. They are there, grotesque, headstrong, gigantic and it seems ridiculous to call them seats or say anything at all about them: I am in the midst of things, nameless things. Alone, without words, defenceless, they surround me, are beneath me, behind me, above me. They demand nothing, they don't impose themselves: they are there. Under the cushion on the seat there is a thin line of shadow, a thin black line running along the seat, mysteriously and mischievously, almost a smile. I know very well that it isn't a smile and yet it exists, it runs under the whitish windows, under the jangle of glass, obstinately, obstinately behind the blue images which pass in a throng, like the inexact memory of a smile, like a half forgotten word of which you can only remember the first syllable and the best thing you can do is turn your eyes away and think about something else, about that man half-lying down on the seat opposite me, there. His blue-eyed, terra cotta face. The whole right side of his body has sunk, the right arm is stuck to the body, the right side barely lives, it lives with difficulty, with avarice, as if it were paralysed. But on the whole left side there is a little parasitic existence, which proliferates; a chance: the arm begins to tremble and then is raised up and the hand at the end is stiff. Then the hand begins to tremble too and when it reaches the height of the skull, a finger stretches out and begins scratching the scalp with a nail. A sort of voluptuous grimace comes to inhabit the right side of the mouth and the left side stays dead. The windows rattle, the arm shakes, the nail scratches, scratches, the mouth smiles under the staring eyes and the man tolerates, hardly noticing it, this tiny existence which swells his right side, which has borrowed his right arm and right cheek to bring itself into being. The conductor blocks my path.

"Wait until the car stops."

But I push him aside and jump out of the tramway. I couldn't stand any more. I could no longer stand things being so close. I push open a gate, go in, airy creatures are bounding and leaping and perching on the peaks. Now I recognize myself, I know where I am: I'm in the park. I drop onto a bench between great black tree-trunks, between the black, knotty hands reaching towards the sky. A tree scrapes at the earth under my feet with a black nail. I would so like to let myself go, forget myself, sleep. But I can't, I'm suffocating: existence penetrates me everywhere, through the eyes, the nose, the mouth. . . .

And suddenly, suddenly, the veil is torn away, I have understood, I have *seen*.

6.00 *p.m.*

I can't say I feel relieved or satisfied; just the opposite, I am crushed. Only my goal is reached: I know what I wanted to know; I have understood all that has happened to me since January. The Nausea has not left me and I don't believe it will leave me so soon; but I no longer have to bear it, it is no longer an illness or a passing fit: it is I.

So I was in the park just now. The roots of the chestnut tree were sunk in the ground just under my bench. I couldn't remember it was a root any more. The words had vanished and with them the significance of things, their methods of use, and the feeble points of reference which men have traced on their surface. I was sitting, stooping forward, head bowed, alone in front of this black, knotty mass, entirely beastly, which frightened me. Then I had this vision.

It left me breathless. Never, until these last few days, had I understood the meaning of "existence." I was like the others, like the ones walking along the seashore, all dressed in their spring finery. I said, like them, "The ocean *is* green; that white speck up there *is* a seagull," but I didn't feel that it existed or that the seagull was an "existing seagull"; usually existence hides itself. It is there, around us, in us, it is *us*, you can't say two words without mentioning it, but you can never touch it. When I believed I was thinking about it, I must believe that I was thinking nothing, my head was empty, or there was just one word in my head, the word "to be." Or else I was thinking . . . how can I explain it? I was thinking of *belonging*, I was telling myself that the sea belonged to the class of green objects, or that the green was a part of the quality of the sea. Even when I looked at things, I was miles from dreaming that they existed: they looked like scenery to me. I picked them up in my hands, they served me as tools, I foresaw their resistance. But that all happened on the surface. If anyone had asked me what existence was, I would have answered, in good faith, that it was nothing, simply an empty form which was added to external things without changing anything in their nature. And then all of a sudden, there it was, clear as day: existence had suddenly unveiled itself. It had lost the harmless look of an abstract category: it was the very paste of things, this root was kneaded into existence. Or rather the root, the park gates, the bench, the sparse grass, all that had vanished: the diversity of things, their individuality, were only an appearance, a veneer. This veneer had melted, leaving soft, monstrous masses, all in disorder—naked, in a frightful, obscene nakedness.

I kept myself from making the slightest movement, but I didn't need to move in order to see, behind the trees, the blue columns and the lamp posts of the bandstand and the Velleda, in the midst of a mountain of laurel. All these objects . . . how can I explain? They inconvenienced me; I would have liked them to exist less strongly, more dryly, in a more abstract way, with more reserve. The chestnut tree pressed itself against my eyes. Green rust covered it half-way up; the bark, black and swollen, looked like boiled leather. The sound of the water in the Masqueret Fountain sounded in my ears, made a nest there, filled them with signs; my nostrils overflowed with a green, putrid odour. All things, gently, tenderly, were letting themselves drift into existence like those relaxed women who burst out laughing and say: "It's good to laugh," in a wet voice; they were parading, one in front of the other, exchanging abject secrets about their existence. I realized that there was no half-way house between non-existence and this flaunting abundance. If you existed, you had to *exist all the way*, as far as mouldiness, bloatedness, obscenity were concerned. In another world, circles, bars of music keep their pure and rigid lines. But existence is a deflection. Trees, night-blue pillars, the happy bubbling of a fountain, vital smells, little heat-mists floating in the cold air, a red-haired man digesting on a bench: all this somnolence, all these meals digested together, had its comic side. . . . Comic . . . no: it didn't go as far as that, nothing that exists can be comic; it was like a floating analogy, almost entirely elusive, with certain aspects of vaudeville. We were a heap of living creatures, irritated, embarrassed at ourselves, we hadn't the slightest reason to be there, none of us, each one, confused, vaguely alarmed, felt in the way in relation to the others. *In the way*: it was the only relationship I could establish between these trees, these gates, these stones. In vain I tried to *count* the chestnut trees, to *locate* them by their relationship to the Velleda, to compare their height with the height of the plane trees: each of them escaped the relationship in which I tried to enclose it, isolated itself, and overflowed. Of these relations (which I insisted on maintaining in order to delay the crumbling of the human world, measures, quantities, and directions)—I felt myself to be the arbitrator; they no longer had their teeth into things. *In the way*, the chestnut tree there, opposite me, a little to the left. *In the way*, the Velleda. . . .

And I—soft, weak, obscene, digesting, juggling with dismal thoughts—I, too, was *In the way*. Fortunately, I didn't feel it, although I realized it, but I was uncomfortable because I was afraid of feeling it (even now I am afraid—afraid that it might catch me behind my head and lift me up like a wave). I dreamed vaguely of killing myself to wipe out at least one of these superfluous lives. But even my death would have been *In the way*. *In the way*, my corpse, my blood on these stones, between these plants, at the back of this smiling garden. And the decomposed flesh would have been *In the way* in the earth which would receive my bones, at last, cleaned, stripped, peeled, proper and clean as teeth, it would have been *In the way*: I was *In the way* for eternity.

The word absurdity is coming to life under my pen; a little while ago, in the garden, I couldn't find it, but neither was I looking for it, I didn't need it: I thought without words, *on* things, *with* things. Absurdity was not an idea in my head, or the sound of a voice, only this long serpent dead at my feet, this wooden serpent. Serpent or claw or root or vulture's talon, what difference does it make. And without formulating anything clearly, I understood that I had found the key to Existence, the key to my Nauseas, to my own life. In fact, all that I could grasp beyond that returns to this fundamental absurdity. Absurdity: another word; I struggle against words; down there I touched the thing. But I wanted to fix the absolute character of this absurdity here. A movement, an event in the tiny coloured world of men is only relatively absurd: by relation to the accompanying circumstances. A madman's ravings, for example, are absurd in relation to the situation in which he finds himself, but not in relation to his delirium. But a little while ago I made an experiment with the absolute or the absurd. This root—there was nothing in relation to which it was absurd. Oh, how can I put it in words? Absurd: in relation to the stones, the tufts of yellow grass, the dry mud, the tree, the sky, the green benches. Absurd, irreducible; nothing—not even a profound, secret upheaval of nature—could explain it. Evidently I did not know everything, I had not seen the seeds sprout, or the tree grow. But faced with this great wrinkled paw, neither ignorance nor knowledge was important. the world of explanations and reasons is not the world of existence. A circle is not absurd, it is clearly explained by the rotation of a straight segment around one of its extremities. But neither does a circle exist. This root, on the other hand, existed in such a way that I could not explain it. Knotty, inert, nameless, it fascinated me, filled my eyes, brought me back unceasingly to its own existence. In vain to repeat: "This is a root"—it didn't work any more. I saw clearly that you could not pass from its function as a root, as a breathing pump, *to that*, to this hard and compact skin of a sea lion, to this oily, callous, headstrong look. The function explained nothing: it allowed you to understand generally that it was a root, but not *that one* at all. This root, with its colour, shape, its congealed movement, was . . . below all explanation. Each of its qualities escaped it a little, flowed out of it, half solidified, almost became a thing; each one was *In the way* in the root and the whole stump now gave me the impression of unwinding itself a little, denying its existence to lose itself in a frenzied excess. I scraped my heel against this black claw: I wanted to peel off some of the bark. For no reason at all, out of defiance, to make the bare pink appear absurd on the tanned leather: to *play* with the absurdity of the world. But, when I drew my heel back, I saw that the bark was still black.

Black? I felt the word deflating, emptied of meaning with extraordinary rapidity. Black? The root *was not* black, there was no black on this piece of wood—there was . . . something else: black, like the circle, did not exist. I looked at the root: was it *more than* black or *almost* black? But I soon stopped questioning myself because I had the feeling of knowing where I was. Yes, I had already scrutinized innumerable objects, with deep uneasiness. I had already tried—vainly—to think something *about* them: and I had already felt their cold, inert qualities elude me, slip through my fingers. Adolphe's suspenders, the other evening in the "Railwaymen's Rendezvous." They *were not* purple. I saw the two inexplicable stains on the shirt. And the stone—the well-known stone, the origin of this whole business: it was not . . . I can't remember exactly just what it was that the stone refused to be. But I had not forgotten its passive resistance. And the hand of the Self-Taught Man; I held it and shook it one day in the library and then I had the feeling that it wasn't quite a hand. I had thought of a great white worm, but that wasn't it either. And the suspicious transparency of the glass of beer in the Café Mably. Suspicious: that's what they were, the sounds, the smells, the tastes. When they ran quickly under your nose like startled hares and you didn't pay too much attention, you might believe them to be simple and reassuring, you might believe that there was real blue in the world, real red, a real perfume of almonds or violets. But as soon as you held on to them for an instant, this feeling of comfort and security gave way to a deep uneasiness: colours, tastes, and smells were never real, never themselves and nothing but themselves. The simplest, most indefinable quality had too much content, in relation to itself, in its heart. That black against my foot, it didn't look like black, but rather the confused effort to imagine black by someone who had never seen black and who wouldn't know how to stop, who would have imagined an ambiguous being beyond colours. It *looked* like a colour, but also . . . like a bruise or a secretion, like an oozing—and something else, an odour, for example, it melted into the odour of wet earth, warm, moist wood, into a black odour that spread like varnish over this sensitive wood, in a flavour of chewed, sweet fibre. I did not simply *see* this black: sight is an abstract invention, a simplified idea, one of man's ideas. That black, amorphous, weakly presence, far surpassed sight, smell and taste. But this richness was lost in confusion and finally was no more because it was too much.

This moment was extraordinary. I was there, motionless and icy, plunged in a horrible ecstasy. But something fresh had just appeared in the very heart of this ecstasy; I understood the Nausea, I possessed it. To tell the truth, I did not formulate my discoveries to myself. But I think it would be easy for me to put them in words now. The essential thing is contingency. I mean that one cannot define existence as necessity. To exist is simply *to be there*; those who exist let themselves be encountered, but you can never deduce anything from them. I believe there are people who have understood this. Only they tried to overcome this contingency by inventing a necessary, causal being. But no necessary being can explain existence: contingency is not a delusion, a probability which can be dissipated; it is the absolute, consequently, the perfect free gift. All is free, this park, this city and myself. When you realize that, it turns your heart upside down and everything begins to float, as the other evening at the "Railwaymen's Rendezvous": here is Nausea; here there is what those bastards—the ones on the Coteau Vert and others—try to hide from themselves with their idea of their rights. But what a poor lie: no one has any rights; they are entirely free, like other men, they cannot succeed in not feeling superfluous. And in themselves, secretly, they are *superfluous*, that is to say, amorphous, vague, and sad.

How long will this fascination last? I *was* the root of the chestnut tree. Or rather I was entirely conscious of its existence. Still detached from it—since I was conscious of it—yet lost in it, nothing but it. An uneasy conscience which, notwithstanding, let itself fall with all its weight on this piece of dead wood. Time had stopped: a small black pool at my feet; it was impossible for something to come *after* that moment. I would have liked to tear myself from that atrocious joy, but I did not even imagine it would be possible; I was inside; the black stump did *not move*, it stayed there, in my eyes, as a lump of food sticks in the windpipe. I could neither accept nor refuse it. At what a cost did I

131

raise my eyes? Did I raise them? Rather did I not obliterate myself for an instant in order to be reborn in the following instant with my head thrown back and my eyes raised upward? In fact, I was not even conscious of the transformation. But suddenly it became impossible for me to think of the existence of the root. It was wiped out, I could repeat in vain: it exists, it is still there, under the bench, against my right foot, it no longer meant anything. Existence is not something which lets itself be thought of from a distance: it must invade you suddenly, master you, weigh heavily on your heart like a great motionless beast—or else there is nothing more at all.

There was nothing more, my eyes were empty and I was spellbound by my deliverance. Then suddenly it began to move before my eyes in light, uncertain motions: the wind was shaking the top of the tree.

It did not displease me to see a movement, it was a change from these motionless beings who watched me like staring eyes. I told myself, as I followed the swinging of the branches: movements never quite exist, they are passages, intermediaries between two existences, moments of weakness, I expected to see them come out of nothingness, progressively ripen, blossom: I was finally going to surprise beings in the process of being born.

No more than three seconds, and all my hopes were swept away. I could not attribute the passage of time to these branches groping around like blind men. This idea of passage was still an invention of man. The idea was too transparent. All these paltry agitations, drew in on themselves, isolated. They overflowed the leaves and branches everywhere. They whirled about these empty hands, enveloped them with tiny whirlwinds. Of course a movement was something different from a tree. But it was still an absolute. A thing. My eyes only encountered completion. The tips of the branches rustled with existence which unceasingly renewed itself and which was never born. The existing wind rested on the tree like a great bluebottle, and the tree shuddered. But the shudder was not a nascent quality, a passing from power to action; it was a thing; a shudder-thing flowed into the tree, took possession of it, shook it and suddenly abandoned it, going further on to spin about itself. All was fullness and all was active, there was no weakness in time, all, even the least perceptible stirring, was made of existence. And all these existents which bustled about this tree came from nowhere and were going nowhere. Suddenly they existed, then suddenly they existed no longer: existence is without memory; of the vanished it retains nothing—not even a memory. Existence everywhere, infinitely, in excess, for ever and everywhere; existence—which is limited only by existence. I sank down on the bench, stupefied, stunned by this profusion of beings without origin: everywhere blossomings, hatchings out, my ears buzzed with existence, my very flesh throbbed and opened, abandoned itself to the universal burgeoning. It was repugnant. But why, I thought, why so many existences, since they all look alike? What good are so many duplicates of trees? So many existences missed, obstinately begun again and again missed—like the awkward efforts of an insect fallen on its back? (I was one of those efforts.) That abundance did not give the effect of generosity, just the opposite. It was dismal, ailing, embarrassed at itself. Those trees, those great clumsy bodies. . . . I began to laugh because I suddenly thought of the formidable springs described in books, full of crackings, burstings, gigantic explosions. There were those idiots who came to tell you about will-power and struggle for life. Hadn't they ever seen a beast or a tree? This plane-tree with its scaling bark, this half-rotten oak, they wanted me to take them for rugged youthful endeavour surging towards the sky. And that root? I would have undoubtedly had to represent it as a voracious claw tearing at the earth, devouring its food?

Impossible to see things that way. Weaknesses, frailties, yes. The trees floated. Gushing towards the sky? Or rather a collapse; at any instant I expected to see the tree-trunks shrivel like weary wands, crumple up, fall on the ground in a soft, folded, black heap. *They did not want* to exist, only they could not help themselves. So they quietly minded their own business; the sap rose up slowly through the structure, half reluctant, and the roots sank slowly into the earth. But at each instant they seemed on the verge of leaving everything there and obliterating themselves. Tired and old, they kept on existing, against the grain, simply because they were too weak to die, because death could only come to them from the outside: strains of music alone can proudly carry their own death within themselves like an internal necessity: only they don't exist. Every existing thing is born without reason, prolongs itself out of weakness and dies by chance. I leaned back and closed my eyes. But the images, forewarned, immediately leaped up and filled my closed eyes with existences: existence is a fullness which man can never abandon.

Strange images. They represented a multitude of things. Not

real things, other things which looked like them. Wooden objects which looked like chairs, shoes, other objects which looked like plants. And then two faces: the couple who were eating opposite to me last Sunday in the Brasserie Vézelise. Fat, hot, sensual, absurd, with red ears. I could see the woman's neck and shoulders. Nude existence. Those two—it suddenly gave me a turn—those two were still existing somewhere in Bouville; somewhere—in the midst of smells?—this soft throat rubbing up luxuriously against smooth stuffs, nestling in lace; and the woman picturing her bosom under her blouse, thinking: "My titties, my lovely fruits," smiling mysteriously, attentive to the swelling of her breasts which tickled . . . then I shouted and found myself with my eyes wide open.

Had I dreamed of this enormous presence? It was there, in the garden, toppled down into the trees, all soft, sticky, soiling everything, all thick, a jelly. And I was inside, I with the garden. I was frightened, furious, I thought it was so stupid, so out of place, I hated this ignoble mess. Mounting up, mounting up as high as the sky, spilling over, filling everything with its gelatinous slither, and I could see depths upon depths of it reaching far beyond the limits of the garden, the houses, and Bouville, as far as the eye could reach. I was no longer in Bouville, I was nowhere, I was floating. I was not surprised, I knew it was the World, the naked World suddenly revealing itself, and I choked with rage at this gross, absurd being. You couldn't even wonder where all that sprang from, or how it was that a world came into existence, rather than nothingness. It didn't make sense, the World was everywhere, in front, behind. There had been nothing *before* it. Nothing. There had never been a moment in which it could not have existed. That was what worried me: of course there was no *reason* for this flowing larva to exist. *But it was impossible* for it is not to exist. It was unthinkable: to imagine nothingness you had to be there already, in the midst of the World, eyes wide open and alive; nothingness was only an idea in my head, an existing idea floating in this immensity: this nothingness had not come *before* existence, it was an existence like any other and appeared after many others. I shouted "filth! what rotten filth!" and shook myself to get rid of this sticky filth, but it held fast and there was so much, tons and tons of existence, endless: I stifled at the depths of this immense weariness. And then suddenly the park emptied as through a great hole, the World disappeared as it had come, or else I woke up—in any case, I saw no more of it; nothing was left but the yellow earth around me, out of which dead branches rose upward.

I got up and went out. Once at the gate, I turned back. Then the garden smiled at me. I leaned against the gate and watched for a long time. The smile of the trees, of the laurel, *meant* something; that was the real secret of existence. I remembered one Sunday, not more than three weeks ago, I had already detected everywhere a sort of conspiratorial air. Was it in my intention? I felt with boredom that I had no way of understanding. No way. Yet it was there, waiting, looking at one. It was there on the trunk of the chestnut tree . . . it was *the* chestnut tree. Things—you might have called them thoughts—which stopped halfway, which were forgotten, which forgot what they wanted to think and which stayed like that, hanging about with an odd little sense which was beyond them. That little sense annoyed me: I *could not* understand it, even if I could have stayed leaning against the gate for a century; I had learned all I could know about existence. I left, I went back to the hotel and I wrote.

Night:

I have made my decision: I have no more reason for staying in Bouville since I'm not writing my book any more; I'm going to live in Paris. I'll take the five o'clock train, on Saturday I'll see Anny; I think we'll spend a few days together. Then I'll come back here to settle my accounts and pack my trunks. By March 1, at the latest, I will be definitely installed in Paris.

Friday:

In the "Railwaymen's Rendezvous." My train leaves in twenty minutes. The gramophone. Strong feeling of adventure.

Saturday:

Anny opens to me in a long black dress. Naturally, she does not put out her hand, she doesn't say hello. Sullenly and quickly, to get the formalities over with, she says:

"Come in and sit down anywhere—except on the armchair near the window."

It's really she. She lets her arms hang, she has the morose face which made her look like an awkward adolescent girl. But she doesn't look like a little girl any more. She is fat, her breasts are heavy.

She closes the door, and says meditatively to herself:

"I don't know whether I'm going to sit on the bed. . . ."

Finally she drops on to a sort of chest covered with a carpet. Her walk is no longer the same: she moves with a majestic heaviness, not without grace: she seems embarrassed at her youthful fleshiness. But, in spite of everything, it's really Anny.

Anny bursts out laughing.

"What are you laughing at?"

As usual, she doesn't answer right away, and starts looking quarrelsome.

"Tell me why you're laughing."

"Because of that wide smile you've been wearing ever since you got here. You look like a father who's just married off his daughter. Come on, don't just stand there. Take off your coat and sit down. Yes, over there if you want."

A silence follows. Anny does not try to break it. How bare this room is! Before, Anny always used to carry an immense trunk full of shawls, turbans, mantillas, Japanese masks, pictures of Epinal. Hardly arrived at an hotel—even if it is only for one night —than her first job is to open this trunk and take out all her wealth which she hangs on the walls, on lamps, spreads over tables or on the floor, following a changeable and complicated order; in less than thirty minutes the dullest room became invested with a heavy, sensual, almost intolerable personality. Perhaps the trunk got lost—or stayed in the check room. . . . This cold room with the door half-open on the bathroom has something sinister about it. It looks like—only sadder and more luxurious— like my room in Bouville.

Anny laughs again. How will I recognize this high-pitched, nasal little laugh?

"Well, you haven't changed. What are you looking for with that bewildered look on your face?"

She smiles, but studies my face with almost hostile curiosity.

"I was only thinking this room doesn't look as if you were living in it."

"Really?" she answers vaguely.

Another silence. Now she is sitting on the bed, very pale in her black dress. She hasn't cut her hair. She is still watching me, calmly, raising her eyebrows a little. Has she got nothing to say to me? Why did she make me come here? This silence is unbearable.

Suddenly, I say pitifully:

"I'm glad to see you."

The last word sticks in my throat: I would have done better to keep quiet. She is surely going to be angry. I expected the first fifteen minutes to be difficult. In the old days, when I saw Anny again, whether after a twenty-four-hour absence or on waking in the morning, I could never find the words she expected, the words which went with her dress, with the weather, with the last words we had spoken the night before. What does she want? I can't guess.

I raise my eyes again. Anny looks at me with a sort of tenderness.

"You haven't changed at all? You're still just as much of a fool?"

Her face shows satisfaction. But how tired she looks!

"You're a milestone," she says, "a milestone beside a road. You explain imperturbably and for the rest of your life you'll go on explaining that Melun is twenty-seven kilometres and Montargis is forty-two. That's why I need you so much."

"Need me? You mean you needed me these four years I haven't seen you? You've been pretty quiet about it."

I spoke lightly: she might think I am resentful. I feel a false smile on my mouth, I'm uncomfortable.

"What a fool you are! Naturally I don't need to see you, if that's what you mean. You know you're not exactly a sight for sore eyes. I need you to exist and not to change. You're like that platinum wire they keep in Paris or somewhere in the neighbourhood. I don't think anyone's ever needed to see it."

"That's where you're mistaken."

"Not I. Anyhow, it doesn't matter. I'm glad to know that it exists, that it measures the exact ten-millionth part of a quarter of a meridian. I think about it every time they start taking measurements in an apartment or when people sell me cloth by the yard."

"Is that so?" I say coldly.

"But you know, I could very well think of you only as an abstract virtue, a sort of limit. You should be grateful to me for remembering your face each time."

Here we are back to these alexandrine discussions I had to go through before when in my heart I had the simplest, commonest desires, such as telling her I loved her, taking her in my arms. Today I have no such desire. Except perhaps a desire to be quiet and to look at her, to realize in silence all the importance of this extraordinary event: the presence of Anny opposite me. Is this day like any other day for her? Her hands are not trembling. She must have had something to tell me the day she wrote—or perhaps it was only a whim. Now there has been no question of it for a long time.

Anny suddenly smiles at me with a tenderness so apparent that tears come to my eyes.

"I've thought about you much more often than that yard of platinum. There hasn't been a day when I haven't thought of you. And I remembered exactly what you looked like—every detail."

She gets up, comes and rests her arms on my shoulders.

"You complain about me, but you daren't pretend you rememebered my face."

"That's not fair," I say, "you know I have a bad memory."

"You admit it: you'd forgotten me completely. Would you have known me in the street?"

"Naturally. It's not a question of that."

"Did you at least remember the colour of my hair?"

"Of course. Blonde."

She begins to laugh.

"You're really proud when you say that. Now that you see it. You aren't worth much."

She rumples my hair with one sweep of her hand.

"And you—your hair is red," she says, imitating me: "the first time I saw you, I'll never forget, you had a mauvish homburg hat and it swore horribly with your red hair. It was hard to look at. Where's your hat? I want to see if your taste is as bad as ever."

"I don't wear one any more."

She whistles softly, opening her eyes wide.

"You didn't think of that all by yourself! Did you? Well, congratulations. Of course! I should have realized. That hair can't stand anything, it swears with hats, chair cushions, even at a wallpaper background. Or else you have to pull your hat down over your ears like that felt you bought in London. You tucked all your hair away under the brim. You might have been bald for all anyone could see."

She adds, in the decisive tone with which you end old quarrels:

"It didn't look at all nice on you."

I don't know what hat she's talking about.

"Did I say it looked good on me?"

"I should say you did! You never talked of anything else. And you were always sneaking a look in the glass when you thought I wasn't watching you."

This knowledge of the past overwhelms me. Anny does not even seem to be evoking memories, her tone of voice does not have the touch of tender remoteness suitable to that kind of occupation. She seems to be speaking of today rather than yesterday; she has kept her opinions, her obstinacies, and her past resentments fully alive. Just the opposite for me, all is drowned in poetic impression; I am ready for all concessions.

Suddenly she says in a toneless voice:

"You see, I'm getting fat, I'm getting old. I have to take care of myself."

Yes. And how weary she looks! Just as I am about to speak, she adds:

"I was in the theatre in London."

"With Candler?"

"No, of course not with Candler. How like you! You had it in your head that I was going to act with Candler. How many times must I tell you that Candler is the orchestra leader? No, in a little theatre, in Soho Square. We played *The Emperor Jones*, some Synge and O'Casey, and *Britannicus*."

"*Britannicus?*" I say, amazed.

"Yes, *Britannicus*. I quit because of that. I was the one who gave them the idea of putting on *Britannicus* and they wanted to make me play Junie."

"Really?"

"Well, naturally I could only play Agrippine."

"And now what are you doing?"

I was wrong in asking that. Life fades entirely from her face. Still she answers at once:

"I'm not acting any more. I travel. I'm being kept."

She smiles:

"Oh, don't look at me in that solicitous way. I always told you it didn't make any difference to me, being kept. Besides, he's an old man, he isn't any trouble."

"English?"

"What does it matter to you?" she says, irritated. "We're not going to talk about him. He has no importance whatsoever for you or me. Do you want some tea?"

She goes into the bathroom. I hear her moving around, rattling cups, talking to herself; a sharp, unintelligible murmur. On the night-table by her bed, as always, there is a volume of Michelet's *History of France*. Now I can make out a single picture hung above the bed, a reproduction of a portrait of Emily Brontë, done by her brother.

Anny returns and suddenly tells me:

"Now you must talk to me about you."

Then she disappears again into the bathroom. I remember that in spite of my bad memory: that was the way she asked those direct questions which annoyed me so much, because I felt a genuine interest and a desire to get things over with at the same time. In any case, after that question, I know for certain that she wants something from me. These are only the preliminaries: you get rid of anything that might be disturbing, you definitely rule out secondary questions: "Now you must talk to me about you." Soon she will talk to me about herself. All of a sudden I no longer have the slightest desire to tell her anything. What good would it be? The Nausea, the fear, existence. . . . It is better to keep all that to myself.

"Come on, hurry up," she shouts through the partition.

She returns with a teapot.

"What are you doing? Are you living in Paris?"

"I live in Bouville."

"Bouville? Why? You aren't married, I hope."

"Married?" I say with a start.

It is very pleasant for me to have Anny think that. I tell her:

"It's absurd. That's exactly the sort of naturalistic imagination you accused me of before. You know: when I used to imagine you a widow and mother of two boys. And all the stories I used to tell about what would happen to us. You hated it."

"And you liked it," she answers, unconcernedly. "You said that to put on a big act. Besides, even though you get indignant in conversation, you're traitor enough to get married one day on the sly. You swore indignantly for a year that you wouldn't see *Violettes Impériales*. Then one day when I was sick you went and saw it alone in a cheap movie."

"I am in Bouville," I say with dignity, "because I am writing a book on the Marquis de Rollebon."

Anny looks at me with studied interest.

"Rollebon? He lived in the eighteenth century?"

"Yes."

ded it did. And now it's gone, disappeared. You
t. Don't you feel more comfortable?"

y to answer no: I am, just as before, sitting on the
air, careful to avoid ambushes, ready to conjure
ble rages.

down again.

he says, nodding her head with conviction, "if you
tand, it's because you've forgotten things. More
ht. Come on, don't you remember your misdeeds
ou came, you spoke, you went: all contrarily. Sup-
ng had changed: you would have come in, there'd
asks and shawls on the wall, I'd have been sitting
and I'd have said (she throws her head back, dilates
and speaks in a theatrical voice, as if in self-mockery):
t are you waiting for? Sit down.' And naturally, I'd
lly avoided telling you: 'except on the armchair near
w.' "

set traps for me."

y weren't traps. . . . So, naturally, you'd have gone
er and sat down."

what would have happened to me?" I ask, turning
ng at the armchair with curiosity.

oks ordinary, it looks paternal and comfortable.

ly something bad," Anny answers briefly.

ave it at that: Anny always surrounded herself with

think," I tell her suddenly, "that I guess something. But
d be so extraordinary. Wait, let me think: as a matter
this room is completely bare. Do me the justice of ad-
that I noticed it right away. All right. I would have
n, I'd have seen these masks on the wall, and the shawls
l that. The hotel always stopped at your door. Your room
mething else. . . . You wouldn't have come to open the
or me. I'd have seen you crouched in a corner, maybe sit-
n that piece of red carpet you always carried with you,
ng at me pitilessly, waiting. . . . I would have hardly said
rd, made a move, taken a breath before you'd have started
ning and I would have felt deeply guilty without knowing
. Then with every moment that passed I'd have plunged
er into error."

"How many times has that happened?"

"A hundred times."

"As a matter of fact
It's a history book, then?"

"Yes."

"Ha, ha!"

If she asks me one mo:
But she asks nothing more
she knows enough about m
listener, but only when she
lowered her eyelids, she is tl
tell me, how she is going to
now? I don't think she expect:
cides it will be good to do so. I

She says suddenly:

"I've changed."

This is the beginning. But :
into the white porcelain cups. Sl
I must say something. Not just a
is expecting. It is torture. Has
gotten heavier, she looks tired: that

"I don't know, I don't think
laugh again, your way of getting up
my shoulders, your mania for talking
ing Michelet's *History*. And a lot of (

This profound interest which sh
sence and her total indifference to all
this life—and then this curious affectati
pedantic—and this way of suppressing
the mechanical formulas of politeness, f
relationships between people easier, fore\
to invent a rôle.

She shrugs:

"Yes, I have changed," she says dryl
every way. I'm not the same person any 1
notice it as soon as you saw me. Instead)
Michelet's *History*."

She comes and stands in front of me.

"We'll see whether this man is as str(
Guess: how have I changed?"

I hesitate; she taps her foot, still smi
annoyed.

"There was something that tormented y

least you prete
should notice

I dare on
edge of the (
away inexpli(
She sits
"Well,"
don't unders
than I thou
any more? \
posing noth
have been
on the bed
her nostrils
'Well, wha
have caref\
the windo
"You
"The
straight o
"An(
and looki
It l(
"O
I l(
taboos.
"I
it wou(
of fact
mitting
come
and al
was s
door
ting
looki
a w(
frow
why
dee(

142

"At least. Are you more adept, sharper now?"

"No!"

"I like to hear you say it. Well then?"

"Well then, it's because there are no more . . ."

"Ha, ha!" she shouts theatrically, "he hardly dares believe it!"

Then she continues softly:

"Well you can believe me: there are no more."

"No more perfect moments?"

"No."

I am dumfounded. I insist.

"You mean you . . . it's all over, those . . . tragedies, those instantaneous tragedies where the masks and shawls, the furniture, and myself . . . where we each had a minor part to play—and you had the lead?"

She smiles.

"He's ungrateful. Sometimes I gave him greater rôles than my own: but he never suspected. Well, yes: it's finished. Are you really surprised?"

"Yes, I'm surprised! I thought that was a part of you, that if it were taken away from you it would have been like tearing out your heart."

"I thought so too," she says, without regret. Then she adds, with a sort of irony that affects me unpleasantly:

"But you see I can live without that."

She has laced her fingers and holds one knee in her hands. She looks with a vague smile which rejuvenates her whole face. She looks like a fat little girl, mysterious and satisfied.

"Yes, I'm glad you've stayed the same. My milestone. If you'd been moved, or repainted, or planted by the side of a different road, I would have nothing fixed to orient myself. You are indispensable to me: I change, you naturally stay motionless and I measure my changes in relation to you."

I still feel a little vexed.

"Well, that's most inaccurate," I say sharply. "On the contrary, I have been evolving all this time, and at heart I . . ."

"Oh," she says with crushing scorn, "intellectual changes! I've changed to the very whites of my eyes."

To the very whites of her eyes. . . . What startles me about her voice? Anyhow, I suddenly give a jump. I stop looking for an Anny who isn't there. This is the girl, here, this fat girl with a ruined look who touches me and whom I love.

"I have a sort of . . . physical certainty. I feel there are no more perfect moments. I feel it in my legs when I walk. I feel it all the time, even when I sleep. I can't forget it. There has never been anything like a revelation; I can't say: starting on such and such a day, at such a time, my life has been transformed. But now I always feel a bit as if I'd suddenly seen it yesterday. I'm dazzled, uncomfortable, I can't get used to it."

She says these words in a calm voice with a touch of pride at having changed. She balances herself on the chest with extraordinary grace. Not once since I came has she more strongly resembled the Anny of before, the Anny of Marseilles. She has caught me again, once more I have plunged into her strange universe, beyond ridicule, affectation, subtlety. I have even recovered the little fever that always stirred in me when I was with her, and this bitter taste in the back of my mouth.

Anny unclasps her hands and drops her knee. She is silent. A concerted silence, as when, at the Opera, the stage is empty for exactly seven measures of music. She drinks her tea. Then she puts down her cup and holds herself stiffly, leaning her clasped hands on the back of the chest.

Suddenly she puts on her superb look of Medusa, which I loved so much, all swollen with hate, twisted, venomous. Anny hardly changes expression; she changes faces; as the actors of antiquity changed masks: suddenly. And each one of the masks is destined to create atmosphere, to give tone to what follows. It appears and stays without modification as she speaks. Then it falls, detached from her.

She stares at me without seeming to see me. She is going to speak. I expect a tragic speech, heightened to the dignity of her mask, a funeral oration.

She does not say a single word.

"I outlive myself."

The tone does not correspond in any way to her face. It is not tragic, it is . . . horrible: it expresses a dry despair, without tears, without pity. Yes, something in her has irremediably dried out.

The masks falls, she smiles.

"I'm not at all sad. I am often amazed at it, but I was wrong: why should I be sad? I used to be capable of rather splendid passions. I hated my mother passionately. And you," she says defiantly, "I loved you passionately."

She waits for an answer. I say nothing.

"All that is over, of course."

"How can you tell?"

"I know. I know that I shall never again meet anything or anybody who will inspire me with passion. You know, it's quite a job starting to love somebody. You have to have energy, generosity, blindness. There is even a moment, in the very beginning, when you have to jump across a precipice: if you think about it you don't do it. I know I'll never jump again."

"Why?"

She looks at me ironically and does not answer.

"Now," she says, "I live surrounded with my dead passions. I try to recapture the fine fury that threw me off the fourth floor, when I was twelve, the day my mother whipped me."

She adds with apparent inconsequence, and a far-away look:

"It isn't good for me to stare at things too long. I look at them to find out what they are, then I have to turn my eyes away quickly."

"Why?"

"They disgust me."

It would almost seem . . . There are surely similarities, in any case. It happened once in London, we had separately thought the same things about the same subjects, almost at the same time. I'd like so much to . . . But Anny's mind takes many turnings, you can never be sure you've understood her completely. I must get to the heart of it.

"Listen, I want to tell you something: you know, I never quite knew what perfect moments were; you never explained them to me."

"Yes, I know. You made absolutely no effort. You sat beside me like a lump on a log."

"I know what it cost me."

"You deserved everything that happened to you, you were very wicked; you annoyed me with your stolid look. You seemed to say: I'm normal; and you practically breathed health, you dripped with moral well-being."

"Still, I must have asked you a hundred times at least what a . . ."

"Yes, but in what a tone of voice," she says, angrily; "you condescended to inform yourself, and that's the whole truth. You were kindly and *distrait*, like the old ladies who used to ask me what I was playing when I was little. At heart," she says dreamily, "I wonder if you weren't the one I hated most."

She makes a great effort to collect herself and smiles, her cheeks still flaming. She is very beautiful.

"I want to explain what they are. I'm old enough now to talk calmly to old women like you about my childhood games. Go ahead, talk, what do you want to know?"

"What they were."

"I told you about the privileged situations?"

"I don't think so."

"Yes," she says with assurance. "It was in Aix, in that square, I don't remember the name any more. We were in the courtyard of a café, in the sun, under orange parasols. You don't remember: we drank lemonade and I found a dead fly in the powdered sugar."

"Ah yes, maybe . . ."

"Well, I talked to you about that in the café. I talked to you about it à propos of the big edition of Michelet's *History*, the one I had when I was little. It was a lot bigger than this one and the pages were livid, like the inside of a mushroom. When my father died, my Uncle Joseph got his hands on it and took away all the volumes. That was the day I called him a dirty pig and my mother whipped me and I jumped out the window."

"Yes, yes . . . you must have told me about that *History of France*. . . . Didn't you read it in the attic? You see, I remember. You see, you were unjust when you accused me of forgetting everything a little while ago."

"Be quiet. Yes, as you remember so well, I carried those enormous books to the attic. There were very few pictures in them, maybe three or four in each volume. But each one had a big page all to itself, and the other side of the page was blank. That had much more effect on me than the other pages where they'd arranged the text in two columns to save space. I had an extraordinary love for those pictures; I knew them all by heart, and whenever I read one of Michelet's books, I'd wait for them fifty pages in advance; it always seemed a miracle to find them again. And then there was something better: the scene they showed never had any relation to the text on the next page, you had to go looking for the event thirty pages farther on."

"I beg you, tell me about the perfect moments."

"I'm talking about privileged situations. They were the ones the pictures told about. I called them privileged, I told myself they must have been terribly important to be made the subject of such rare pictures. They had been chosen above all the others, do you understand: and yet there were many episodes which had a greater plastic value, others with a greater historical interest. For example, there were only three pictures for the whole sixteenth century: one for the death of Henri II, one for the assassination of the Duc de Guise and one for the entry of Henri IV into Paris. Then I imagined that there was something special about these events. The pictures confirmed the idea: the drawings were bad, the arms and legs were never too well attached to the bodies. But it was full of grandeur. When the Duc de Guise was assassinated, for example, the spectators showed their amazement and indignation by stretching out their hands and turning their faces away, like a chorus. And don't think they left out any pleasant details. You could see pages falling to the ground, little dogs running away, jesters sitting on the steps of the throne. But all these details were treated with so much grandeur and so much clumsiness that they were in perfect harmony with the rest of the picture: I don't think I've ever come across pictures that had such a strict unity. Well, they came from there."

"The privileged situations?"

"The idea I had of them. They were situations which had a rare and precious quality, style, if you like. To be king, for example, when I was eight years old, seemed a privileged situation to me. Or to die. You may laugh, but there were so many people drawn at the moment of their death, and so many who spoke such sublime words at that moment that I quite genuinely thought . . . well, I thought that by dying you were transported above yourself. Besides, it was enough just to be in the room of a dying person: death being a privileged situation, something emanated from it and communicated itself to everyone there. A sort of grandeur. When my father died, they took me up to his room to see him for the last time. I was very unhappy going up the stairs, but I was also drunk with a sort of religious ecstasy; I was finally entering a privileged situation. I leaned against the wall, I tried to make the proper motions. But my aunt and mother were kneeling by the bed, and they spoiled it all by crying."

She says these last words with anger, as if the memory still scorched her. She interrupts herself; eyes staring, eyebrows raised, she takes advantage of the occasion to live the scene once more.

"I developed all that later on: first I added a new situation, love (I mean the act of love). Look, if you never understood why I refused . . . certain of your demands, here's your opportunity to understand now: for me, there was something to be saved. Then I told myself that there should be many more privileged situations than I could count, finally I admitted an infinite number of them."

"Yes, but what were they?"

"But I've told you," she says with amazement, "I've been explaining to you for fifteen minutes."

"Well, was it especially necessary for people to be impassioned, carried away by hatred or love, for example; or did the exterior aspect of the event have to be great, I mean—what you could see of it. . . ."

"Both . . . it all depended," she answers ungraciously.

"And the perfect moments? Where do they come in?"

"They came afterwards. First there are annunciatory signs. Then the privileged situation, slowly, majestically, comes into people's lives. Then the question whether you want to make a perfect moment out of it."

"Yes," I say, "I understand. In each one of these privileged situations there are certain acts which have to be done, certain attitudes to be taken, words which must be said—and other attitudes, other words are strictly prohibited. Is that it?"

"I suppose so. . . ."

"In fact, then, the situation is the material: it demands exploitation."

"That's it," she says. "First you had to be plunged into something exceptional and feel as though you were putting it in order. If all those conditions had been realized, the moment would have been perfect."

"In fact, it was a sort of work of art."

"You've already said that," she says with irritation. "No: it was . . . a duty. You *had* to transform privileged situations into perfect moments. It was a moral question. Yes, you can laugh if you like: it was moral."

I am not laughing at all.

"Listen," I say spontaneously, "I'm going to admit my shortcomings, too. I never really understood you, I never sincerely tried to help you. If I had known . . ."

"Thank you, thank you very much," she says ironically. "I hope you're not expecting recognition for your delayed regrets. Besides, I hold nothing against you; I never explained anything to you clearly, I was all in knots, I couldn't tell anyone about it, not even you—especially not you. There was always something that rang false at those moments. Then I was lost. But I still had the feeling I was doing everything I could."

"But what had to be done? What actions?"

"What a fool you are. I can't give you any examples, it all depends."

"But tell me what you were trying to do."

"No, I don't want to talk about it. But here's a story if you like, a story that made a great impression on me when I was in school. There was a king who had lost a battle and was taken prisoner. He was there, off in a corner, in the victor's camp. He saw his son and daughter pass by in chains. He didn't weep, he didn't say anything. Then he saw one of his servants pass by, in chains too. Then he began to groan and tear out his hair. You can make up your own examples. You see: there are times when you mustn't cry—or else you'll be unclean. But if you drop a log on your foot, you can do as you please, groan, cry, jump around on the other foot. It would be foolish to be stoical all the time: you'd wear yourself out for nothing."

She smiles:

"Other times you must be *more* than stoical. Naturally, you don't remember the first time I kissed you?"

"Yes, very clearly," I say triumphantly, "it was in Kew Gardens, by the banks of the Thames."

"But what you never knew was that I was sitting on a patch of nettles: my dress was up, my thighs were covered with stings, and every time I made the slightest movement I was stung again. Well, stoicism wouldn't have been enough there. You didn't bother me at all, I had no particular desire for your lips, the kiss I was going to give you was much more important, it was an engagement, a pact. So you understand that this pain was irrelevant, I wasn't allowed to think about my thighs at a time like that. It wasn't enough not to show my suffering: it was necessary not to suffer."

She looks at me proudly, still surprised at what she had done.

"For more than twenty minutes, all the time you were insisting on having the kiss I had decided to give you, all the time I had you begging me—because I had to give it to you according to form—I managed to anaesthetize myself completely. And God knows I have a sensitive skin: I felt *nothing* until we got up."

That's it. There are no adventures—there are no perfect moments . . . we have lost the same illusions, we have followed the same paths. I can guess the rest—I can even speak for her and tell myself all that she has left to tell:

"So you realized that there were always women in tears, or a red-headed man, or something else to spoil your effects?"

"Yes, naturally," she answers without enthusiasm.

"Isn't that it?"

"Oh, you know, I might have resigned myself in the end to the clumsiness of a red-headed man. After all, I was always interested in the way other people played their parts . . . no, it's that . . ."

"That there are no more privileged situations?"

"That's it. I used to think that hate or love or death descended on us like tongues of fire on Good Friday. I thought one could radiate hate or death. What a mistake! Yes, I really thought that 'Hate' existed, that it came over people and raised them above themselves. Naturally, I am the only one, I am the one who hates, who loves. But it's always the same thing, a piece of dough that gets longer and longer . . . everything looks so much alike that you wonder how people got the idea of inventing names, to make distinctions."

She thinks as I do. It seems as though I had never left her.

"Listen carefully," I say, "for the past moment I've been thinking of something that pleases me much more than the rôle of a milestone you generously gave me to play: it's that we've changed together and in the same way. I like that better, you know, than to see you going farther and farther away and being condemned to mark your point of departure forever. All that you've told me—I came to tell you the same thing—though with other words, of course. We meet at the arrival. I can't tell you how pleased I am."

"Yes?" she says gently, but with an obstinate look. "Well, I'd still have liked it better if you hadn't changed; it was more convenient. I'm not like you, it rather displeases me to know that someone has thought the same things I have. Besides, you must be mistaken."

I tell her my adventures, I tell her about existence—perhaps at too great length. She listens carefully, her eyes wide open and her eyebrows raised.

When I finish, she looks soothed.

"Well, you're not thinking like me at all. You complain

because things don't arrange themselves around you like a bouquet of flowers, without your taking the slightest trouble to do anything. But I have never asked as much: I wanted action. You know, when we played adventurer and adventuress: you were the one who had adventures, I was the one who made them happen. I said: I'm a man of action. Remember? Well, now I simply say: one can't be a man of action."

I couldn't have looked convinced because she became animated and began again, with more energy:

"Then there's a heap of things I haven't told you, because it would take too long to explain. For example, I had to be able to tell myself at the very moment I took action that what I was doing would have . . . fatal results. I can't explain that to you very well. . . ."

"It's quite useless," I say, somewhat pedantically," "I've thought that too."

She looks at me with scorn.

"You'd like me to believe you've thought exactly the same way I have: you really amaze me."

I can't convince her, all I do is irritate her. I keep quiet. I want to take her in my arms.

Suddenly she looks at me anxiously:

"Well, if you've thought about all that, what can you do?"

I bow my head.

"I . . . I outlive myself," she repeats heavily.

What can I tell her? Do I know any reasons for living? I'm not as desperate as she is because I didn't expect much. I'm rather . . . amazed before this life which is given to me—given for nothing. I keep my head bowed, I don't want to see Anny's face now.

"I travel," she goes on gloomily; "I'm just back from Sweden. I stopped in Berlin for a week. This man who's keeping me . . ."

Take her in my arms? What good would it do? I can do nothing for her; she is as solitary as I.

"What are you muttering about?"

I raise my eyes. She is watching me tenderly.

"Nothing. I was thinking about something."

"Oh? Mysterious person! Well, talk or be quiet, but do one or the other."

I tell her about the "Railwaymen's Rendezvous," the old ragtime I had played on the phonograph, the strange happiness it gives me.

"I was wondering if, in that direction, one couldn't find or look for . . ."

She doesn't answer, I don't think she was much interested in what I told her.

Still, after a moment, she speaks again—and I don't know whether she is following her own ideas or whether it is an answer to what I have just told her.

"Paintings, statues can't be used: they're lovely *facing* me. Music . . ."

"But the theatre . . ."

"What about the theatre? Do you want to enumerate all the fine arts?"

"Before, you used to say you wanted to act because on the stage you had to realize perfect moments!"

"Yes, I realized them: for the others. I was in the dust, in the draught, under raw lights, between cardboard sets. I usually played with Thorndyke. I think you must have seen him at Covent Garden. I was always afraid I'd burst out laughing in his face."

"But weren't you ever carried away by your part?"

"A little, sometimes: never very strongly. The essential thing, for all of us, was the black pit just in front of us, in the bottom of it there were people you didn't see; obviously you were presenting them with a perfect moment. But, you know, they didn't live in it: it unfolded in front of them. And we, the actors, do you think we lived inside it? In the end, it wasn't anywhere, not on either side of the footlights, it didn't exist; and yet everybody thought about it. So you see, little man," she says in a dragging, almost vulgar tone of voice, "I walked out on the whole business."

"I tried to write a book . . ."

She interrupts me.

"I live in the past. I take everything that has happened to me and arrange it. From a distance like that, it doesn't do any harm, you'd almost let yourself be caught in it. Our whole story is fairly beautiful. I give it a few prods and it makes a whole string of perfect moments. Then I close my eyes and try to imagine that I'm still living inside it. I have other characters, too. . . . You have to know how to concentrate. Do you know what I read? Loyola's *Spiritual Exercises*. It has been quite useful for me. There's a way of first setting up the background, then making characters appear. You manage to *see*," she adds with a maniacal air.

"Well," I say, "that wouldn't satisfy me at all."

"Do you think it satisfies me?"

We stay silent for a moment. Evening is coming on; I can hardly make out the pale spot of her face. Her black dress melts with the shadow which floods the room. I pick up my cup mechanically, there's a little tea left in it and I bring it to my lips. The tea is cold. I want to smoke but I don't dare. I have the terrible feeling that we have nothing more to say to one another. Only yesterday I had so many questions to ask her: where she had been, what she had done, whom she had met. But that interested me only in so far as Anny gave her whole heart to it. Now I am without curiosity: all these countries, all these cities she has passed through, all the men who have courted her and whom she has perhaps loved—she clung to none of that, at heart she was indifferent to it all: little flashes of sun on the surface of a cold, dark sea. Anny is sitting opposite to me, we haven't seen each other for four years and we have nothing more to say.

"You'll have to leave now," Anny says suddenly, "I'm expecting someone."

"You're waiting for . . ."

"No, I'm waiting for a German, a painter."

She begins to laugh. This laugh rings strangely in the dim room.

"There's someone who isn't like us—not yet. He acts, he spends himself."

I get up reluctantly.

"When shall I see you again?"

"I don't know, I'm leaving for London tomorrow evening."

"By Dieppe?"

"Yes, and I think I'll go to Egypt after that. Maybe I'll be back in Paris next winter, I'll write you."

"I'll be free all day tomorrow," I say timidly.

"Yes, but I have a lot to do," she answers dryly. "No, I can't see you. I'll write you from Egypt. Just give me your address."

"Yes."

In the shadow I scribble my address on an envelope. I have to put down Hotel Printania so they can forward my letters when I leave Bouville. Yet I know very well that she won't write. Perhaps I shall see her again in ten years. Perhaps this is the last time I shall see her. I am not only overwhelmed at leaving her; I have a frightful fear of going back to my solitude again.

She gets up; at the door she kisses me lightly on the mouth.

"To remember your lips," she says, smiling. "I have to refresh my memories for my spiritual exercises."

I take her by the arm and draw her to me. She does not resist but she shakes her head.

"No. That doesn't interest me any more. You can't begin again. . . . And besides, for what people are worth, the first good-looking boy that comes along is worth as much as you."

"What are you going to do, then?"

"I told you, I'm going to England."

"No, I mean . . ."

"Nothing!"

I haven't let go of her arms, I tell her gently:

"Then I must leave you after finding you again."

I can see her face clearly now. Suddenly it grows pale and drawn. An old woman's face, absolutely frightful; I'm sure she didn't put that one on purposely: it is there, unknown to her, or perhaps in spite of her.

"No," she says slowly, "no. You haven't found me again."

She pulls her arms away. She opens the door. The hall is sparkling with light.

Anny begins to laugh.

"Poor boy! He never has any luck. The first time he plays his part well, he gets no thanks for it. Get out."

I hear the door close behind me.

Sunday:

This morning I consulted the Railway Guide: assuming that she hasn't lied to me, the Dieppe train will leave at 5.38. But maybe her man will be driving her. I wandered around Menilmontant all morning, then the quays in the afternoon. A few steps, a few walls separate me from her. At 5:38 our conversation of yesterday will become a memory, the opulent woman whose lips brushed against my mouth will rejoin, in the past, the slim little girl of Meknes, of London. But nothing was past yet, since she was still there, since it was still possible to see her again, to persuade her, to take her away with me forever. I did not feel alone yet.

I wanted to stop thinking about Anny, because, imagining

her body and her face so much, I had fallen into a state of extreme nervousness: my hands trembled and icy chills shook me. I began to look through the books on display at second-hand stalls, especially obscene ones because at least that occupies your mind. When the Gare d'Orsay clock struck five I was looking at the pictures in a book entitled *The Doctor with the Whip*. There was little variety: in most of them, a heavy bearded man was brandishing a riding whip over monstrous naked rumps. As soon as I realized it was five o'clock, I threw the book back on the pile and jumped into a taxi which took me to the Gare Saint-Lazare.

I walked around the platform for about twenty minutes, then I saw them. She was wearing a heavy fur coat which made her look like a lady. And a short veil. The man had on a camel's-hair coat. He was tanned, still young, very big, very handsome. A foreigner, surely, but not English; possibly Egyptian. They got on the train without seeing me. They did not speak to each other. Then the man got off and bought newspapers. Anny had lowered the window of her compartment; she saw me. She looked at me for a long time, without anger, with inexpressive eyes. Then the man got back into the compartment and the train left. At that moment I clearly saw the restaurant in Piccadilly where we used to eat, before, then everything went blank. I walked. When I felt tired I came into this café and went to sleep. The waiter has just wakened me and I am writing this while half-asleep.

Tomorrow I shall take the noon train back to Bouville. Two days there will be enough to pack my bags and straighten out my accounts at the bank. I think the Hotel Printania will want me to pay two weeks extra because I didn't give them notice. Then I have to return all the books I borrowed from the library. In any case, I'll be back in Paris before the end of the week.

Will I gain anything by the change? It is still a city: this one happens to be cut in two by a river, the other one is by the sea, yet they look alike. One takes a piece of bare sterile earth and one rolls big hollow stones on to it. Odours are held captive in these stones, odours heavier than air. Sometimes people throw them out of the windows into the streets and they stay there until the wind breaks them apart. In clear weather, noises come in one end of the city and go out the other, after going through all the walls; at other times, the noises whirl around inside these sun-baked, ice-split stones.

I am afraid of cities. But you mustn't leave them. If you go too far you come up against the vegetation belt. Vegetation has crawled for miles towards the cities. It is waiting. Once the city is dead, the vegetation will cover it, will climb over the stones, grip them, search them, make them burst with its long black pincers; it will blind the holes and let its green paws hang over everything. You must stay in the cities as long as they are alive, you must never penetrate alone this great mass of hair waiting at the gates; you must let it undulate and crack all by itself. In the cities, if you know how to take care of yourself, and choose the times when all the beasts are sleeping in their holes and digesting, behind the heaps of organic debris, you rarely come across anything more than minerals, the least frightening of all existants.

I am going back to Bouville. The vegetation has only surrounded three sides of it. On the fourth side there is a great hole full of black water which moves all by itself. The wind whistles between the houses. The odours stay less time there than anywhere: chased out to sea by the wind, they race along the surface of the black water like playful mists. It rains. They let plants grow between the gratings. Castrated, domesticated, so fat that they are harmless. They have enormous, whitish leaves which hang like ears. When you touch them it feels like cartilage, everything is fat and white in Bouville because of all the water that falls from the sky. I am going back to Bouville. How horrible!

I wake up with a start. It is midnight. Anny left Paris six hours ago. The boat is already at sea. She is sleeping in a cabin and, up on deck, the handsome bronze man is smoking cigarettes.

Tuesday, in Bouville:

Is that what freedom is? Below me, the gardens go limply down towards the city, and a house rises up from each garden. I see the ocean, heavy, motionless, I see Bouville. It is a lovely day.

I am free: there is absolutely no more reason for living, all the ones I have tried have given way and I can't imagine any more of them. I am still fairly young, I still have enough strength to start again. But do I have to start again? How much, in the strongest of my terrors, my disgusts, I had counted on Anny to save me I realized only now. My past is dead. The Marquis de Rollebon is dead, Anny came back only to take all hope away.

I am alone in this white, garden-rimmed street. Alone and free. But this freedom is rather like death.

Today my life is ending. By tomorrow I will have left this town which spreads out at my feet, where I have lived so long. It will be nothing more than a name, squat, bourgeois, quite French, a name in my memory, not as rich as the names of Florence or Bagdad. A time will come when I shall wonder: whatever could I have done all day long when I was in Bouville? Nothing will be left of this sunlight, this afternoon, not even a memory.

My whole life is behind me. I see it completely, I see its shape and the slow movements which have brought me this far. There is little to say about it: a lost game, that's all. Three years ago I came solemnly to Bouville. I had lost the first round. I wanted to play the second and I lost again: I lost the whole game. At the same time, I learned that you always lose. Only the rascals think they win. Now I am going to be like Anny, I am going to outlive myself. Eat, sleep, sleep, eat. Exist slowly, softly, like these trees, like a puddle of water, like the red bench in the streetcar.

The Nausea has given me a short breathing spell. But I know it will come back again: it is my normal state. Only today my body is too exhausted to stand it. Invalids also have happy moments of weakness which take away the consciousness of their illness for a few hours. I am bored, that's all. From time to time I yawn so widely that tears roll down my cheek. It is a profound boredom, profound, the profound heart of existence, the very matter I am made of. I do not neglect myself, quite the contrary: this morning I took a bath and shaved. Only when I think back over those careful little actions, I cannot understand how I was able to make them: they are so vain. Habit, no doubt, made them for me. They aren't dead, they keep on busying themselves, gently, insidiously weaving their webs, they wash me, dry me, dress me, like nurses. Did they also lead me to this hill? I can't remember how I came any more. Probably up the Escalier Dautry: did I really climb up its hundred and ten steps one by one? What is perhaps more difficult to imagine is that I am soon going to climb down again. Yet I know I am: in a moment I shall find myself at the bottom of the Coteau Vert, if I raise my head, see in the distance the lighting windows of these houses which are so close now. In the distance. Above my head; above my head; and this instant which I cannot leave, which locks me in and limits me on every side, this instant I am made of will be no more than a confused dream.

I watch the grey shimmerings of Bouville at my feet. In the sun they look like heaps of shells, scales, splinters of bone, and gravel. Lost in the midst of this debris, tiny glimmers of glass or mica intermittently throw off light flames. In an hour the ripples, trenches, and thin furrows which run between these shells will be streets, I shall walk in these streets, between these walls. These little black men I can just make out in the Rue Boulibet—in an hour I shall be one of them.

I feel so far away from them, on the top of this hill. It seems as though I belong to another species. They come out of their offices after their day of work, they look at the houses and the squares with satisfaction, they think it is *their* city, a good, solid, bourgeois city. They aren't afraid, they feel at home. All they have ever seen is trained water running from taps, light which fills bulbs when you turn on the switch, half-breed, bastard trees held up with crutches. They have proof, a hundred times a day, that everything happens mechanically, that the world obeys fixed, unchangeable laws. In a vacuum all bodies fall at the same rate of speed, the public park is closed at 4 p.m. in winter, at 6 p.m. in summer, lead melts at 335 degrees centigrade, the last streetcar leaves the Hotel de Ville at 11.05 p.m. They are peaceful, a little morose, they think about Tomorrow, that is to say, simply, a new today; cities have only one day at their disposal and every morning it comes back exactly the same. They scarcely doll it up a bit on Sundays. Idiots. It is repugnant to me to think that I am going to see their thick, self-satisfied faces. They make laws, they write popular novels, they get married, they are fools enough to have children. And all this time, great, vague nature has slipped into their city, it has infiltrated everywhere, in their house, in their office, in themselves. It doesn't move, it stays quietly and they are full of it inside, they breathe it, and they don't see it, they imagine it to be outside, twenty miles from the city. I *see* it, I *see* this nature . . . I know that its obedience is idleness, I know it has no laws: what they take for constancy is only habit and it can change tomorrow.

What if something were to happen? What if something suddenly started throbbing? Then they would notice it was there and they'd think their hearts were going to burst. Then what good would their dykes, bulwarks, power houses, furnaces and pile drivers be to them? It can happen any time, perhaps right now: the omens are present. For example, the father of a family might go out for a walk, and, across the street, he'll see something like a red rag, blown towards him by the wind. And when the rag has gotten close to him he'll see that it is a side of rotten meat, grimy with dust, dragging itself along by crawling, skipping, a piece of writhing flesh rolling in the gutter, spasmodically shooting out spurts of blood. Or a mother might look at her child's cheek and ask him: "What's that—a pimple?" and see the flesh puff out a little, split, open, and at the bottom of the split an eye, a laughing eye might appear. Or they might feel things gently brushing against their bodies, like the caresses of reeds to swimmers in a river. And they will realize that their clothing has become living things. And someone else might feel something scratching in his mouth. He goes to the mirror, opens his mouth: and his tongue is an enormous, live centipede, rubbing its legs together and scraping his palate. He'd like to spit it out, but the centipede is a part of him and he will have to tear it out with his own hands. And a crowd of things will appear for which people will have to find new names—stone-eye, great three-cornered arm, toe-crutch, spider-jaw. And someone might be sleeping in his comfortable bed, in his quiet, warm room, and wake up naked on a bluish earth, in a forest of rustling birch trees, rising red and white towards the sky like the smokestacks of Jouxtebouville, with big bumps half-way out of the ground, hairy and bulbous like onions. And birds will fly around these birch trees and pick at them with their beaks and make them bleed. Sperm will flow slowly, gently, from these wounds, sperm mixed with blood, warm and glassy with little bubbles. Or else nothing like that will happen, there will be no appreciable change, but one morning people will open their blinds and be surprised by a sort of frightful sixth sense, brooding heavily over things and seeming to pause. Nothing more than that: but for the little time it lasts, there will be hundreds of suicides. Yes! Let it change just a little, just to see, I don't ask for anything better. Then you will see other people, suddenly plunged into solitude. Men all alone, completely alone with horrible monstrosities, will run through the streets, pass heavily in front of me, their eyes staring, fleeing their ills yet carrying them with them, open-mouthed, with their insect-tongue flapping its wings. Then I'll burst out laughing even though my body may be covered with filthy, infected scabs which blossom into flowers of flesh, violets, buttercups. I'll lean against a wall and when they go by

I'll shout: "What's the matter with your science? What have you done with your humanism? Where is your dignity?" I will not be afraid—or at least no more than now. Will it not still be existence, variations on existence? All these eyes which will slowly devour a face—they will undoubtedly be too much, but no more so than the first two, Existence is what I am afraid of.

Evening falls, the first lamps are lit in the city. My God! How *natural* the city looks despite all its geometries, how crushed it looks in the evening. It's so . . . so evident, from here; could I be the only one to see it? Is there nowhere another Cassandra on the summit of a hill, watching a city engulfed in the depths of nature? But what difference does it make? What could I tell her?

My body slowly turns eastward, oscillates a little and begins to walk.

Wednesday: My last day in Bouville:

I have looked all over town for the Self-Taught Man. He surely hasn't gone home. He must be walking at random, filled with shame and horror—this poor humanist whom men don't want. To tell the truth, I was hardly surprised when the thing happened: for a long time I had thought that his soft, timid face would bring scandal on itself. He was so little guilty: his humble, contemplative love for young boys is hardly sensuality— rather a form of humanity. But one day he had to find himself alone. Like M. Achille, like me: he is one of my race, he has good will. Now he has entered into solitude—forever. Everything suddenly crumbled, his dreams of culture, his dreams of an understanding with mankind. First there will be fear, horror, sleepless nights, and then after that, the long succession of days of exile. In the evening he will come back to wander around the Cour des Hypothèques; from a distance he will watch the glowing windows of the library and his heart will fail him when he remembers the long rows of books, their leather bindings, the smell of their pages. I am sorry I didn't go along with him, but he didn't want me to; he begged me to let him alone: he was beginning his apprenticeship in solitude. I am writing this in the Café Mably. I went in with great ceremony, I wanted to study the manager, the cashier, and forcibly feel that I was seeing them for the last time. But I can't stop thinking about the Self-Taught Man, I still have his open face before my eyes, his face full of reproach, his blood-stained collar. So I asked for some paper and I am going to tell what happened to him.

I went to the library about two o'clock this afternoon. I was thinking: "The library. I am going in here for the last time."

The room was almost deserted. It hurt me to see it because I knew I would never come back. It was light as mist, almost unreal, all reddish; the setting sun rusted the table reserved for women, the door, the back of the books. For a second I had the delightful feeling that I was going into underbrush full of golden leaves; I smiled. I thought: I haven't smiled for a long time. The Corsican was looking out of the window, his hands behind his back. What did he see? The skull of Impétraz? I shall never see that skull again, or his top hat or his morning coat. In six hours I will have left Bouville. I put the two books I borrowed last month on the assistant librarian's desk. He tore up a green slip and handed me the pieces:

"There you are, Monsieur Roquetin."

"Thank you."

I thought: now I owe them nothing more. I don't owe anything more to anybody here. Soon I'm going to say good-bye to the woman in the "Railwaymen's Rendezvous," I am free. I hesitated a few instants: would I use these last moments to take a long walk through Bouville, to see the Boulevard Victor-Noir again, the Avenue Galvani, and the Rue Tournebride. But this forest was so calm, so pure: it seemed to me as though it hardly existed and that the Nausea had spared it. I went and sat down near the stove. The *Journal de Bouville* was lying on the table. I reached out and took it.

"Saved by His Dog."

"Yesterday evening, M. Dubosc of Remiredon, was bicycling home from the Naugis Fair . . ."

A fat woman sat down at my right. She put her felt hat beside her. Her nose was planted on her face like a knife in an apple. Under the nose, a small, obscene hole wrinkled disdainfully. She took a bound book from her bag, leaned her elbows on the table, resting her face against her fat hands. An old man was sleeping opposite me. I knew him: he was in the library the evening I was so frightened. I think he was afraid too. I thought: how far away all that is.

At four-fifteen the Self-Taught Man came in. I would have

liked to shake hands and say good-bye to him. But I thought our last meeting must have left him with unpleasant memories: he nodded distantly to me and, far enough away, he set down a small white package which probably contained, as usual, a slice of bread and a piece of chocolate. After a moment, he came back with an illustrated book which he placed near his package. I thought: I am seeing him for the last time. Tomorrow evening, the evening after tomorrow, and all the following evenings, he will return to read at this table, eating his bread and chocolate, he will patiently keep on with his rat's nibbling, he will read the works of Nabaud, Naudeau, Nodier, Nys, interrupting himself from time to time to jot down a maxim in his notebook. And I will be walking in Paris, in Paris streets, I will be seeing new faces. What could happen to me while he would still be here, with the lamp lighting up his heavy pondering face. I felt myself drifting back to the mirage of adventure just in time. I shrugged my shoulders and began reading again.

"Bouville and neighbouring areas:

Monistiers:

Activities of the gendarmerie for the year. The sergeant-major Gaspard, commanding the Monistiers brigade and its four gendarmes, Messrs. Lagoutte, Nizan, Pierpont, and Ghil, were hardly idle during the past year. In fact, our gendarmes have reported 7 crimes, 82 misdemeanours, 159 contraventions, 6 suicides and 15 automobile accidents, three of which resulted in death.

Jouxtebouville:

Friendly Society of Trumpet Players of Jouxtebouville. General rehearsal today; remittance of cards for the annual concert.

Compostel:

Presentation of the Legion of Honour to the Mayor.

Bouville Boy Scouts:

Monthly meeting this evening at 8.45 p.m., 10 Rue Ferdinand-Byron, Room A.
Programme: Reading of minutes. Correspondence. Annual banquet. 1932 assessment, March hiking schedule. Questions. New members.

Society for the Prevention of Cruelty to Animals:
Next Thursday, from 3 to 5 p.m., Room C, 10 Rue Ferdinand-Byron, Bouville, Public meeting. Send inquiries and
correspondence to the President, to the main office or to 154
Avenue Galvani.

*Bouville Watchdog Club . . . Bouville Association of Dis-
abled Veterans . . . Taxi-Owners' Union . . . Bouville Com-
mittee for the Friends of the Board-Schools. . . .*

Two boys with satchels come in. Students from the High-
school. The Corsican likes students from the High-school because
he can exercise a paternal supervision over them. Often, for his
own pleasure, he lets them stir around on their chairs and talk,
then suddenly tiptoes up behind them and scolds: "Is that the
way big boys behave? If you don't behave yourselves, the librarian
is going to complain to your headmaster."

And if they protest, he looks at them with terrible eyes:
"Give me your names." He also directs their reading: in the
library certain volumes are marked with a red cross; Hell: the
works of Gide, Diderot, Baudelaire and medical texts. When a
student wants to consult one of these books, the Corsican makes
a sign to him, draws him over to a corner and questions him. After
a moment he explodes and his voice fills the reading-room: "There
are a lot of more interesting books for a boy of your age. Instruc-
tive books. Have you finished your homework? What grade are
you in? And you don't have anything to do after four o'clock?
Your teacher comes in here a lot and I'm going to tell him about
you."

The two boys stay near the stove. The younger one has
brown hair, a skin almost too fine and a tiny mouth, wicked and
proud. His friend, a big heavy-set boy with the shadow of a
moustache, touched his elbow and murmured a few words. The
little brown-haired boy did not answer, but he gave an imper-
ceptible smile, full of arrogance and self-sufficiency. Then both
of them nonchalantly chose a dictionary from one of the shelves
and went over to the Self-Taught Man who was staring wearily
at them. They seemed to ignore his existence, but they sat down
right next to him, the brown-haired boy on his left and the thick-
set one on the left of the brown-haired boy. They began looking
through the dictionary. The Self-Taught Man's look wandered
over the room, then returned to his reading. Never had a library

offered such a reassuring spectacle: I heard no sound, except the short breathing of the fat woman, I only saw heads bent over books. Yet, at that moment, I had the feeling that something unpleasant was going to happen. All these people who lowered their eyes with such a studious look seemed to be playing a comedy: a few instants before I felt something like a breath of cruelty pass over us.

I had finished reading but hadn't decided to leave: I was waiting, pretending to read my newspaper. What increased my curiosity and annoyance was that the others were waiting too. It seemed as though my neighbour was turning the pages of her book more rapidly. A few minutes passed, then I heard whispering. I cautiously raised my head. Both boys had closed their dictionaries. The brown-haired one was not talking, his face, stamped with deference and interest, was turned to the right. Half-hidden behind his shoulder, the blond was listening and laughing silently. Who's talking? I thought.

It was the Self-Taught Man. He was bent over his young neighbour, eye to eye, smiling at him; I saw his lips move and, from time to time, his long eyelashes palpitate. I didn't recognize this look of youthfulness; he was almost charming. But, from time to time, he interrupted himself and looked anxiously behind him. The boy seemed to drink his words. There was nothing extraordinary about this little scene and I was going to go back to my reading when I saw the boy slowly slide his hand behind his back on the edge of the table. Thus hidden from the Self-Taught Man's eyes it went on its way for a moment, and began to feel around, then, finding the arm of the bigger boy, pinched it violently. The other, too absorbed in silent enjoyment of the Self-Taught Man's words, had not seen it coming. He jumped up and his mouth opened widely in surprise and admiration. The brown-haired boy had kept his look of respectful interest. One might have doubted that this mischievous hand belonged to him. What are they going to do to him? I thought. I knew that something bad was going to happen, and I saw too that there was still time to keep it from happening. But I couldn't guess what there was to prevent. For a second, I had the idea of getting up, slapping the Self-Taught Man on the shoulder and starting a conversation with him. But just at that moment he caught my look. He stopped speaking and pinched his lips together with an air of irritation. Discouraged, I quickly lowered my eyes and made a show of reading my paper. However, the fat woman had set down her book and raised her head. She seemed hypnotized. I felt sure the woman was going to burst: they all *wanted* something to burst. What could I do? I glanced at the Corsican: he wasn't looking out of the window any more, he had turned half-way towards us.

Fifteen minutes passed. The Self-Taught Man had begun his whispering again. I didn't dare look at him any more, but I could well imagine his young and tender air and those heavy looks which weighed on him without his knowing it. Once I heard his laugh, a fluted, childish little laugh. It gripped my heart: it seemed as though the two kids were going to drown a cat. Then the whispers stopped suddenly. This silence seemed tragic to me: it was the end, the deathblow. I bowed my head over my newspaper and pretended to read; but I wasn't reading: I raised my eyes as high as I could, trying to catch what was happening in this silence across from me. By turning my head slightly, I could see something out of the corner of my eye: it was a hand, the small white hand which slid along the table a little while ago. Now it was resting on its back, relaxed, soft and sensual, it had the indolent nudity of a woman sunning herself after bathing. A brown hairy object approached it, hesitant. It was a thick finger, yellowed by tobacco; inside this hand it had all the grossness of a male sex organ. It stopped for an instant, rigid, pointing at the fragile palm, then suddenly, it timidly began to stroke it. I was not surprised, I was only furious at the Self-Taught Man; couldn't he hold himself back, the fool, didn't he realize the risk he was running? He still had a chance, a small chance: if he were to put both hands on the table, on either side of the book, if he stayed absolutely still, perhaps he might be able to escape his destiny this time. But I *knew* he was going to miss his chance: the finger passed slowly, humbly, over the inert flesh, barely grazing it, without daring to put any weight on it: you might have thought it was conscious of its ugliness. I raised my head brusquely, I couldn't stand this obstinate little back-and-forth movement any more: I tried to catch the Self-Taught Man's eye and I coughed loudly to warn him. But he closed his eyes, he was smiling. His other hand had disappeared under the table. The boys were not laughing any more, they had both turned pale. The brown-haired one pinched his lips, he was afraid, he looked as though what was happening had gone beyond his control. But he did not draw his hand away, he left it on the table, motionless, a little curled. His friend's mouth was open in a stupid, horrified look.

Then the Corsican began to shout. He had come up without anyone hearing him and placed himself behind the Self-Taught Man's chair. He was crimson and looked as though he were going to laugh, but his eyes were flashing. I started up from my chair, but I felt almost relieved: the waiting was too unbearable. I wanted it to be over as soon as possible. I wanted them to throw him out if they wanted, but get it over with. The two boys, white as sheets, seized their satchels and disappeared.

"I saw you," the Corsican shouted, drunk with fury, "I saw you this time, don't try and tell me it isn't true. Don't think I'm not wise to your little game, I've got eyes in my head. And this is going to cost you plenty. I know your name, I know your address, I know everything about you, I know your boss, Chuillier. And won't he be surprised tomorrow morning when he gets a letter from the librarian. What? Shut up!" he said, his eyes rolling. "And don't think it's going to stop there. We have courts in France for people like you. So you were studying, so you were getting culture! So you were always after me to get books for you. Don't think you were kidding me."

The Self-Taught Man did not look surprised. He must have been expecting this for years. He must have imagined what would happen a hundred times, the day the Corsican would slip up behind him and a furious voice would resound suddenly in his ears. Yet he came back every evening, he feverishly pursued his reading and then, from time to time, like a thief, stroked a white hand or perhaps the leg of a small boy. It was resignation that I read on his face.

"I don't know what you mean," he stammered, "I've been coming here for years. . . ."

He feigned indignation and surprise, but without conviction. He knew quite well that the event was there and that nothing could hold it back any longer, that he had to live the minutes of it one by one.

"Don't listen to him," my neighbour said, "I saw him." She got up heavily: "And that isn't the first time I've seen him; no later than last Monday I saw him and I didn't want to say anything because I couldn't believe my eyes and I'd never have thought that in a library, a serious place where people come to learn, things like that would happen; things that'd make you blush. I haven't any children, but I pity the mothers who send their own to work here thinking they're well taken care of, and all the time there are monsters with no respect for anything and who keep them from doing their homework."

The Corsican went up to the Self-Taught Man:

"You hear what the lady says?" he shouted in his face. "You don't need to try and make fools of us. We saw you, you swine!"

"Monsieur, I advise you to be polite," the Self-Taught Man said with dignity. It was his part. Perhaps he would have liked to confess and run, but he had to play his part to the end. He was not looking at the Corsican, his eyes were almost closed. His arms hung limply by his sides; he was horribly pale. And then a flush of blood rose to his face.

The Corsican was suffocating with fury:

"Polite? Filth! Maybe you think I didn't see you. I was watching you all the time. I've been watching you for months!"

The Self-Taught Man shrugged his shoulders and pretended to drop back into his reading. Scarlet, his eyes filled with tears, he had taken on a look of supreme interest and looked attentively at a reproduction of a Byzantine mosaic.

"He goes on reading. He's got a nerve," the woman said, looking at the Corsican.

The Corsican was undecided. At the same time, the assistant librarian, a timid, well-meaning young man whom the Corsican terrorised, slowly raised himself from his desk and called: "Paoli, what's the matter?" There was a moment of irresolution and I hoped the affair would end there. But the Corsican must have thought again and found himself ridiculous. Angry, not knowing what more to say to this mute victim, he drew himself up to his full stature and flung a great fist into the air. The Self-Taught Man turned around, frightened. He looked at the Corsican open-mouthed; there was a horrible fear in his eyes.

"If you strike me I shall report you," he said with difficulty, "I shall leave of my own free will."

I got up but it was too late: the Corsican gave a voluptuous little whine and suddenly crashed his fist against the Self-Taught Man's nose. For a second I could only see his eyes, his magnificent eyes, wide with shame and horror above a sleeve and swarthy fist. When the Corsican drew back his fist the Self-Taught Man's nose began pouring blood. He wanted to put his hands to his face but the Corsican struck him again on the corner of the mouth. The Self-Taught Man sank back in his chair and stared in front of him with gentle, timid eyes. The blood ran from his nose onto his coat. He groped around with his left hand, trying to find his package, while with his right he stubbornly tried to wipe his dripping nostrils.

"I'm going," he said, as if to himself.

The woman next to me was pale and her eyes were gleaming.

"Rotter," she said, "serves him right."

I shook with rage. I went round the table and grabbed the little Corsican by the neck and lifted him up, trembling: I would have liked to break him over the table. He turned blue and struggled, trying to scratch me; but his short arms didn't reach my face. I didn't say a word, but I wanted to smash in his nose and disfigure him. He understood, he raised his elbow to protect his face: I was glad because I saw he was afraid. Suddenly he began to rattle:

"Let go of me, you brute. Are you a fairy too?"

I still wonder why I let him go. Was I afraid of complications? Had these lazy years in Bouville rotted me? Before, I wouldn't have let go of him without knocking out his teeth. I turned to the Self-Taught Man who had finally got up. But he fled from my look, head bowed, and went to take his coat from the hanger. He passed his left hand constantly over his nose, as if to stop the bleeding. But the blood was still flowing and I was afraid he would be sick. Without looking at anyone, he muttered:

"I've been coming here for years. . . ."

Hardly back on his feet, the little man had become master of the situation again. . . .

"Get the hell out," he told the Self-Taught Man, "and don't ever set foot in here again or I'll have the police on you."

I caught up with the Self-Taught Man at the foot of the stairs. I was annoyed, ashamed at his shame, I didn't know what to say to him. He didn't seem to notice I was there. He had finally taken out his handkerchief and he spat continuously into it. His nose was bleeding a little less.

"Come to the drugstore with me," I told him awkwardly.

He didn't answer. A loud murmur escaped from the reading-room.

"I can never come back here," the Self-Taught Man said. He turned and looked perplexedly at the stairs, at the entrance to the reading-room. This movement made the blood run between his collar and his neck. His mouth and cheeks were smeared with blood.

"Come on," I said, taking him by the arm.

He shuddered and pulled away violently.

"Let me go!"

"But you can't stay by yourself, someone has to wash your face and fix you up."

He repeated:

"Let me go, I beg you, sir, let me go."

He was on the verge of hysterics: I let him go. The setting sun lit his bent back for a moment, then he disappeared. On the threshold there was a star-shaped splash of blood.

One hour later:

It is grey outside, the sun is setting; the train leaves in two hours. I crossed the park for the first time and I am walking down the Rue Boulibet. I *know* it's the Rue Boulibet but I don't recognize it. Usually, when I start down it I seem to cross a deep layer of good sense: squat and awkward, the Rue Boulibet, with its tarred and uneven surface, looked like a national highway when it passes through rich country towns with solid, three-storey houses for more than half a mile; I called it a country road and it enchanted me because it was so out of place, so paradoxical in a commercial port. Today the houses are there but they have lost their rural look: they are buildings and nothing more. I had the same feeling in the park a little while ago: the plants, the grass plots, the Olivier Masqueret Fountain, looked stubborn through being inexpressive. I understand: the city is the first one to abandon me. I have not left Bouville and already I am there no longer. Bouville is silent. I find it strange that I have to stay two more hours in this city which, without bothering about me any more, has straightened up its furniture and put it under dust-sheets so as to be able to uncover it in all its freshness, to new arrivals this evening, or tomorrow. I feel more forgotten than ever.

I take a few steps and stop. I savour this total oblivion into which I have fallen. I am between two cities, one knows nothing of me, the other knows me no longer. Who remembers me? Perhaps a heavy young woman in London. . . . And is it really of *me* that she thinks? Besides, there is that man, that Egyptian. Perhaps he has just gone into her room, perhaps he has taken her in his arms. I am not jealous; I know that she is outliving herself. Even if she loved him with all her heart, it would still be the love of a dead woman. I had her last living love. But there is still something he can give her: pleasure. And if she is fainting and sinking into enjoyment, there is nothing more which attaches her to me. She takes her pleasure and I am no more for her than if I had never met her; she has suddenly emptied herself of me, and all other consciousness in the world has also emptied itself of me. It seems funny. Yet I know that I exist, that I am here.

Now when I say "I," it seems hollow to me. I can't manage to feel myself very well, I am so forgotten. The only real thing left in me is existence which feels it exists. I yawn, lengthily. No one. Antoine Roquentin exists for on one. That amuses me. And just what is Antoine Roquentin? An abstraction. A pale reflection of myself wavers in my consciousness. Antoine Roquentin . . . and suddenly the "I" pales, pales, and fades out.

Lucid, forlorn, consciousness is walled-up; it perpetuates itself. Nobody lives there any more. A little while ago someone said "me," said *my* consciousness. Who? Outside there were streets, alive with known smells and colours. Now nothing is left but anonymous walls, anonymous consciousness. That is what there is: walls, and between the walls, a small transparency, alive and impersonal. Consciousness exists as a tree, as a blade of grass. It slumbers, it grows bored. Small fugitive presences populate it like birds in the branches. Populate it and disappear. Consciousness forgotten, forsaken between these walls, under this grey sky. And here is the sense of its existence: it is conscious of being superfluous. It dilutes, scatters itself, tries to lose itself on the brown wall, along the lamp post or down there in the evening mist. But it *never* forgets itself. That is its lot. There is a stifled voice which tells it: "The train leaves in two hours," and there is the consciousness of this voice. There is also consciousness of a face. It passes slowly, full of blood, spattered, and its bulging eyes weep. It is not between the walls, it is nowhere. It vanishes; a bent body with a bleeding face replaces it, walks slowly away, seems to stop at each step, never stops. There is a consciousness of this body walking slowly in a dark street. It walks but it gets no further away. The dark street does not end, it loses itself in nothingness. It is not between the walls, it is nowhere. And there is consciousness of a stifled voice which says: "The Self-Taught Man is wandering through the city."

Not the same city, not between these toneless walls, the Self-Taught Man walks in a city where he is not forgotten. People are thinking about him; the Corsican, the fat woman; perhaps everybody in the city. He has not yet lost, he cannot lose himself, this tortured bleeding self they didn't want to kill. His lips and nostrils hurt him; he thinks: "It hurts." He walks, he must walk. If he stopped for one instant the high walls of the library would suddenly rise up around him and lock him in; the Corsican would spring from one side and the scene would begin again, exactly alike in all the details, and the woman would smirk: "They ought to be in jail, those rotters." And the scene would begin again. He thinks: "My God, if only I hadn't done that, if only that could not be true."

The troubled face passes back and forth through my consciousness: "Maybe he is going to kill himself." No: this gentle, baited soul could never dream of death.

There is knowledge of the consciousness. It sees through itself, peaceful and empty between the walls, freed from the man who inhabited it, monstrous because empty. The voice says: "The luggage is registered. The train leaves in two hours." The walls slide right and left. There is a consciousness of macadam, a consciousness of the ironmongers, the loopholes of the barracks and the voice says: "For the last time."

Consciousness of Anny, of Anny, fat old Anny in her hotel room, consciousness of suffering and the suffering is conscious between the long walls which leave and will never return: "Will there never be an end to it?" the voice sings a jazz tune between the walls "some of these days," will there never be an end to it? And the tune comes back softly, insidiously, from behind, to take back the voice and the voice sings without being able to stop and the body walks and there is consciousness of all that and consciousness of consciousness. But no one is there to suffer and wring his hands and take pity on himself. No one, it is a suffering of the crossroads, a forgotten suffering—which cannot forget itself. And the voice says: "There is the 'Railwaymen's Rendezvous'," and the *I* surges into the consciousness, it is I, Antoine Roquentin, I'm leaving for Paris shortly; I am going to say good-bye to the patronne.

I'm coming to say good-bye to you."

"You're leaving, Monsieur Roquentin?"

"I'm going to Paris. I need a change."

"Lucky!"

How was I able to press my lips against this large face? Her body no longer belongs to me. Yesterday I was able to imagine it under the black wool dress. Today the dress is impenetrable. This white body with veins on the surface of the skin, was it a dream?

"We'll miss you," the patronne says. "Won't you have something to drink? It's on the house."

We sit down, touch glasses. She lowers her voice a little.

"I was used to you," she says with polite regret," we got along together."

"I'll be back to see you."

"Be sure to, Monsieur Antoine. Stop in and say hello to us the next time you're in Bouville. You just tell yourself: 'I'm going to say hello to Mme Jeanne, she'll like that.' That's true, a person really likes to know what happens to others. Besides, people always come back here to see us. We have sailors, don't we, working for the Transat: sometimes I go for two years without seeing them, they're either in Brazil or New York or else working on a transport in Bordeaux. And then one fine day I see them again. 'Hello, Madame Jeanne.' And we have a drink together. You can believe it or not, but I remember what each one likes. From two years back! I tell Madeleine: Give a dry vermouth to M. Pierre, a Noilly Cinzano to M. Léon. They ask me: How can you remember that? It's my business, I tell them."

In the back of the room there is a thick-set man who has been sleeping with her recently. He calls her:

"Patronne!"

She gets up:

"Excuse me, Monsieur Antoine."

The waitress comes over to me:

"So you're leaving us just like that?"

"I'm going to Paris."

"I lived in Paris," she says proudly. "For two years. I worked in Siméon's. But I was homesick."

She hesitates a second, then realizes she has nothing more to say to me:

"Well, good-bye, Monsieur Antoine."

She wipes her hand on her apron and holds it out to me.

"Good-bye, Madeleine."

She leaves. I pull the *Journal de Bouville* over to me, then push it away again: I read it in the library a little while ago, from top to bottom.

The patronne does not come back: she abandons her fat hands to her boy friend, who kneads them with passion.

The train leaves in three-quarters of an hour.

I count my money to pass the time.

Twelve hundred francs a month isn't enormous. But if I hold myself back a little it should be enough. A room for 300 francs, 15 francs a day for food: that leaves 450 francs for petty cash, laundry, and movies. I won't need underwear or clothes for a long while. Both my suits are clean, even though they shine at the elbows a little: they'll last me three or four years if I take care of them.

Good God! Is it I who is going to lead this mushroom existence? What will I do all day long? I'll take walks. I'll sit on a folding chair in the Tuileries—or rather on a bench, out of economy. I'll read in the libraries. And then what? A movie once a week. And then what? Can I smoke a Voltigeur on Sunday? Shall I play croquet with the retired old men in the Luxembourg? Thirty years old! I pity myself. There are times when I wonder if it wouldn't be better to spend all my 300,000 francs in one year—and after that . . . . But what good would that do me? New clothes? Women? Travel? I've had all that and now it's over, I don't feel like it any more: for what I'd get out of it! A year from now I'd find myself as empty as I am today, without even a memory, and a coward facing death.

Thirty years! And 14,400 francs in the bank. Coupons to cash every month. Yet I'm not an old man! Let them give me something to do, no matter what . . . I'd better think about something else, because I'm playing a comedy now. I know very well that I don't want to do anything: to do something is to create existence—and there's quite enough existence as it is.

The truth is that I can't put down my pen: I think I'm going to have the Nausea and I feel as though I'm delaying it while writing. So I write whatever comes into my mind.

Madeleine, who wants to please me, calls to me from the distance, holding up a record:

"Your record, Monsieur Antoine, the one you like, do you want to hear it for the last time?"

"Please."

I said that out of politeness, but I don't feel too well disposed to listen to jazz. Still, I'm going to pay attention because, as Madeleine says, I'm hearing it for the last time: it is very old, even too old for the provinces; I will look for it in vain in Paris. Madeleine goes and sets it on the gramophone, it is going to spin; in the grooves, the steel needle is going to start jumping and grinding and when the grooves will have spiralled it into the centre of the disc it will be finished and the hoarse voice singing "Some of these days" will be silent forever.

It begins.

To think that there are idiots who get consolation from the fine arts. Like my Aunt Bigeois: "Chopin's Preludes were such a help to me when your poor uncle died." And the concert halls overflow with humiliated, outraged people who close their eyes and try to turn their pale faces into receiving antennæ. They imagine that the sounds flow into them, sweet, nourishing, and that their sufferings become music, like Werther; they think that beauty is compassionate to them. Mugs.

I'd like them to tell me whether they find this music compassionate. A while ago I was certainly far from swimming in beatitudes. On the surface I was counting my money, mechanically. Underneath stagnated all those unpleasant thoughts which took the form of unformulated questions, mute astonishments and which leave me neither day nor night. Thoughts of Anny, of my wasted life. And then, still further down, Nausea, timid as dawn. But there was no music then, I was morose and calm. All the things around me were made of the same material as I, a sort of messy suffering. The world was so ugly, outside of me, these dirty glasses on the table were so ugly, and the brown stains on the mirror and Madeleine's apron and the friendly look of the gross lover of the patronne, the very existence of the world so ugly that I felt comfortable, at home.

Now there is this song on the saxophone. And I am ashamed. A glorious little suffering has just been born, an exemplary suffering. Four notes on the saxophone. They come and go, they seem to say: You must be like us, suffer in rhythm. All right! Naturally, I'd like to suffer that way, in rhythm, without complacence, without self-pity, with an arid purity. But is it my fault if the beer at the bottom of my glass is warm, if there are brown stains on the mirror, if I am not wanted, if the sincerest of my sufferings drags and weighs, with too much flesh and the skin too wide at the same time, like a sea-elephant, with bulging eyes, damp and touching and yet so ugly? No, they certainly can't tell me it's compassionate—this little jewelled pain which spins around above the record and dazzles me. Not even ironic: it spins gaily, completely self-absorbed; like a scythe it has cut through the drab intimacy of the world and now it spins and all of us, Madeleine, the thick-set man, the patronne, myself, the tables, benches, the

174

stained mirror, the glasses, all of us abandon ourselves to existence, because we were among ourselves, only among ourselves, it has taken us unawares, in the disorder, the day to day drift: I am ashamed for myself and for what exists *in front* of it.

It does not exist. It is even an annoyance; if I were to get up and rip this record from the table which holds it, if I were to break it in two, I wouldn't reach *it*. It is beyond—always beyond something, a voice, a violin note. Through layers and layers of existence, it veils itself, thin and firm, and when you want to seize it, you find only existants, you butt against existants devoid of sense. It is behind them: I don't even hear it, I hear sounds, vibrations in the air which unveil it. It does not exist because it has nothing superfluous: it is all the rest which in relation to it is superfluous. It *is*.

And I, too, wanted to *be*. That is all I wanted; this is the last word. At the bottom of all these attempts which seemed without bonds, I find the same desire again: to drive existence out of me, to rid the passing moments of their fat, to twist them, dry them, purify myself, harden myself, to give back at last the sharp, precise sound of a saxophone note. That could even make an apologue: there was a poor man who got in the wrong world. He existed, like other people, in a world of public parks, bistros, commercial cities and he wanted to persuade himself that he was living somewhere else, behind the canvas of paintings, with the doges of Tintoretto, with Gozzoli's Florentines, behind the pages of books, with Fabrizio del Dongo and Julien Sorel, behind the phonograph records, with the long dry laments of jazz. And then, after making a complete fool of himself, he understood, he opened his eyes, he saw that it was a misdeal: he was in a bistro, just in front of a glass of warm beer. He stayed overwhelmed on the bench; he thought: I am a fool. And at that very moment, on the other side of existence, in this other world which you can see in the distance, but without ever approaching it, a little melody began to sing and dance: "You must be like me; you must suffer in rhythm."

The voice sings:

> *Some of these days*
> *You'll miss me, honey*

Someone must have scratched the record at that spot because it makes an odd noise. And there is something that clutches the heart: the melody is absolutely untouched by this tiny coughing of the needle on the record. It is so far—so far behind. I understand that too: the disc is scratched and is wearing out, perhaps the singer is dead; I'm going to leave, I'm going to take my train. But behind the existence which falls from one present to the other, without a past, without a future, behind these sounds which decompose from day to day, peel off and slip towards death, the melody stays the same, young and firm, like a pitiless witness.

The voice is silent. The disc scrapes a little, then stops. Delivered from a troublesome dream, the café ruminates, chews the cud over the pleasure of existing. The patronne's face is flushed, she slaps the fat white cheeks of her new friend, but without succeeding in colouring them. Cheeks of a corpse. I stagnate, fall half-asleep. In fifteen minutes I will be on the train, but I don't think about it. I think about a clean-shaven American with thick black eyebrows, suffocating with the heat, on the twenty-first floor of a New York skyscraper. The sky burns above New York, the blue of the sky is inflamed, enormous yellow flames come and lick the roofs; the Brooklyn children are going to put on bathing drawers and play under the water of a fire-hose. The dark room on the twenty-first floor cooks under a high pressure. The American with the black eyebrows sighs, gasps and the sweat rolls down his cheeks. He is sitting, in shirtsleeves, in front of his piano; he has a taste of smoke in his mouth and, vaguely, a ghost of a tune in his head. "Some of these days." Tom will come in an hour with his hip-flask; then both of them will lower themselves into leather armchairs and drink brimming glasses of whisky and the fire of the sky will come and inflame their throats, they will feel the weight of an immense, torrid slumber. But first the tune must be written down. "Some of these days." The moist hand seizes the pencil on the piano. "Some of these days you'll miss me, honey."

That's the way it happened. That way or another way, it makes little difference. That is how it was born. It is the worn-out body of this Jew with black eyebrows which it chose to create it. He held the pencil limply, and the drops of sweat fell from his ringed fingers on to the paper. And why not I? Why should it need precisely this fat fool full of stale beer and whisky for the miracle to be accomplished?

"Madeleine, would you put the record back? Just once, before I leave."

Madeleine starts to laugh. She turns the crank and it begins again. But I no longer think of myself. I think of the man out there who wrote this tune, one day in July, in the black heat of his room. I try to think of him *through* the melody, through the white, acidulated sounds of the saxophone. He made it. He had troubles, everything didn't work out for him the way it should have: bills to pay—and then there surely must have been a woman somewhere who wasn't thinking about him the way he would have liked her to—and then there was this terrible heat wave which turned men into pools of melting fat. There is nothing pretty or glorious in all that. But when I hear the sound and I think that that man made it, I find this suffering and sweat . . . moving. He was lucky. He couldn't have realized it. He must have thought: with a little luck, this thing will bring in fifty dollars. Well, this is the first time in years that a man has seemed moving to me. I'd like to know something about him. It would interest me to find out the type of troubles he had, if he had a woman or if he lived alone. Not at all out of humanity; on the contrary—besides, he may be dead. Just to get a little information about him and be able to think about him from time to time, listening to the record. I don't suppose it would make the slightest difference to him if he were told that in the seventh largest city of France, in the neighbourhood of a station, someone is thinking about him. But I'd be happy if I were in his place; I envy him. I have to go. I get up, but I hesitate an instant, I'd like to hear the Negress sing. For the last time.

She sings. So two of them are saved: the Jew and the Negress. Saved. Maybe they thought they were lost irrevocably, drowned in existence. Yet no one could think of me as I think of them, with such gentleness. No one, not even Anny. They are a little like dead people for me, a little like the heroes of a novel; they have washed themselves of the sin of existing. Not completely, of course, but as much as any man can. This idea suddenly knocks me over, because I was not even hoping for that any more. I feel something brush against me lightly and I dare not move because I am afraid it will go away. Something I didn't know any more: a sort of joy.

The Negress sings. Can you justify your existence then? Just a little? I feel extraordinarily intimidated. It isn't because I have much hope. But I am like a man completely frozen after a trek through the snow and who suddenly comes into a warm room. I think he would stay motionless near the door, still cold, and that slow shudders would go right through him.

Some of these days
You'll miss me, honey

Couldn't I try. . . . Naturally, it wouldn't be a question of a tune . . . but couldn't I, in another medium? . . . It would have to be a book: I don't know how to do anything else. But not a history book: history talks about what has existed—an existant can never justify the existence of another existant. My error, I wanted to resuscitate the Marquis de Rollebon. Another type of book. I don't quite know which kind—but you would have to guess, behind the printed words, behind the pages, at something which would not exist, which would be above existence. A story, for example, something that could never happen, an adventure. It would have to be beautiful and hard as steel and make people ashamed of their existence.

I must leave, I am vacillating. I dare not make a decision. If I were sure I had talent. . . . But I have never—never written anything of that sort. Historical articles, yes—lots of them. A book. A novel. And there would be people who would read this book and say: "Antoine Roquentin wrote it, a red-headed man who hung around cafés," and they would think about my life as I think about the Negress's: as something precious and almost legendary. A book. Naturally, at first it would only be a troublesome, tiring work, it wouldn't stop me from existing or feeling that I exist. But a time would come when the book would be written, when it would be behind me, and I think that a little of its clarity might fall over my past. Then, perhaps, because of it, I could remember my life without repugnance. Perhaps one day, thinking precisely of this hour, of this gloomy hour in which I wait, stooping, for it to be time to get on the train, perhaps I shall feel my heart beat faster and say to myself: "That was the day, that was the hour, when it all started." And I might succeed —in the past, nothing but the past—in accepting myself.

Night falls. On the second floor of the Hotel Printania two windows have just lighted up. The building-yard of the New Station smells strongly of damp wood: tomorrow it will rain in Bouville.